The Man
Who Never Lived

KEVIN IRELAND was born in Mt Albert, Auckland, but his
family moved across the harbour to Devonport in 1938.
In that seaside village, after what seems like a lifetime of
further shifts around the world, he now lives and works
as a fulltime writer.

The Man Who Never Lived

KEVIN IRELAND

V

VINTAGE

Random House New Zealand Ltd
(An imprint of the Random House Group)

18 Poland Road
Glenfield
Auckland 10
NEW ZEALAND

Sydney   New York   Toronto
London   Auckland   Johannesburg
and agencies throughout the world

First published 1997
© Kevin Ireland 1997
The moral rights of the Author have been asserted.

Printed in Wellington by GP Print

ISBN 1 86941 325 3

Publication is assisted by

ARTS COUNCIL OF NEW ZEALAND *TOI AOTEAROA*

Chapters

for Jack and Frederika

1

Everything began from the moment I discovered the body on the beach. Just small, puzzling changes at first. Slippery ones that you couldn't get a grip on. Then in a matter of a few days my whole existence took a skate. The solid world on which I thought I stood simply slid away from underneath me.

Yet at the time, finding a body held no deep significance. How could it? All I thought was that the whole encounter had a kind of disturbing *oddity*. By which I mean, it's not every day you go out for a stroll and walk straight up to a corpse, is it? In fact, how should it surprise anyone to learn that it had never happened to me before?

But that's not all I'm getting at when I use the word oddity. Perhaps the strangest sensation I remember was that the experience didn't throw me one little bit. I just looked a short way ahead and matter-of-factly noticed a hump on the sand, and thought to myself it had to be a dead body. It was a corpse, beyond any question or doubt.

There it lay, in a heap of seaweed and two sea-blackened tree branches, on a tiny spill of sand that the outgoing tide had left, high and dry among the rocks that marked the top end of the reef just where it disappears into the sand dunes.

The scene is like a photograph. I have tried to develop the memory from different angles, yet what I've always ended up with is the same body on the same beach. Nothing about it will ever change.

Even now, if I close my eyes, I can still see it lying there, exactly as it was. And I can recall with perfect clarity how I knew instantly there was no way the thing was going to shake the sand and seaweed off, get up and start leaping about.

So how come I was so certain, from a few yards off, that I was walking directly in line towards a dead body, when it was half covered up and I'd never seen a corpse before – except the cosmetically improved ones you pay your last respects to in their funeral caskets?

The police asked me that, too. They said, how come I could see through all the camouflage and why didn't I think it was a shop dummy or a practical joke? And the only thing I could answer was, it's what's commonly called a gut reaction. I've always trusted mine. Sometimes you just know something for a fact.

After all, there was the extraordinary position and shape of the body to go by – the way it was humped up in the sand, utterly still, as if it had been trapped while trying to swim underneath the two bits of driftwood, with seaweed streaming away from it like a torn skirt.

The face, chest and arms were half-obscured by sand and weed, and the feet were entirely buried. Only the back of its head, from which there hung several long limp hanks of hair, its hunched and slightly bloated shoulders, its narrow feminine waist and the two smooth and swollen mounds of its backside, could be seen clearly.

Anyone would have noticed that the body couldn't have just walked there, then keeled over and died. And neither did it seem likely that it had been carried there by someone and carefully arranged beside the rocks. It simply didn't seem humanly possible. And besides, the only footprints in the crust of sand were mine.

I wasn't in the slightest bit fazed or afraid. But the one thing that did make me cautious as I stood there was the possibility that the thing might smell. There was only a light breeze that day, and it came from the north-east, over my shoulder. So I bent warily to sniff and I didn't pick up the first nauseating whiff of the thing until I actually gave it a prod with a finger. And yes, it really was stomach-wrenching. Flies were dive-bombing the mound of its back and buzzing its ears. It's a wonder the gulls hadn't begun to picnic on it. I've often seen them scoffing the odd bits of rotten fish that get washed up on the beach.

There had been a seven o'clock tide that morning, so I had no trouble figuring out that the body would have come bobbing in when it was dark, then it would have got caught in a backwash and stranded high and dry among the rocks, out of sight of the joggers, at about that time. Which means it could have been lying there for nearly four hours. And for at least the past hour, and possibly quite a bit longer, the sun would have risen over the surrounding reef and been on it full-blast. Late summers in Mt Matheson are among the warmest in the whole country.

I've got the timing near enough to right, because I looked at my watch almost straight away, and it was a few minutes past eleven. For years I had made a habit of taking a constitutional walk an hour or two before lunch. It's good exercise, and it's one of those daily routines you need to establish to keep going after retirement.

Of course, I also realised that the corpse could have been brought in on the high tide before seven the previous night, but we hadn't yet changed to daylight saving, so it stays fairly light in Mt Matheson till about eight, and all evening there are quite a few strollers and children wandering and horsing about on the reef, and the sand dunes behind it. And, of course, there are the young lovers. At night they pop out like sandhoppers and swarm about the place where I found the body. Someone would have been bound to have tripped over it, if it had been washed up then.

So I had no doubt that it came in on the morning tide. But there's another good reason why no one had noticed the body before I got there.

Not only was it partly hidden in sand and seaweed, but as I said, it had been cast up at the upper, broken part of the

11

reef. The beach runs right up against the abrupt wall of the reef a short way further down and the sand is packed hard all the way. When there's a fine morning, a light breeze and an outgoing tide, most people prefer the hard smooth stretch of the beach, within a short distance of the waves.

It's only the older residents, such as myself, who sometimes stump along the high-tide line, just below the dunes, pausing here and there to examine debris and shells – and also to get away on our own. It's our daytime territory, our strip of the seaside. We feel we own it. If we can possibly avoid doing so, we don't go down among the teenage hooligans, or the blowsy young mums with their appalling broods of screaming little riffraff, or the rolling tottering pain-racked demon athletes – just as we don't wander any higher up in the dunes, where the sand is too soft and the going gets heavy and difficult, not to mention the hazards of beer cans, broken bottles and french letters everywhere.

Those are the unadorned details of the observations I made at the time and later. All the gossip about the two branches being locked together at the head of the corpse like a cross, and the seaweed being wreathed carefully along its full length like a tribute from the sea makes me angry. It's a load of absolute drivel.

The body had floated in on the tide where the rocks always create a tiny enclosed backwater, and it had been dumped there where sticks and seaweed collect every day of the year. It's as straightforward and uncomplicated as that.

2

Of course, I didn't waste any time getting straight on to the police. Using a bit of the local knowledge I've gathered over seventy years of visiting and living in Mt Matheson, I doubled back as quickly as I could to where Fairbreeze Avenue swings in close to the beach, at exactly the same spot where once upon a time there was a shortcut that came down beside the boundary of Smoyle's farm.

Straight away I spotted Bert Matthews in his front garden, so I told him – no doubt a bit dramatically – that I needed to use his phone to get in touch with the local police station. Bert happened to be one of my top managers from way back in the old days, so I didn't have to put my needs to him twice or translate it into grunt-speak, as you seem to be obliged to do these days whenever you ring the council and ask them to send around their cherry-picker to change a dud light-bulb in a street lamp. He said 'It's in the hallway, sir!' without a moment's hesitation.

That phone call now seems to me to mark the beginning of the next stage – when everything started to go wrong. It was precisely from the time that I picked up Bert's handset that I got involved, though I wasn't to notice till several days later that there was a definite pattern to it all.

I'm not a prickly or over-sensitive person, but I'm proud to say I'm nobody's mug either, so let me very briefly describe the next lot of strange events this way: the police were okay to start with, there were just two of them, both in uniform, and they arrived quickly from the Mt Matheson police station, and followed me back to the beach. The important thing to remember is that they treated me with average respect – which is all I'd ordinarily ask for. So far, so good. But a whole new contingent arrived from their headquarters, across the harbour at Rownley, and the difference in their behaviour was nothing short of bloody remarkable.

This new pack of bright sparks asked me at least five times if my name was Arthur Henry Gransey – though the first lot, from Mt Matheson, had written that down in a notebook half an hour earlier – and when I repeated that indeed my name was *Mister* Arthur Henry Gransey, they kept on looking at me in a strangely unsettling way. It was just an impression, but it was an unmistakable one – and it was very weird. They kept going into little huddles then looking me over. And there was no way of telling what was going on inside their heads.

At which point let me be the first person to step forward and say that we've got a great police force. I'm not criticising them. They're probably the least corrupt and most helpful in the world. But that doesn't mean to say there isn't the odd corkscrew among them. Know what I mean?

So, I suddenly got brassed off with the way they were carrying on, and I decided to leave them to their investigations. I told them politely that since I had things to get on with at home, they could make an appointment to visit me there later, if they had any further questions.

You'd have thought I was planning to make a run for it. Two of them moved straight in front of me and another, a small thick-set man with a Mexican moustache and bristling grey hair like a wire brush, caught the sleeve of my shirt and snarled – yes, actually snarled, 'You don't go anywhere, Fred. You just hang on, okay.'

He gave me a hell of a fright. He wasn't being funny. I was up against a hard little pit-bull of a man who gave orders and got his way. A dangerous sharp-eyed man who was not to be crossed.

I know the type well. I've employed one or two of them in my day. You hire them like cattle-dogs, and you place them in positions where the rest of the people you have working for you have been slacking and getting into bad habits, and need a good snapping at around the ankles, just to show who's boss. This type never says please, or sorry for the inconvenience, or thank you sir. They call other people 'Fred' and bark at them to hang on. And they get results.

So, the next thing that happened was that I found myself being taken back to a car, where I was asked to hop in and repeat everything I'd said, and more notes were taken. Then I was told I would be required – yes, 'required' was the word – to go to the police station to make a formal statement.

Half an hour must have gone by before this actually happened, a time in which I watched from my grandstand seat in the police car a helicopter arrive, presumably all the way from Rownley. It unloaded several mysterious packages wrapped neatly in silver foil, then away it went again, making a hell of a racket. Several more vans also turned up, with a photographer and so on.

The body was shielded off and stakes were pushed into the beach with tape strung between them to keep out the gawkers who were drifting in all the time like plastic bottles on a spring tide. I don't know why the police don't charge the public a dollar a look. In these days of user pays, surely it would help cover expenses.

It was all mildly interesting to watch, though nothing very decisive seemed to be happening. The police came and went and milled about, the helicopter returned with more silver packages and a launch appeared from around the Mt Matheson headland and coasted up and down near the reef.

Eventually, I was given a cup of tea in a polystyrene cup by a very nice smiling policewoman, then everyone seemed to start walking away, and suddenly the main part of the show just packed up, as if those concerned had become bored with it. Most of the vans moved off in one direction and the car I was in went off in another.

It soon turned out that we were followed by a small convoy of cars heading for the tiny Mt Matheson police station. At the time I guessed they were coming with us to establish an inquiry team, but it was another case of false expectancy.

I'd seen too many police serials in the days when Grace and I used to watch a lot of television. Everyone was actually on their way to make a fresh cup of tea and to eat the ham sandwiches which had been delivered by the helicopter. I discovered that they were what lay inside the packages when the silver foil was unwrapped.

3

It was after we'd all had a snack at the police station that I learned the body was that of a man. Funny how I'd assumed it was a woman.

What must have put me off track were the several longish hanks of hair I'd noticed hanging down the nape of the neck, while the rest of the hair, plus the face – which I was never to see – had been buried right up to the ears. In addition to which, as I've mentioned, his waist was narrow and his backside was impressively smooth, though extremely unattractive.

The softness and bloated roundness of his shape had also deceived me. The condition he was in – remember, he was far from being what you could call on the fresh side – had made him seem curved and womanly, and I hadn't been helped by the way that sand and seaweed had concealed the feet and smoothed out the legs. It was an easy mistake to have made.

'Do you have an idea who it could be?' I couldn't stop myself from asking. After all, I'd found the body and I assumed I had the next best thing to an interest in knowing its name.

'We're conducting inquiries,' came the frosty reply from the large and raw-boned young constable who sat across from me at the worktable at which he'd taken my formal statement.

'Well,' I said, without thinking I may be saying something of any consequence. 'I'd be interested to know. When you find out.'

A voice close behind me spoke almost directly into my ear, 'So, what's it to you?'

We were in the small open office at the back of the main counter of the station and a lot of people had been coming and going. Everything was a hell of a squeeze. I hadn't noticed another policeman, in plainclothes, just about breathing down my neck.

'You surprised me,' I said – though that must have been

obvious. Why is it that prominent, law-abiding, peaceful people like me get so twitchy when they go into a police station? It's not as if we have anything to fear or hide. The few previous contacts I'd had with the police in Mt Matheson and Rownley had always made me believe they were definitely on the side of people like me and the values I stood for. After all, I'd always supported the cause of law and order. Indeed, there had once been a time when a policeman merely had to discover who I was and he would've thought twice before daring to book me even for a parking offence. I'm not boasting or exaggerating, just recording a fact.

There was even the famous occasion when we got our first yellow lines in the gutters of the Rownley shopping centre. I didn't know what the bloody things were for, so I drove the Daimler into my usual illegal parking spot and Jim Barker, who was the very obliging Rownley sergeant, came up, looked in the window, saluted and went around behind the car to give me hand signals to help me back my outside wheels right over a strip of bright new yellow paint. Those were the days.

'Surprised?' the cop repeated and stared doubtfully, as if he was trying to work out whether there was something about me that was not quite on the level.

'Sitting like that, behind me,' I tried to explain, as patiently as I could. 'I didn't know you were there.'

'I'm always here, when I come over from Rownley,' he said, and shook his head slowly to indicate that I had to be either extraordinarily stupid or untrustworthy.

I didn't bother to reply, so he leaned back in his chair, tapped his biro on his desktop and asked loudly, 'It's my Mt Matheson desk. Why wouldn't I be here?'

It really was becoming a very silly example of talking at cross purposes, so I said with only the faintest edge of sarcasm, 'I expect I was just being conversational. It doesn't really matter.' And I got up to go.

'Hang on,' the plainclothes man said. Hanging on seemed to be one of their favourite expressions. 'Why were you being conversational about me sitting at my own desk? How's that?'

He glanced with big round eyes at the uniformed man, who now also shook his head. They looked and sounded like a couple of galoots at their little game, but how do you say that to the police – in their own territory, so to speak?

'I didn't make any comment at all about you sitting there,' I corrected. 'You seem to have got the wrong end of everything. I was merely enquiring as to the man's name. But don't bother. I expect I'll read it in the paper.'

Then I added, 'Anyway, since you've finished taking my statement, I'd like to go home.'

This made the plainclothes man smile very slightly and very briefly. He held his right arm out in front of me and opened the palm of his hand in a stop sign.

'What makes you think you know him?' he asked, all deadpan and ingenuous.

'I don't,' I said wearily. By now I must have spent almost two hours doing my public duty and helping the police, and these were all the thanks I got. A lot of playground hamming about, with weird looks and a touch of bullying. Just like schoolboys. It was all so obvious and tiresome. 'As a matter of fact I don't know him from Adam.'

What I meant to imply, of course, was that he'd been face down and pretty well camouflaged, but the way it must have sounded gave the dick his cue.

'How would you expect to?'

'How? What?' I said.

'Know him from Adam.'

'It's an expression,' I explained. 'Like doing your onion or getting as mad as a meat-axe.' For the first time I was beginning to feel very annoyed. I'd had quite enough and I didn't need to be pushed any further.

'Hold on to your walking frame,' the policeman said. 'All I was suggesting is how would you expect to know him from Adam when his face was battered to a pulp, his teeth were smashed out and every one of his fingers was chopped off? Even his own mother wouldn't know him, would she?'

There was a terrible silence in which, for a second or two, I simply couldn't breathe. Then I said, 'Oh God . . .' and couldn't think of another word to add.

4

There seemed to be a sudden, brief outburst of arguing, which I felt too tired to tune in to. Then I distinctly heard an excited and very authoritative voice asking what the hell everyone thought they were playing at.

This was followed by a silence, broken by the same voice which now announced flatly and firmly that there could be hell to pay unless they stopped pushing the old bastard around and got him home double-quick.

As I've already intimated, I'm usually pretty smart on the uptake. In fact, I pride myself on not having lost any of my marbles, but I swear that was the very first time it dawned on me that the police weren't just being oafish and obstreperous, but seemed to have something definite against me.

How silly could I get? I'd put their general behaviour down to the casual surly sloppiness of modern youth – more evidence of bad manners and a general breakdown in standards of public conduct – but it was actually a whole sight more sinister.

Something was definitely wonky with the way I'd been treated. Yet how could it have happened? All I'd done was find a body, report it – and now there was all this mysterious hostility. It didn't add up.

The whole experience had been humiliating, especially for a person of my seniority and considerable past standing in the community. So I'm not too proud to admit now that I was pretty confused when immediately afterwards I was taken out to a car and told once again to 'hop in'.

Hop? At my age?

For a while, in the back of the car, it even crossed my mind that I was not really being given a lift home at all. Indeed, it occurred to me that we may have been heading towards Rownley, across the harbour, for the driver took the long way round to my place instead of the connecting dog-leg across Fairbreeze Avenue.

I suppose that's why it took me quite a time to notice who I was travelling with. And that, too, was a surprise. There were three people in the car, besides myself. A driver in uniform and two others, both of whom wore extremely scruffy clothing.

One was a man, in a T-shirt, jeans and a brown leather jacket. He sat in the front, twiddling with a machine that I could only guess was some sort of computer. The other was a young blonde woman, who sat beside me in the back. She wore a pathetically short skirt, presumably to show off her skinny legs, and I thought at first she looked so waif-like and under-nourished that she must have been picked up for truancy and was being taken back to school. She was chewing gum, a moronic habit I detest.

It startled me when she tapped the shoulder of the plain-clothes man in front and said, 'Tell us again. What did you say this guy's name was, Tenky?'

The man called Tenky half-turned and replied, 'Gransey. Arthur Henry Gransey.'

'Huh,' was all the woman said. She went back to her munching and didn't even spare me a sideways glance.

Not so many years previously the mere sound of my name would have made her sit up, stop chewing and take notice. Every single soul in Rownley and Mt Matheson, without exception, responded to those syllables, most of them in pleasurable anticipation of favours and rewards, though a few may've been soiling their britches. The whole shooting match around here knew that Arthur Gransey was the man at the top.

Which gives me an opportunity to emphasise, for the benefit of those with failing memories, that I was often referred to – in my own hearing, and with a great deal of truth – as the king of this place. King Arthur of the Rownley table was the joke that tells you everything. After all, when I burst on the scene here, Rownley was a one-horse hick town at the end of the road to nowhere, and as for the general area under the shadow of Mt Matheson, just across the harbour, well, that was all farmland. A rural waste. It was me who set about transforming Rownley and Mt Matheson into the prize double-yolker of the goose that laid the golden eggs. I as good as made it all happen, through the good offices of Greater Gransey Holdings Ltd – or GGH as countless appreciative investors used to refer to the firm before it was not so much taken over as highjacked and devoured by Trupper's Enterprises.

Yet now, it seemed, I had become one of the great forgotten. Just another nobody. I was a hunk of ancient mould that some bit of a kid in the police force could talk across without adjusting her skirt to cover her knees or hooking the filthy wad of muck out of her mouth.

At the top of the drive I expected them to drop me off and go away, but the pair instructed the driver to bring me to the door, where they also insisted on what the young blonde called seeing me inside, 'Mister Dandly'.

What that turned out to be was, just as I thought, a good nosy around. They were like a couple of puppies, wandering about, sniffing here and there, not even pretending to conceal their interest in what my kitchen, downstairs living area and den looked like.

So far I had managed to keep my temper, but I was now back in my own territory and that made a big difference. I put the kettle on for a cup of tea and rather ostentatiously placed one cup and saucer on the kitchen table, rattling the china loudly. Second by second, I was getting more than just riled by everything that had happened – I was beginning to get very, very mad at the whole carry on, and I told myself that I'd wait only till I'd finished making the tea, after which

I'd order them to get the hell out of my home and, if that didn't work, I'd threaten them with Frank Pelley, my lawyer. I was building up into a proper explosive rage at last. I'd had enough.

It was pretty good timing. They left just before the kettle and I reached boiling point. Naturally, the anorexic blonde looked back over her shoulder and said, 'We'll be seein' ya, Mister Grandee.'

So when Nathan phoned about an hour later, I told him yes, I'd be at home and I would appreciate his coming around to see me far more than he would ever know. I definitely needed someone to talk to.

5

Nathan was my oldest and wisest friend. We had known each other for a long way past half a century – in fact, ever since we were twelve, when our paths met in the third form at Rownley High School. All through our school years we were constant companions, until Nathan had to leave, when his father died – in harness, so to speak – in the act of selling a one-way ticket to the end of the line from his little cubbyhole behind a wire grille at the old Rownley railway station, where the Flying Noodle Takeaway now stands.

The Labour Party had just come to power, strings of compassion were pulled, and Nathan walked in where they'd carried his father out, as an office boy in the Railways. It was a prized 'secure job for life' in the 1930s, when times were so tough there's no point in talking about them any more, for no one would ever believe you. Which is why, even though I chose subsequently to follow a different path and take my chances in the real world of property investment and development, I never blamed him for playing safe in the civil service. We knew, in those days, what life was all about.

Nathan had several long periods in various departments in Auckland and Wellington after he shifted sideways from the Railways and clambered up the civil service ladder to the top grades, but in between he managed to wangle some important postings in or near Rownley and we never lost touch.

Destiny, I suppose, is what most people would call it, though there were other factors. My first wife Belle was a distant cousin of his, he was godfather to my first child, Ralph, and I was godfather to his daughter Daphne. It was almost as if we were blood relations.

In fact, Ralph and Daphne had nearly got married at one stage many years ago, though both Nathan and I were extremely relieved when they didn't go through with the idea. The pair of them were bad enough news at the time without doubling the damage they could do us. The thought of it could still bring me out in a sweat years afterwards.

The best side of Nathan came out the instant he arrived. 'Look, before you tell me what's on your mind, Arthur,' he said, straight off, 'Just sit down for a minute and let me put a great thought to you.'

'A great thought?'

'I know I don't have many these days. But this one came to me right out of the blue as I drove over here – though I've a feeling it may have been lodged, unexpressed, just at the back of my mind, for a very long while indeed.'

I sat down and waited. It's a funny thing, but just having Nathan there made me feel quite a bit better.

'Good,' he went on. 'Now just spare me a moment to let me phrase this great thought in the form of a question. And I venture to say it's one you'll agree we both should have been asking ourselves some time ago.'

He waited for me to give some sort of little 'Hmmm' to show I was listening, then he went on, 'Have you ever asked yourself what's the point of us always sitting around conserving our resources, when we should be saying to hell with it, let's have a good time while we're still able to?'

I didn't know quite what to answer to that. I had no quarrel with the quiet satisfactions of retirement, except, perhaps, the isolation I had often experienced after Grace, my second wife, departed to wait for me on the Other Side. I led a fairly active life, walking, taking the occasional swim, gardening and so on. And I listened to the radio and looked through the papers, which meant I took a broad interest in people and events. What did he mean by talking about having a good time, anyway? Travel, bars, nightclubs, bowls, ballroom dancing? They'd never interested me. Never on your sweet life. A waste of precious money, time and energy. Trivial distractions from the business side of life, all of them.

But Nathan gave me what I'd always described as his quizzical look. He furrowed up his forehead, half-closed his eyes and attempted a crooked smile. It was a comical expression, though Grace never liked it. She said it made him look like a gnome, and he was too old and tricky to convince her on that score – except perhaps set in concrete, with a fishing rod, next to a goldfish pond. People often underestimated Grace. She was never outspoken, as Belle had been – and still is. Belle could be plain bloody crude, and a complete social liability when she felt like it, but Grace could be pretty sharp at times in her own subtle way.

'No comment?' he asked. 'Arthur, I've got to warn you. You're getting more and more like a civil servant each time I see you.'

I laughed for the first time that day and asked him what was on his mind.

'Well,' he said. 'Fact number one is that you've got an exceptional cellar. Fact number two is that we never seem to take time off to enjoy it. And fact number three is a point I've been meaning to put to you for the past three or four years – you ought to make a serious start soon on some of those Frog specials you've got rotting away down there.'

'Rotting away? *Rotting*?' I had to laugh again.

'For all you know, they could be turning to vinegar – or

corked. You should own up. You've become a shocking old miser. A wine hoarder.'

'What are you getting at? Would you like me to crack a bottle?' I asked. I had made it a fixed rule, all my working life, never to have a drink before five o'clock, and there seemed no good reason to change that in my retirement, so I suppose there could have been just a particle of truth in what he said. I guess I could have been seen as a hoarder, though the fact of the matter was I could seldom be bothered having a drink now I had all the opportunity in the world – after all, what was there to gain from getting shickered on my own? And it was far too late to educate my palate. My tastebuds had burnt out long ago.

But suddenly I got Nathan's point. I could think of a couple of good reasons for breaking every rule in existence. 'What are you suggesting?' I asked.

Nathan looked back at me with the bland stare of a cat that's got its eye on the gravy boat. He didn't need to say a word.

'A bordeaux? A burgundy?' I asked, laughing. 'You're welcome to a bottle of anything you like.'

'A whole bottle?' He opened his eyes theatrically. 'I don't know about that, but we could start with a couple of glasses.'

'You realise it won't have breathed?'

'Look at it this way, Arthur. So far as the breathing bit goes, we're still capable of doing that for ourselves. But if we let much more time go by, the only drinking we'll manage will be out of a medicine bottle.'

That was as much persuasion as I needed. I got up and fetched a bottle of Pomerol – well, a Latour–Pomerol actually – from the cellar, opened it and said, with what I admit was a slightly painful bravado, to hell with the experts, a little chill on the red wouldn't hurt us on a warm day like this.

Actually, I know damn all about the finer points of wine – but I certainly remember the basic drill and I am definitely incapable of ever forgetting what the labels cost.

So we sipped away, and slowly Nathan encouraged me to unload the burden of the whole dreadful saga of the mutilated corpse. And I also went on a bit about the odd and bloody rude behaviour of the police.

'I could tell you were upset straight away, as soon as I rang,' Nathan said quietly.

'Well, you were right, as usual, in these matters,' I said. 'The thing I can't get used to is the way I've always been a respectable sort of person. I've always abided by the laws of the land – or so near to them that it doesn't matter. I don't go around making a criminal nuisance of myself. In fact, as you very well know, the Rownley police used to treat me with a great deal of respect . . .'

'I'd call it *deference* – deference is the word I'd choose,' Nathan corrected.

'Yet the day I find a body on the beach,' I went on, 'I'm made to feel as though I'm somehow tainted by the crime. I feel . . . Well, I feel . . .'

'*Disillusioned,* Arthur?'

'Exactly,' I said. 'Disillusioned – grossly disillusioned. It's as if my own side had let me down.'

'And no one else in the family knows what's happened, I suppose?'

'Who would I be likely to tell? It's all been so bloody humiliating.'

'Well, there's . . .' He paused and gazed over his glass at me, swilling it gently and sniffing. Then he merely grinned sheepishly.

'Belle?' I said, looking straight back at him.

'You do get in touch still,' he reminded me.

'She rings and I answer. You know that as well as I do,' I told him. 'It's never the other way around.'

'Or James or Bruce. You could have rung them.'

'Where? At their offices? On a busy day?'

James and Bruce were outstanding boys. They were two of my three sons by Grace, and they made up, to a considerable extent, for the single rotten apple – their younger brother – whom I had been forced to cut down from the family tree. The boy whose name I had forbidden ever to be uttered in my house. The one who, by comparison, made Ralph look like a plaster Jesus.

'Or Deenie.'

Nathan was pushing things by bringing up the subject of Geraldine. She was Ralph's full sister, my only daughter – the girl I'd had by Belle.

'She's in Wellington,' I said, 'as you are well aware.'

Nathan raised his eyebrows and finished his glass before speaking. 'Oh dear, Arthur,' he said. 'It has turned out to be a bad day for you. That was the reason I rang you earlier, though with all the drama you've been through, I haven't so far been able to tell you. It was all to do with Deenie.'

'What about her? What's happened?' I asked – and felt my heart pounding harder and faster.

'A friend of mine swears he saw her across the harbour in Rownley yesterday.'

I looked carefully at him, but managed to hold my breath for a few seconds and say nothing.

'She didn't seem to see my friend, incidentally – and, in fact, he only recognised Deenie after she'd gone past. He said she had her hair done up differently and she was wearing sunglasses. She seemed to be making some sort of ineffectual attempt at disguising herself. But it was her all right, looking very swish. So, well . . . I thought I'd ask if you knew – and at least let you know, if you didn't.'

I refilled our glasses and we sat there in silence for a while. I tried to stop my mind from focusing on Deenie. It brought too much pain. Then, abruptly, Nathan told me that we were enjoying the pleasure of a most remarkable wine – 'glamorous' was the word he used for it: 'Not quite a Petrus, but good enough to hold its own with the rest of the region.'

That's when the memories stormed through me. There was no resisting them. I wasn't like this usually. I'd built up too many secret defences over the years. But I'd had one hell of a stressful day. On top of which, I'd had wine – and now there was all this talk about Deenie. It was all too much.

Trust Nathan to hit the button, I thought. The mention of

that word 'glamorous' simply did for me. It was the exact word for Deenie. Even taking into account, or perhaps because of, the small scar at the corner of her mouth. No wonder she'd been recognised. She had style and she had class. Deenie was good enough to hold her own with the most glamorous women on this or any other planet in the whole universe. She could never successfully hide herself away. You would pick her out anywhere. And it wasn't just a simple condition of beauty – she was clever, distinctive, intoxicating, magnetic.

I know I'm her father, and all that, but I'm speaking the truth. I would always love her more than the others. Even James and Bruce. There was no way I could help myself. Even in spite of her one terrible defect of character.

But I'm not just referring here to her disastrous choice of men. The fact of the matter was that Deenie had never been able to help herself. She was always her own undoing. She was more than just irresponsible. When it came to getting by in life, she was a danger to herself and to those around her. And here she was, back in town. Why hadn't she rung me?

6

Then Belle rang – which may sound a bit of a cheap joke, when it's put that way, but there's an undeniable precision to the words. As long as bells have clappers and Belle has a finger she can bang on the buttons of a phone, there will be no stopping them both from ringing. God knows how she would have got by in ages past, when there were no telephones. Shouted from the rooftops, I expect.

As soon as I heard her voice, I pressed the voice-standby button so Nathan could listen in to the conversation. I didn't want any dealings with Belle that could make me look or sound furtive. You had to come right out in the open with her, or she'd wrong-foot you every time.

'What've you done to the phone?' she shouted straight away. 'Your voice's gone all hollow. You sound like you're down a pit.'

'You can say that again,' I agreed, though she didn't pick me up on the point. She hardly ever paid attention to what anyone said, unless she could fit it into one of the grand designs in life she was currently working on.

'Never mind,' she shouted. 'The big news is that Deenie's back. Here in Rownley. I know because Rachael spotted her in town today and she told me the minute she saw her. So why didn't you ring to tell me, that's what I want to know? She always gets in touch with you.'

'Who? Rachael?'

'Don't try to bullshit with me, Arthur. I'm not some poor simple tart like that other wife of yours you worried and tormented into an early grave. You know what I bloody mean.'

'As a matter of fact, by sheer coincidence, I'd just heard a few moments ago that someone had seen her over on your side.'

'Oh yeah? Nathan, I expect.'

'In a sort of way . . . But how ever did you guess?'

'Don't try your pathetic sarcasm on me. It rolls right off,' she said. 'You two have been in cahoots since the cradle. I should know, shouldn't I? I've been trampled all over by the pair of you. With hobnails. I'm number one victim when it comes to you two, aren't I?'

'You were talking about Deenie,' I reminded her.

'You should be on *Mastermind* with a memory like that,' she snapped. 'In fact, now I think about it, the two of you should be in the movies, like Laurel and Hardy. You could do the Oliver Hardy bits and Nathan's the spitting image of that skinny little . . .'

'You mentioned Deenie,' I said patiently. 'You said someone saw her.'

'It was Rachael – Rachael Black. I've told you that once

already, haven't I? Or have you got amnesia? Alzheimers? Blenheimer's?'

'Blenheimer's?'

Belle laughed raucously. 'Yes, Blenheimer's – the cask wine, you old nitwit. It's a joke – Blenheimer's is a wine.'

'Very funny,' I said. 'And now you've got it off your chest, do you think we could get back to the subject of Deenie?'

'Oh my giddy Gawd,' she yelled. 'Have you really got completely untied in your top-knot? What else do you think I rang you up about, but Deenie? Haven't you listened to a single word I've been saying? Rachael Black saw Deenie right in the middle of Rownley. Deenie, our daughter . . . Remember her? Here, in Rownley . . . Savvy? Or do I have spell it out to you, letter by letter? And what I'd like to know, if you could spare me two minutes of your valuable time, King Bloody Arthur, is just what we're going to do with her. I thought she was safely out of the way in Wellington. Why did she pack up and leave this time?'

There was no point in arguing with the woman. On and off, I'd suffered half a century of this kind of babble. 'Clean the wax out of your ears, Belle,' was all I said. 'And listen for once in your life, will you? I'm telling you I haven't seen her. I haven't even spoken to her yet. And I've only just heard she was here, too. Have you got that?'

'Well, I want you to do something. You're her father.'

'Pay attention carefully, Belle, while I say it in words an infant should be able to understand. I haven't spoken to Deenie.'

There was a heavy sigh from the other end of the line. A very Belle-ish exasperated sound, which I'm probably doomed to recognise to my dying day. It's a sigh that seems to echo: Why doesn't the whole stupid world pull itself together and organise things the way I want them when I pick up the telephone?

Speaking very slowly and carefully, I went on, 'However, there's hardly any doubt she'll get in touch – when she feels she needs me. Which means when she needs a handout.'

There was a brief silence, then Belle shouted, 'Well, I think it's very odd that she hasn't got in touch with either of us. What's she up to? Is she hiding in shame or something?'

'Possibly. It wouldn't be the first time.'

'That's a nasty remark, coming from you of all people.'

'It's the truth. And, in any case, she really is hard to recognise apparently. Nathan's friend – the one who spotted her – had to take a second squizz before he was sure it was her.'

'That's what Rachael said. She thought Deenie was in disguise. That's not like her. She's never gone incognito before. She loves everyone to know who she is.'

'She may have changed hairdressers.'

'Is that a joke?'

'Look Belle, I'm worried too. It's not like her not to get in touch. It's a mystery to me why she's here and keeping her distance.'

'I wish you didn't sound like you're speaking from inside a coffin,' she protested. 'You should ring Telecom and have them check your line. There's something wrong with it.'

'Thank you, Belle. You've made my day. First a body on Ocean Beach, then Deenie's sighted, and now you're telling me I'm speaking from a box in the ground – that's all I need.'

'A body?' she yelled excitedly. 'Did you say a body – on Ocean Beach?'

'I'm surprised you listened.'

'That must be the one on the radio. I heard about it on the news.'

'I wish that's as near as I'd got to it.'

At last I had her attention, though it had taken a corpse to work the trick.

'Did you really see it?' she shouted. 'The body? God, that must've been a turn up for the books. You ought to go out and buy a Lotto ticket. Why didn't you tell me before? Who was it, Arthur? The radio said it was unidentified.'

'If it was unidentified, then how would I be expected to know who it was? Anyway, someone had gone to a lot of trouble so it wouldn't be recognised.'

'What do you mean? What on earth are you talking about?'

'It was a Jack the Ripper job from the sound of it. The fingers were torn off, the teeth were hammered out and the face was mushed up – like a suet pudding, I expect. That's what I *mean*, Belle.'

I heard what sounded like a hiccup on the other end of the line. Then Belle got her breath back. 'That's disgusting, Arthur,' she yelled. 'I'm sorry I rang you. You always were a dirty little bastard. You should be fined for talking filth like that over a public telephone.'

'It's a private one.'

Belle's phone went click, though I could have laid a safe bet that she had tried to make me jump by slamming it down. It would never have occurred to her that I couldn't hear the thump it made at her end.

'More wine?' I asked Nathan as I poured, gripping the bottle in both hands so I wouldn't shake the contents all over the table. Nathan didn't move a muscle in reply; he just stared ahead, grinning smugly.

After a few seconds he picked up his glass and took a sip. 'It gets better with every drop. We must do more of this. Your cellar deserves it,' he said.

Then his expression became serious. 'Now tell me, Arthur. What in God's name did we ever see in that woman? I mean, we must have come pretty close to murdering each other over her. I definitely had homicidal thoughts about you. Gruesome ones. For just a few weeks, of course – until I realised that if anyone ought to be put down it was Belle.'

'There was capital punishment at the time. At the very least, she could have got one of us – perhaps both of us – put away for a very long time,' I agreed. 'They'd have had us cracking rocks all the prime years of our lives.'

'Amazing what they can do to you when you're young,' Nathan said, grinning once more. 'At least we're over that, thank God.'

'I wonder,' I said. 'I wonder if we ever really recover . . .'

'Oh, yes,' he replied. 'Oh, very definitely yes. We've been

through all that long ago, and we've come out the other side very nicely, thank you. We're not going to let ourselves ever get stirred up over a bit of skirt again.'

But I didn't mean Nathan and me. I was thinking of Geraldine – my little Deenie. I wondered if that went for her too – that now I had advanced so far into the realms of age and understanding I'd draw a line at the extreme edges of reason when it came to the things I'd still do for her.

7

When Nathan left, just after four, I went upstairs to the master bedroom and had a nap. The wine had drugged me pleasantly and I had a deep blissful dreamless rest – for a change. Sleep usually comes fitfully these days, full of bizarre conjunctions of the imagination, and racked with aches in the marrow of my bones, prolonged coughing fits, plus bladder and other problems. So it was like a gift. I felt stunned with the pure pleasure of it.

But when I woke it was a huge effort to get up from the bed again. For ten or fifteen minutes I must have lain there on my back, half sitting up on a stack of pillows, trying not to worry about Deenie or puzzle at the weird behaviour of the police or dwell on images of mutilated corpses being thrown up on the beach just down the road.

I forced myself to stare out of the landscape window, across the sand dunes to the sea and the horizon, then I turned back to contemplate the massive, unavoidable lump of Mount Matheson, which gave the whole area its name. The Mount glowed in the afternoon sun at the end of the peninsula like a giant golden syrup pudding. In certain lights, and especially late in the day, it seemed to swell and loom right over the settlement at its feet. It sometimes appeared to be so close that you could hurl a stone at it from my place and clock it right in the middle – though it must have been almost half a mile distant.

The house I live in is right on the spot from which Nathan and I often used to set out shooting rabbits when we were boys. We used to come across from Rownley on the launch, which was the usual way of getting to Mt Matheson before the bridge was built that now connects the two sides of the long meandering upper reaches of the harbour. We'd rig up a ridgepole, throw a piece of tarpaulin over it, wrap ourselves in blankets or giant-sized pollard bags stuffed with screwed-up newspapers – no sleeping bags in those days – then get up at the crack of dawn with our single-shot BSA twenty-twos and sneak along the fencelines for miles between the farms and the dunes picking off the furry little buggers.

Rabbits had the run of Mt Matheson in those days. They were all over the place – hundreds of them everywhere. Mt Matheson was part-farmland, part-wilderness and an absolute boys' paradise. Funny how in one lifetime it could change from a sprinkling of farmhouses, a few holiday baches, a camping ground and a single general store that only opened its shutters in summer into the most desirable and expensive stretch of sea-enclosed suburban living anywhere south of Auckland.

I can actually claim to have led the march of history that transformed every square inch of the territory around me. There's nothing old as far as the eye can see. The streets, houses, lawns and gardens of Mt Matheson have all appeared, as if by a magic wand, in the past half-century. It's all brand spanking new and almost every feature of the old derelict landscape is now perfectly manicured – though it's a pity that not all the people who visit the district are aware of the civilising change that people like me have wrought. A lot of them, especially some of the bludging long-haired greasy degenerates on their motorbikes, don't want to live up to our bold self-made image.

The house I live in is built on what the estate agents call a

34

commanding site, and its design is one of the most impressive on this side of the harbour, inside and out. Some years ago, when Grace was here to care about such things, it even featured in *House and Garden* and a couple of other top national magazines.

Of course, it has become quite expensive to maintain, but I built it to fulfil a dream, and I love the place. It has five upstairs bedrooms, two with en-suite bathrooms, plus one separate bathroom. And downstairs there is a generously proportioned open living area, which leads into a dining alcove – both of which I hardly ever go into now – and a wonderful roomy kitchen.

There are also the usual laundry amenities, plus a small back room which Grace and I used to call the sewing room, because it was where she kept the sewing machine that was hardly ever used from the day I bought it for her. She had no need to. After all, the wife of Arthur Gransey could easily afford the services of a dressmaker.

But the main downstairs feature is a large central den, which has always been my own private territory. Even Grace seldom intruded there, and she would never have thought of entering without knocking.

The den is the soul of the place, so far as I'm concerned. With its wood-panelled walls and ceiling, stone fireplace and breastwork, and its slate floor, it's a bit like a cross between an executive office and a country club. It holds a full-sized billiard-table, surrounded by leather chairs and sofas. And between the bar and a large roll-top desk, there's a door that leads off to the cellar. I use the kitchen and den throughout the day. I virtually live in them.

Outside, there are all the expected facilities, including a long split-level patio, with raised flowerbeds and a barbecue. There's also a swimming pool, gazebo and a quarter of an acre of garden front and back, and I can park three cars in the garage without a squeeze.

Several people, including James and Bruce – increasingly – have hinted that I don't really need it all. And I have no trouble admitting that they're right. But the short answer I always rely on to knock their argument over is to say that my house is my castle. It is the definitive statement I make about myself. The symbol of my achievements. It bears witness to my life's triumphs and exploits – and God knows, enough people seem otherwise to have forgotten them.

What also goes almost without saying is this: there is another huge benefit in owning a large house, for a man like me. I am permanently occupied, tidying up and looking after the gardens and so on. It gives me something to do in my retirement. It's more than just a job – it provides me with a creative sense of purpose.

Though now that I write those words, after all the crazy and bewildering events that occurred in the days that followed my finding of the body on the beach, I will make no secret of the realisation that it does amount to a bit of a comedown. Here I am, at the age of seventy-five, more or less hale and hearty, still alert, yet not all that much different in my real situation in life to John and Elsie Luckham, who can't afford the property prices in Mt Matheson-proper, and who catch a bus from three or four miles away twice a week to help with the garden and tidying up the house.

It has even struck me recently as a curiosity of existence that after the extraordinary life I've led, I seem to have ended up as nothing more than a kind of exalted handyman-gardener. A kind of senior potterer. A fulltime dithering, if pretty well-heeled, nobody. Someone the police feel free to treat like an old idiot, push around and call Fred.

As I've said already, and will probably say again, I'd been what you might could call boss dog in Rownley. And that was a mere ten or so years ago. Top of the dung heap, as Deenie liked to put it. She has always had a crude side to her, which she has obviously inherited from Belle, that contrasts oddly with those pale-blue innocent eyes and long sleepy lashes and the delicate moulding of her mouth.

I too can call a spade a spade – or a bloody shovel, if need be. But I'm not talking about Deenie's hard-punching language and the occasional swear word she uses so effectively. What I'm getting at is a kind of mutilation of character – a way of talking that suddenly makes you wince.

It's a bit like the scar on her face, the physical impairment that blazes in a thin rip of white, which begins at the left of her upper lip, just as it comes in at the corner, then runs in a jagged line like a miniature bolt of lightning for a few centimetres across the lower cheek. When she uses make-up, it's almost impossible to see, then suddenly you get a tiny flash of it, when she smiles. It's ugly and it can make you shudder, but it's hypnotic and beautiful at the same time.

Ralph, too, has always carried a defect. In fact, I have to admit that both my children by Belle turned out strangely.

There Ralph was, marvellously proportioned, handsome, chiselled out like one of those marble statues I saw when Grace and I did our big OE trip around Europe – and a bit of a lady-killer, so I'm ashamed to acknowledge – yet, inside it all, as rough as guts. No style, no refinements of character, no redeeming qualities that I had ever noticed. I had come to think of Ralph, whenever I could be bothered to make the effort, as a no-hoper, a wastrel, a drunkard and a yobbo.

I've forgotten the exact date of his birth, but Ralph must be just about knocking on fifty, yet despite the way he has abused his body he usually looks a good deal younger, depending on how much he's had to drink. Deenie, who is five years his junior, was spot-on when she once described her brother to me as a middle-aged juvenile delinquent. And that's a phrase – juvenile delinquent – that you don't hear much any more. There's so many of them about that no one bothers to make the distinction.

I have no trouble in agreeing that Ralph and she got their good looks – as well as the strange twists to their personalities – from Belle. I wouldn't deny that I may appear to some as an ugly little bastard, though I'm definitely no tub-of-guts. I bear no resemblance whatsoever to Oliver Hardy, as Belle suggested over the telephone. I go to a lot of trouble to keep myself firm and trim.

The truth is that Belle was a real knock-out, right up to her fifties, and the few times I've seen her recently haven't changed my opinion that she's still got an impressive presence, despite the ridiculous blue rinse. When I was in my early twenties she only had to turn her switches on and she blinded me. I would have done anything for her. I was her slave. I discovered I would even have killed for her, when she and Nathan had their affair.

It was totally different with Grace. She was everything that Belle could never be. Grace was quiet yet amusing; a bit on the plain side, certainly, but kind and thoughtful and companionable. She supported me in everything I did, and she was a great organiser and comforter. She got me through what could have been a very messy divorce with Belle, smoothly and painlessly, and though I wouldn't exactly say I loved her in the way I had once loved Belle, I was truly, deeply fond of her. She was a real friend, an ideal old-fashioned stay-at-home New Zealand housewife – modest, agreeable, supportive of her husband and a wonderful mother.

Look at the way James and Bruce turned out. Both of them are a glowing testimonial to Grace. Not quite forty and they're right at the top, James in Auckland and Bruce in Christchurch. And even though I did help them get started and provided the financial base to underpin them, they put their own brains and abilities to work, and achieved the rest. I didn't do it for them. They just made up their minds and went for it. The credit is theirs.

That Grace was so suddenly snatched away from the three of us was something I still think about often. You don't get over a thing like that. The loss is there forever.

Cancer is a strange disease. So little is known about it, though it strikes down thousands every year, but I can't help feeling that there's a psychological factor in its onset, a mental trigger that sets it off. And, in Grace's case, I have always laid the blame for that entirely with our third child, the one I came to think of as rotten to the core, a piece of human filth who contaminated everyone and everything around him.

I didn't have scientific evidence, but I acquired a certainty in my bones that it was the monster we had bred who brought cancer into our house. I was convinced there just had to be a connection. The way I saw it, he killed his own mother.

I couldn't help going over all these things for the umpteen-hundredth time as I lay there on my bed in the late afternoon of the day I found the body on the beach – just before all hell broke loose – unsuccessfully willing myself to get up. Then the phone rang again.

It turned out to be a call from Radio R, our local commercial station. But I was too quick for them. They never had a chance.

'I have a considerable shareholding in your company,' I said, without messing about with preliminaries, 'so if you don't bugger off I'll see you get the sack. Got that?' And I lowered the phone with considerable satisfaction.

The pleasure lasted a few minutes, then the bloody phone went again. 'Is that Mister Gransey?' a voice said.

'Yes,' I replied.

'Arthur Gransey?'

'Yes.'

'This is the *Rownley Echo*. I'd just like to ask a few questions about the corpse on Ocean Beach. I believe you were the first to the scene and I'd like you to describe in your own words how . . .'

After the voice from the radio comes the bloody *Echo* . . .

Had they forgotten, in the dream world these little scumbags inhabit, that only a few years ago it was me who made the biggest echo in Rownley? A bloody newsrag would never have *dared* ring me up in this way. I'd have had the toe of the editor's boot applied to the reporter's arse before he'd had time to put the phone down.

This time I got really mad. 'Listen, young man,' I bawled. 'As far as I'm concerned, you can drop your britches and shove your *Echo* right back where it came from.' And I slammed the phone down.

Then I thought about what I'd just said.

'Oh, no,' I groaned to myself. 'Just like Belle. Slamming down the telephone. I'm getting just like her.'

And I had to laugh at what a silly old bastard that made me.

8

It was the last time I was to laugh that day. When I got downstairs I looked from the door of the kitchen out across the patio to my sun sofa and saw the unmistakable shape of Ralph gazing back at me. There he was, as bold as a young buck on the bash, stretched out full length, in jandals, mottled jeans and a garish long-sleeved beach shirt – all fifty years of him, give or take.

On the table within close reach was a bottle of Glenmoranjie. And he held a cigar in one hand and a glass in the other.

'Cheers, daddy-o,' he said, blowing out a doughnut-sized smoke ring.

'That's my whisky,' was all I could think of to say. 'How did you get in?'

Another plump and perfectly shaped smoke ring followed, then he said, 'The man who sells the tickets must have left the zoo gates wide open. So I waltzed in and saw you taking your afternoon nap . . .'

'You just walked in? You went upstairs? Here, in my house? You saw me asleep?'

'Like a little babe, tucked up in your cot. Far away in the Land of Nod.'

'You could have been . . .'

Ralph shook his head in mock solemnity. 'Yes, daddy-o. It doesn't bear thinking about, does it? I could have been one of your local villains, rascals, miscreants or felons, couldn't I?' He smiled at me and wiped a hand back through his curls, just as Belle used to when she was young and putting pressure on me to do her a favour or buy something expensive for her.

'Or a cold-blooded psychopathic killer, with a crazed hang-up about the rich old bastards of Mt Matheson,' he added. 'Just as well I'm your average normal product of your average normal family, isn't it?'

'You had no right to . . .'

He shook his head again. 'Oh, climb down off the bloody ceiling will you. Of course I've bloody got the right. I'm your son. The door was open. No one answered when I called out. You could have had a heart attack or choked on your own vomit or any bloody thing. Were you pissed or something? There's an empty wine bottle on the coffee table in the den.'

'You went in there too?'

'Naw,' he said in a lazy drawl. 'I just dreamed it up. I've got this weird imagination I inherited from me dad.'

'Well, you can put down your father's whisky right this minute and clear the hell out of here. We've been through this sort of thing before and I'm not standing for any more of it. Have you got that?'

'You're a senile old fart and a feeble bloody fool,' he said with a sigh. 'You shouldn't be living in a place this big. Do you ever think about it? It's like the Sheraton-bloody-Hotel. There must be rooms in this place you never go into from one year's end to another. Apart from the fact that it's a gross indecency for one rich old capitalist to own so much of the world's wealth, you're becoming a liability to us all – and I really mean it. The way you left the whole place wide open while you went upstairs to bed makes you a danger to yourself, do you know that?'

'Get out,' I said.

'Mt Matheson happens to be a high crime area,' he replied, without moving. 'Has no one ever bothered to tell you? All these rottweilers and alsatians and burglar alarms and brick fences and thorn hedges don't mean a thing to the pros. What they see is posh houses full of blow-in doddering arseholes, who've sold up their farms or their businesses and don't know each other, and care even less, because they've only ever learned to look after Number One. It's the perfect place for pickings. Do you realise there's carloads of thieves cruising through here every day on the lookout for places like this?'

I couldn't help telling him, 'You ought to know all about that.'

'Now, now, daddy-o. Don't make me get on the blower to Jamie-boy or Brucie-boy. In five minutes flat they'll swoop down from the skies in one of their executive jets and they'll whistle you straight off to an old people's home where they'll take you to your cell, knock you out with forget-me tablets, lock the door and throw the key away. They'd get a really big sense of achievement out of doing it to you, too − have you ever thought of that? They'd love to pay you back that way for everything you've done for them.'

'Get out,' I repeated.

'I'll go,' he said, 'when I'm ready to go, dad. And not a minute sooner. Because what I've come for is some information.'

'I'm not telling you anything, except get out.'

'Oh yes you will.'

The way he lay there, so handsome and so full of himself, and so pathetically flawed, filled me with rage. It was unfair that Ralph had turned out like this. I had adored him when he was a very little boy. He had been like an angel, with his smiles and dimples and curls.

So what had happened? How could all that wonder and male beauty have been so wasted and corrupted? It was as though a demon had got into him. He was a lost soul. In spite of my own scepticism, I had really begun to believe he was possessed by the forces of darkness.

Ralph flicked a long solid tube of ash onto the patio tiles. He knew how I would hate that single insolent gesture more than anything he had so far said − and how I would boil up inside and long to hit him.

With a yawn he went on, 'It's actually about that poor

waterlogged prick they say you tripped over down on the beach. I want to know about him.'

'Get out,' I said for the umpteenth time.

'Nope,' he replied, helping himself to more of my single malt. 'Not any more, daddy dear. We're going to have a proper little question and answer session for the first time in our lives. We don't have any option, and there's going to be no bullshitting.'

'I'm calling the police,' I threatened. And I was serious.

'Go ahead.'

I went towards the phone, just inside the kitchen door, determined to get rid of him even if I had to have him marched off in handcuffs, but before I could get there Ralph added, 'Deenie wants to know, too. She's very interested in corpses is Deenie. Bloody morbid of her, don't you think?'

'You bastard.'

'You're wrong there, too. You know only too bloody well I've got a full hand of fair-dinkum birth and baptism certificates. I was conceived and born in holy wedlock. I've counted the months on the fingers of both hands and I can prove I'm your real kosher legitimate little Rownley high achiever.'

That was a typical stupid Ralph remark. Thought he was being a smart-alec, as usual, with his puerile drivel, while all the time he was showing what a stunted little kid he was inside.

As he watched me glare at him and seethe, Ralph lowered one leg from the sofa, but not to get off. He just set himself swinging slowly backwards and forwards. If I'd been thirty or forty years younger I'd have dragged him off the cushions and knocked him to the ground.

'Okay,' I said, when I'd steadied myself. 'You've made me curious. But you can stop acting the maggot. You've got exactly one minute to put that glass down and get your arse off my patio furniture and explain to me what you're getting at about Deenie. Then you're on your way again.'

'Thought you'd come around, father dear,' Ralph said, taking a long sip at his glass, then blowing yet another perfect smoke ring. 'Deenie's right in it this time . . .'

His voice paused for a moment. He knew how to get at me through Deenie, and he really enjoyed making me wait and watching me suffer.

'Yes, she's right in it, is our Deenie . . . Right in it up to here . . .' The hand that held the cigar made a languid little wave in the air above him. 'Now what about we plot a raid on the pantry and devour a spot of sustenance while we try to catch up on recent events involving dead bodies. I'm bloody starving.'

I looked at my watch. I usually ate at about seven-thirty or eight, and now it was only a quarter past six. Children felt hungry at that hour, not grown men of fifty. It tells you quite a lot about the person Ralph was deep down inside, doesn't it?

9

Ralph and I had shared a meal? Fifteen years? Twenty? The last time I'd even let him step inside the house for a few minutes would have been round about five years previously, when I'd listened to his latest pathetic plea for capital, just after Grace had passed on.

He had put the acid on me for a loan when he thought, wrongly, I'd be at my most vulnerable. I've forgotten the exact details of that latest miserable little flea-bitten scheme. But you can bet it would have been something along the lines of taking up a door-to-door franchise for washing powder, or buying into a no-hope rotten firewood deal, or leasing a corner section to flog second-hand engine parts or stolen surfboards.

I could picture him among all those garish pennants and balloons and whirling plastic propellers. Small-time was Ralph all over, despite the huffing and puffing and big-talk. When it came to business ambition, he had neither the savvy nor the imagination to think past earning a fast buck to splash out on a beer and a pie for his next lunch.

When Belle and I parted, not long after Deenie was born in 1951, naturally she held on to Ralph and Deenie. I also made sure she kept the house in Rownley where we had lived, plus a regular fixed maintenance payment while the children needed help with their upbringing. If I say so myself – and I do – it was a generous settlement, considering her betrayals.

But I took damned careful precautions to see Belle had no financial comeback at me as I went about achieving my plans and ambitions in the Rownley business world. And I also made sure she couldn't snoop or get to me while I started a new family with Grace. I bought Smoyle's farm, which was right at the back of Ocean Beach, at Mt Matheson – a move that turned out to be not just a good way of putting a safe distance between myself and the past, but a brilliant stroke propertywise and moneywise, even if I say so myself.

Any mug should have been able to see that a bridge was going to have to be built to connect the two sides of the harbour, and then there'd be a bonanza in sub-divisions that would be like striking a vein of pure platinum. It was staring everyone in the face and the amazing thing was so very few people could pick it out.

Ralph used to come across on the launch to Mt Matheson with Deenie on weekend visits – once a month, at first – but when Grace had James and Bruce in quick succession, followed by the third one, who was such a grizzly little piss-a-bed that it's no wonder he turned out to be a creature who seemed not to be of our flesh and blood, all that had to stop. Instead, I applied a lot of ingenuity to make time for Deenie, but I could only manage to see Ralph for the odd week once or twice a year during school holidays.

Yet I can never justly be accused of having neglected him as a boy. As time went by, I can honestly claim to have gone miles out of my way to offer Ralph an opportunity to tag along with Grace, myself, Deenie and his half-brothers to our bach at Taupo, whenever I could afford the time to give him proper attention.

I suppose that's when I began to notice that somehow Ralph wasn't growing up on the straight and narrow. It was hard for me to put my finger on it at first, because, of course, I was forever rushing around here, there and everywhere, frantically building up the firm.

Rownley was like a frontier town in those days. I have heard Aucklanders in the know refer to the place as Dodge City, and they had a point. If you had the cheek and you could create the merest impression of wealth you could set your sights on anything or anyone around here you wanted. Yet it seemed on the surface like Sleepy Hollow. The streets were neat and tidy, the mayor of Rownley, so help me God, was a corner-shop grocer, the churches were chocka all day on Sunday, the sergeant of police rode around on a pushbike and people with money and the very highest standards of decency were starting to move into the district because they knew they could retire here in respectability.

All this was a valid picture of the place, but it was only half the truth. Underneath the placid reassuring calm, and behind the lace curtains, good manners and hand-shaking, Rownley was actually jumping. The stakes were high, there were fortunes to be made and there was no rulebook. You could shoot the lights out in the streets – provided you had nerve, you wore a three-piece suit and a dark blue tie, and you never forgot to raise your hat to a lady while keeping your arse well covered.

Rownley was wide open and I suppose you could say I rode right through it, flashing a smile, looking a bit of a dude perhaps – but blazing away with both barrels.

It kept me so busy I had to be half-awake even when I slept, in case some crooked bastard was trying to creep up on me – so how the hell could I have been expected to keep an eye on a small boy with the devil in him, when I only had control of him for a few days of the year? Ralph was Belle's responsibility, absolutely and entirely.

Even if I was willing to accept some of the blame – which I'm certainly not – the trouble was there was no early incident that provoked a crisis, just a whole lot of little shocks, minor things. Like the occasion at Taupo when I picked up Ralph's clothes.

He was asleep and I found he had a little embroidered bag in one of his pants pockets. It was stuffed under a snotty handkerchief and it was the bag that Grace kept spare change in. It was empty, of course, and when I bent over the boy and sniffed I could smell tobacco on his breath and in his hair.

Eventually I did come to recognise the unavoidable fact that Ralph was growing up to be nothing but a sneak and a liar. But I kept it private for far too long, and when I finally got around to talking to Belle about it, she said it was only a stage that all boys went through, and they always grew out of it.

I do have to admit that I blame myself now for going along with Belle – but, as I said, I had my nose to the grindstone at the time, she was directly in charge of the boy, and it was simply easier to accept what she said and leave the problem for the years to sort out.

Then Belle rang me one afternoon and said I had to come down to the police station with her. They wanted to talk to us about a spate of car conversions in which Ralph was involved, along with a lot of the worst street scum in Rownley.

It turned out that Jim Barker had had his eye on Ralph for a few months without being able to nail him, as he put it. But since in those days the Rownley police knew exactly who I was and treated me with the respect that was due to a person of my standing, he let it be known off the cuff that if I felt I was in a position to do something positive about the boy he'd allow me every opportunity to deal with him before the courts got their hooks into him.

It wasn't a pleasant interview for someone like me to have to go through, but I took the hint. Given the strict public values of the time – as opposed to the private ones – there is absolutely no doubt that if I'd let the matter get further out of hand it would almost certainly have damaged me in business. Civic rectitude was one of the names of the game I was involved in.

Ralph was seventeen at the time, so I plucked him out of his final year at Rownley High School and the very next day flew him straight over to Sydney, then up by train to Brisbane. The boy needed discipline and, though Belle bitched blue murder and screamed at me, I wasn't having any more messing about. So off he went like shit from a goose.

I'd established some useful connections in Oz and one of them was able to place him right out of harm's way on a station in central Queensland. And things came within an ace of working out for the best.

Ralph was always a natural with animals. Dogs, cats, horses – he could communicate with them as though he spoke their language. Alsatians, for instance. Ralph could go right up to them, and even though they'd bristle and snarl and show him a jawful of fangs, they'd never go for him. He'd talk to them and they'd avoid his eyes, growl a bit, then quieten down. It was a remarkable thing to witness.

What went wrong in Queensland was the old, old story – temptation. He got some woman in the family way, when he'd been keeping a perfectly clean record for a whole six years, and just at the time he'd marked himself out to move on to bigger things. Ralph would have become a manager. He was a certainty. With his abilities he could easily have ended up taking on his own station. He had genuine prospects and I may very well have invested in him myself.

The trouble was the woman who tempted him was married already, though she was living apart from her husband, and it just so happened that he was some kind of manic-depressive prize nutcase. So, when this bastard found out about his wife being full of arms and legs that Ralph had planted in her he got drunk and blew her brains all over the kitchen wall, then turned the gun on himself.

That's why I didn't blame Ralph at first for slipping downhill again. It was a terrible thing to have happened, especially at that age. And when I later discussed the whole thing with Nathan he tried to convince me that it must have traumatised the boy. But in the end I couldn't abide the bullshit. What burnt me up was that Ralph just caved in without resisting. He should have shown more backbone and put up a fight for his soul.

Willpower and integrity were the missing ingredients in his nature. He never had an ounce of either in him.

Then, when he eventually drifted back to Rownley – to borrow money, of course – I couldn't give him the time he needed. I was the hardest working man in town. I had to slave at my business twenty-five hours a day, and on top of all that I had the responsibility of Grace and a young family, including the one I eventually came to think of as a scumbag sent by Satan to blight my life. Besides which, Deenie was beginning to give me nightmares.

By this time I'd become very involved in Deenie's problems, and for good reason. Let me remind the world again that, if I say I loved Ralph as a tiny tot, and if I also say that James and Bruce soon turned out to be the pride of my life, I'd also have to admit that I've never given my secret self to a child as I did to Deenie.

Even though I wasn't able to see as much of her as I wanted to, I thought of her every day. That's no exaggeration. Often, when I was overstrained and overworked and overtired, and just about stretched to breaking point, I'd think privately of Deenie, and I'd pull myself together and commit myself to her and the future.

It wasn't just the fact that she was my only daughter, she represented everything that was beautiful about the world. She was my secret symbol of love. A magic talisman.

She was small and delicate-looking and pretty – and she had this glowing presence that used to mystify me and send me into . . . Well, raptures is a corny word when you write it down, but it conveys the general idea.

Yet, with everything in the wide world going for her, why was it that she had to take trips down to the gutter to find her men? She could have crooked her little finger and had the pick of Rownley, Auckland, Sydney, London, the whole of Planet Earth . . . She was more than beautiful, she was radiant. She would light up and make you feel warm and good to be near her. Belle had the same gift to some extent, but Deenie had it a hundred times over. She was queen of the universe. She could have been a goddess.

So, suddenly here I was again, just as if nothing had happened, eating vegetarian lasagne I'd heated in the microwave, and sitting across the table from Ralph, even though I'd ordered him off the doorstep several times that day – and on at least two or three other occasions over the previous few years.

I was trapped yet again by the mention of Deenie. Ralph knew he only had to dangle her in front of me like bait and he'd hook me like a silly big fish.

You never escape from children. They're always there. They can come back to haunt you even in your dreams.

10

'You ought to be looking after yourself a bloody sight better than this,' Ralph told me, taking such an obvious gloating pleasure in the way he was turning the tables and offering me advice for a change, that I had to turn away from him for a while to cool off.

'It's no good buying all this crap you've got in the freezer and whacking it full of microwaves,' he said. 'You should be bulldozing your way through big juicy inch-thick T-bone steaks. Why don't you fire-up that bloody great barbecue you've got rusting away outside? It's the size of a church organ, and it doesn't look or smell as if it's been used in years. And it's not as if you can't afford to eat off the fat of the land. What a bloody awful waste. These are perfect evenings for a barbie . . . Slab or two of the arse-end of a steer or a couple of hogget chops in one hand, and a foaming glass of turps in the other . . .'

Trust Ralph to recommend dietary tips from his days on the station beyond the black stump. 'That crap, as you call it,' I couldn't help answering, even though I knew it was not only a waste of time, but I'd be giving Ralph more ammunition to use against me, 'costs a bomb in the Mt Matheson health food shop. Grace put me onto it and, God knows, it has probably saved my life.'

'Didn't save hers,' he said.

I ignored the crass insensitivity of the remark, and went on, 'It's made out of one hundred percent natural ingredients. The cheese is fat reduced and the meat isn't real, it's made from some sort of beans. Soya, I think.'

Ralph snorted at me. 'How in buggery can you make meat out of beans?' he asked mock-seriously, so I knew one of his feeble jokes was coming. 'Or did you say *beings*? Don't tell me we're eating human beans? Geddit? Human beings – human beans?'

'Ha, ha – see how you've amused me,' I said angrily. Then I took a deep breath and went on as patiently as I could manage. I was determined to talk some clear thinking into him, for my own sense of dignity as much as anything. 'It's actually quite a miracle of technology, making this stuff. It goes through a complex knitting process to create an imitation meaty texture. And it happens to be very good for you. Grace studied the whole subject thoroughly.'

Ralph spluttered, then roared with laughter. 'Christ Almighty, dad. Knitted soya beans,' he said. 'I've heard everything now. Have you seen the way the milk factories are selling skimmed-dick in the dairies – when you know as good as me it's nothing but pigfood? Once upon a time the cockies couldn't give skimmed-dick away. They used to tip it down the creeks and poison the poor bloody eels. Now they've got the effrontery to put it in the same refrigerator as real milk and charge you the same fuckin' price. The world's gone bloody dippy.'

'Milk is actually good for you, without all that cream,' I said.

''Good for you? Good? How the hell can bloody pigfood be good for you?'

'Well, it seemed to be good for the pigs.'

Ralph stopped laughing and shook his head sadly at me. 'That's exactly what I've been telling you, if only you'd listen, daddy-o — it's good for the pigs. And it's the bloody consumers that're being swindled. Do you know, the cheeky bastards are flogging off all sorts of gutless food you wouldn't read about? Cheeseless cheese. Milkless milk. Meatless meat. It's unreal — but it's bloody fascinating, the way they always ask you to part with real money for it, isn't it? They won't take moneyless money, will they? I thought something was up with that grub you threw on my plate, besides coming out of a homemade paper wrapper, without a proper plastic packet. It's got no taste, no nourishment, no fuel power, nothing. That crap goes in one end and out the other, and there's no difference you can notice. It never sticks to your ribs. What are you up to? Are you really trying to avoid dying? Or are you seriously trying to kill yourself through boredom and misery?'

His cheeks were flushed now with the whisky and his eyes were going watery. It occurred to me that at fifty the good looks that had got him into so much trouble wouldn't last him more than a year or two longer. His face was sagging as if it was beginning to melt off his skull. I noticed, too, that his temples had a liberal dusting of grey. If that didn't have him worried already every time he looked in a mirror, it soon would.

'And as for knitted meatless meat, that takes the bloody biscuit . . .'

He stopped to laugh again, then wiped his mouth disgustingly on his sleeve. If he'd still been a boy I would have clipped him around the ear for that. 'Just think. If only I'd rung up before I dropped in on you, I could've brought my knitting needles and we could have purled and plained some tucker for tomorrow.'

I wasn't standing for any more of his half-drunken babble, so I changed the subject back to the real issues.

'Geraldine,' I said to him. 'That's the only excuse you've got for stepping inside this house. It's the only subject you and I have got to discuss. And if you want to know, the only reason why I gave you food was to fill you up with blotting paper to stop you passing out on me.'

'Geraldine?' he repeated with a wink, ignoring the rest of what I'd said. 'Now I'd agree that's a fine name for a girl. But what I've always wanted to know is, if you were going to call your only daughter after a tin-pot town in the South Island, why didn't you go the whole hog and call her Christchurch or Timaru or Invercargill? Or what about Westport? Something solid and substantial about Westport. Of course, I suppose you would've had to've drawn the line at towns like Nelson – Nelson Gransey would've confused everyone badly, wouldn't it? Including the dear little baby girl.'

It was the same stale old joke he'd been boring the family with for nearly forty years. In fact, it was past being boring, it was a crude and unforgivable insult. Geraldine was actually the name of my mother, who'd died giving birth to me, and Ralph knew that only too well, and what it meant to me.

But there was more at stake than just the way my best whisky was taking him, so I managed to control my contempt, and merely said, 'Deenie then. What kind of trouble is she in?'

Ralph poured himself another drink. Two thirds of the bottle had gone, so I got a glass to help him finish it off. It was mine after all. My money had paid for it.

'And don't reach for your fags,' I told him, seeing his hand diving for a pocket. 'You know the rules. I let you smoke that filthy lump of rolled cabbage leaf on the patio, but there's no smoking inside this house.'

'No drugs, no sex, no rock 'n' roll,' he replied with a fat and aggressive smile, as if he was going to pick an argument, though luckily the amazing originality and wit of the remark must have pleased him so much that he returned his hand to the whisky glass and didn't get out more cigars or cigarettes.

Then he frowned as if he was struggling to remember something. The whisky had obviously fuddled his brain at last. He sat there for a couple of minutes, with what I'd describe as a brain-damaged look, then at last he gazed up at me and said, surprisingly flatly and weakly, 'Yes, poor old Deenie. She's worse news than ever these days, daddy-o. I've got to tell you she's become a walking disaster, has Deenie. I suppose I was going to have to tell you sooner or later she's had this thing going in Wellington with one of the real sick villains of the century.'

I made an effort to bottle up the next question, but failed as always. I simply had to ask, 'Well, I expect I ought to know the worst. Who is it this time?'

'A friggin' arsehole called Tuggy Sullivan. And now he's got himself in more faecal matter than he can handle. And Deenie's in it with him.'

'And where do you fit in, Ralph? How come you're supposed to know all about everything? How come you've got an interest in this body on the beach?'

'Wrong again, Mister Gransey. You've got it all wrong again, as usual. I don't know bugger-all about nothing. All I've got to do is find things out, and that's the whole strength of it.'

'Got to?'

'Yes sirree, yes sirree,' he mumbled, emptying the bottle into both our glasses, which was unexpectedly generous of him. 'There are certain people in Auckland and Wellington who wouldn't need much convincing that Deenie's dear old pal Tuggy has to be the man you found on the beach. And I've been asked to keep an eye on things and find out all the whys and wherefores, plus the etceteras.'

'Why you?' Despite everything that had happened between

Ralph and me, it was impossible for me to forget that he was my son, or that I'd watched him stagger and stumble through almost half-a-century of living, and it angered me that anyone thought they could just come up and try to push him around. 'Are you in some kind of trouble?'

'Well, let's put it this way, dad,' he said with a laugh that was more like a series of spluttering coughs than the real thing. 'I'd rather be me than Deenie. And I'm not too sure I'd like to be you either. You've got a hard time coming from everyone, including the blue heelers.'

'Don't be silly,' I said. 'It was a coincidence, finding that body. There must have been half a dozen or more regulars walking along the beach at the time. Any one of us could have found it.'

'But it so happened it wasn't anyone else, it was you. You, you. *You*. And if it turns out that corpse is Tuggy, dad, it'll look very bad. There's the Deenie connection, and then there's me, and to top it all off there's you as well. Like it or not, you're in it right up to your garters. See what I mean?'

'No.'

'Too many family connections, wouldn't you say? It doesn't look good for the Granseys, does it? He's been a very bad boy, has our Tuggy. There's a whole lot of angry people want to know what he's been up to, what's happened to him and what he's done with certain possessions he was rumoured to be lugging around the countryside.'

'You mean drugs, I suppose?' For the first time I felt uneasy and got up to look across the front lawn to the road. I had a sudden prickly sensation that I was being snooped on.

Of course, there was no one in sight. But there was a car I'd never seen before at the top of the drive, parked in the street right in front of my house, and there was also a van on the other side of the road.

The car was a grimy blue Ford Falcon with a patch-painted door and boot, and it was empty. But you couldn't tell with the van. It was leaning away on the far camber of the road. It was a clean and shiny white, and you could only just see the rear windows, but it was too far away to make out anything inside them.

'You've been reading *Truth* again,' Ralph said. 'Drugs is the first thing everyone thinks these days, but Tuggy wasn't really what you'd call your average dealer. He was bigger than that. He wasn't just drugs, he was dollars. He was a money man. And if you're wondering about the Falcon out there, it's mine. I want any passing traffic to see I'm here.'

I didn't get the point of that remark and put it down to the booze. Instead, I asked, 'And the van?'

Ralph got up unsteadily and looked out the window. 'For God's sake,' he said. 'If you're going to worry about all the white vans in Mt Matheson you'll go off your chump in two hours flat. Second-hand Jap imports. There's second-hand white vans everywhere. The roads are clogged up with them. Bastards've got them who wouldn't otherwise raise the readies to own a pedal-car or a bloody apple box on cast-iron trolley wheels.'

Trust Ralph to hate others for being able to share the pleasures of the roads with him. The way he said 'second-hand', breaking it up into two separate words, with an outraged lift of the voice and a sneer, gave him away completely. His old Falcon, with its pale green front passenger door, so obviously a scrapyard replacement, and its splodge of bright blue paint over the boot where a major reconstruction job had been done, was probably eighth, ninth or tenth-hand.

'And Deenie?' I asked. 'What's her position exactly?'

'Her position? That's a good one, when you think about it,' he said holding his glass up and squinting through it at the last red glow of sunset, as darkness began to move in on us from the hedge around the swimming pool. 'Her position's flat on her back and what you'd call seriously compromised.'

'Stop that filth this minute,' I said in fury, banging the table. Ralph was stewed, but there was no excuse for talking about his sister like that.

Naturally, he just laughed stupidly at the rise he'd got out of me, then went on, 'She and Tuggy were supposed to go to

Auckland for some reason or other connected with Tuggy's business dealings. But they turned off to come here, because there was some kind of problem he was having, and they were spotted near here three days ago. Then Deenie turns up in the middle of Rownley yesterday wearing a Woolworths disguise. God knows what they were both up to, except there's a suggestion that someone owes someone else a lot of money and there's a whisper that someone's been shot. And just to top things off, Tuggy has disappeared and Deenie is rumoured to have gone into hiding after ringing Auckland to shriek that she doesn't know Tuggy's whereabouts or what's happened to his possessions, and then there's this corpse floats in on the tide and Deenie's old man finds it. And suddenly everyone's talking about the Granseys and how they look like they're the only ones with the answers. Complicated, eh?'

'But you know I'm down on the beach twice a day, summer and winter, rain or shine, taking my walk.'

'Bad luck, daddy-o. I said you were overdoing it. All this knitted food and exercise is doing you no bloody good at all. James and Bruce are right. You'd be much better off in an old people's home instead of digging up cadavers.'

'Don't talk like a drunken idiot, Ralph,' I snapped. 'You haven't told me where Deenie is yet. I've got to see her. I've got to help her.'

'Deenie isn't seeing anyone till the pathologists or the coroners or the cops tie Tuggy's name to one of that corpse's big toes.'

'Stop talking silly drivel,' I demanded. 'Where is she? You've got to tell me.'

'Now listen, dad. And listen carefully, because no one is going to bother to explain this to you again. No one is going to tell you anything. They want your information, and they don't trade. And . . .'

Ralph stopped suddenly to throw the last drop of whisky down his throat, then he gasped, thumped his chest and went on, 'I don't know where the hell Deenie is and no one's going to tell me unless it suits them. I've only spoken to certain people I know on the telephone. Look, I don't know anything else or I'd let you in on it.'

'Then, where's Roger?'

Roger was Deenie's son by a violent yob who was – thank God – now doing time in Paremoremo. He'd be out of the way for at least another three years, even with remission for good behaviour, if that was possible.

'I dunno. Wellington, maybe. But honestly, I dunno.'

'They wouldn't touch him, would they?'

'Naw. Why would they touch a kid?'

'Well, I want Deenie back here, Ralph. So you tell whoever it is that rings I want her here, and I want her now. Is that clear?'

'Sure, I will. But just for this actual moment in time, I'm going to catch up on my beauty sleep.'

'Not here, you're not.'

'I'm too pissed to drive.'

'I'll pay for a taxi. I want you out of here and back home on your own perch in your own fowlshed – wherever that is. You're going home now to wait for the next call about Deenie, is that understood?'

Ralph yawned, then he swept back his curls and smiled. 'I'll park the car in the garage when I wake. My responsibility in life as a good son is to stay here, keep an eye on my father and protect him, for his own good.'

Then he went to the den, grabbed a rug, kicked off his disgusting jandals and flopped full length on one of my best leather sofas.

'If I haven't woken up by ten tonight,' he said, 'Give us a shake, will you? I've told certain parties all the calls are coming here from now on. There's nothing you can do about it. This is the Greater Gransey Holdings Information Centre, okay?'

He yawned, then just before he closed his eyes and snored off he said, 'Lock the garage, lock the doors and windows, and leave the outside lights on, will you? I can pick up a distinct whiff of very nasty crime in the night air. So we're going to have to think a bit more about security, aren't we, father?'

11

Security has haunted me all my life and I see no point in denying it now, though I certainly used to go to some trouble to keep my fears concealed from those who may have used them against me. But I'm talking about the real thing, not the kind of security that Ralph was referring to. I've never cared a toss about shutting windows or turning a key in the doors of the house, though I do admit to one exception. I've always been particular about locking up the garage.

The reason for this is simple. I used to run Jags and Daimlers before I moved over eventually to a little Japanese tin-can to do the shopping in – which is all I've needed a car for these past five years. And the point about Jags and Daimlers is that James and Bruce would have loved to have taken them out and wrapped them around a power pole, the way boys of fifteen or sixteen can't help doing. So the garage door got double locked, though, if the responsibility was mine, the front door of the house was left swinging open in the breeze all day and to all comers.

Grace told me once that she'd gone out to the garage and caught James, when he was only ten or twelve, behind the steering wheel of the new Jag I'd taken delivery of only a day or two earlier. She reckoned he must have been sitting there for a good hour, just gripping the wheel, staring straight ahead, as if he'd been hypnotised.

It took Grace all her strength to prise his fingers away, one by one. They were wrinkled and bloodless, and she was terrified she might break them, for they seemed to be cemented there in a kind of paralysis.

That did it for me. I wasn't going to have a boy of mine think my cars were dream chariots or dinky toys. Yet even at the time I wasn't comfortable with what I felt forced to do. The way I looked at it, I was betraying a code of honour by training myself in the unnatural act of locking up the garage.

You see, in the far-off days when I grew up, people didn't bother much about keys. Men of property didn't lock their doors, as a matter of pride as well as policy. It wasn't dignified to show that much distrust of your neighbours and associates.

Grace, however, always used to check the doors whenever we went out. She had a routine that she would recite aloud, in a funny little jingle:

> When you have to go to town,
> Check the windows, upstairs, down.
> Wireless playing, switch on lights,
> Lock the doors, you'll be all right.

She used to walk around the house reciting this nonsense like a little prayer, though I never criticised her for it. The truth was, her nerves were shot to hell in her last years, before she departed to rest, so since running through this kind of drill seemed to keep her happy, I went along with it.

Anyway, I'm pleased to say I've relapsed, so far as doors are concerned. It has always seemed to me to be a bit useless. Turning a key in a lock may make you feel safe, but all you are keeping out are the small fry – street kids, kleptos and impulse thieves. A determined robber (and are there any who aren't?) will simply ghost his way through your average locks and burglar alarms.

Anyway, what have I got to pinch? A couple of old transistor radios and a wonky television set that I hardly ever switch on these days, and which works only when you curse it and kick it. That's about all. I don't own expensive tools or gadgets. The single thing of value is a fairly new-model microwave – I paid a bit over five hundred bucks for it two years ago – but there are no jewels, precious ornaments or oil paintings in the house, and I never keep much cash lying about. And I don't suppose many thieves have the expertise to ransack a cellar effectively, though I guess they would probably get down on the spirits.

What I mean by real security is something quite different. It's being able to look at your image in the mirror and congratulate yourself in secret that you're in no one's debt, that you're one of the few people on the planet who has fulfilled their human destiny, that you've won your battles and achieved every goal in life, and that you don't owe a return of favour or a single brass razoo to anyone.

You're the master of your destiny. You're free of all liabilities, personal, financial or otherwise. No one can climb on top and trample on you. That's what I'm getting at.

Let me put it another way. I would go so far as to say that I may well be the only man living in the shadow of Mt Matheson who can hold his hand to his heart and say he doesn't have a debt of any kind – not just in money terms, but in obligations, gifts or services. The way I've arranged the personal details of my retirement – setting up a trust, spreading my investments assiduously and wisely, and watching over my interests – there is nothing that can touch me, unless the whole of civilisation falls, and even then I think I'd make out longer than most.

I've always been a bit of a wily old stoat in my business philosophy. I have covered every inch of the ground tirelessly, I have seized my opportunities without hesitation, and I have always kept my eyes peeled for the slightest flicker of a shadow.

That's exactly how a stoat does it, and that's why it's a successful predator. The so-called conservationists who call a stoat vermin don't know half of it. They're employing a very loaded word that distorts the essential truth. They forget they're referring to a masterpiece of creation. A superb living instrument of secrecy, style, security, efficiency and stealth.

I was lucky to have learned my lesson at an early age. It was one of those experiences that change your life forever. It provides a vital clue to the way things were to turn out over the next few days, so I suppose I may as well confess how it came about. After all, I've kept it locked up inside me for sixty years.

12

It all dates from when I was about fourteen. Nathan and I had taken the evening launch over from Rownley. We'd brought our rifles – no one seemed to bother much about asking for a look at your licence in those days, supposing you ever had one, provided you had the common sense to wrap your gear around the rifle so that it didn't look threatening, and you always took the bolt out – and we'd set up camp beside a hedge on Smoyle's farm, as usual.

The following day is so perfectly clear to me that even now I can run it over the screen of my memory like an old movie. It was a final brief outing, right at the very end of the school holidays, so there weren't many people over in the camping ground or out on the dunes, and that meant everything was peaceful and the early-morning conditions were perfect for shooting.

Because we only had open-sight single-shot rifles, we were bloody accurate. The Mt Matheson bunnies seldom gave you a second go when you got a chance to get a bead on them, and we were pretty good on the snap-shot too.

You develop an instinct with a rifle, so it becomes part of you. You get so you don't think about it being there. The rifle becomes an extension of your nervous system. It's the place the message arrives at when it gets sent from eye to brain to arm and then to the first finger of your right hand, the one that squeezes the trigger. A hunter gets so familiar with his rifle that when he spots a bunny out of the corner of his eye it's on its back kicking its legs in the air before he consciously realises he's shot it.

We must have got six or seven that morning, which was bloody good shooting with open sights and with all that sand-dune cover for the bunnies to dive into. And you have to remember that we'd already picked off so many that summer that the others were getting a bit gun-shy.

We were pretty pleased with ourselves, so after we'd skinned and gutted them, we wrapped them up with our gear, hid them in the shade, and went out on the reef to catch fish. We often did that, if there was a good incoming tide, for it meant we'd catch the afternoon launch back to Rownley and take fresh fish home, as well as rabbits, and more often than not we'd have a few left over to flog off to our regulars. Remember, all this happened during the Depression, so the fresh food we brought back with us was always welcome, and the surplus helped pay for lines and ammo, and even the luxury of a bit of extra pocket-money.

The reef was fairly consistent fishing, without ever being what you'd call great, so the rabbit guts always came in handy to chuck out for berley. It'd encourage some good fish to come in to our lines and we'd sometimes take home snapper, gurnard, trevally, rock cod, sea bream and even an occasional kahawai or kingfish. But the real magic of it was that there were one or two places where you could stand high on a jutting rock ledge, right over the fish, and actually watch them come in against the rocks, cruising slowly through crystal water across the sand and pebbles, and among the waving weeds three or four fathoms below. You could study the pattern of their coming and going then drop a line right alongside them.

But this particular day, for the first time, there were no fish to be seen, not even the bream that always lazed in the weeds.

'Those bastards at the camping ground must have caught them all. We may as well piss off and catch the early launch,' I remember saying. We despised campers, hated them for intruding into our territory and blamed them for everything that went wrong, a lack of rabbits, poor fishing, even rain in the night.

However, Nathan had promised his mother fish for dinner so he insisted that since we had a good heap of rabbit guts we ought to hang on and see if we could bring something around. And after perhaps half an hour a few little reef fish did come noseying about, though they weren't worth wasting time on.

Then Nathan shouted out, 'Christ Almighty. Look over there.' And when I followed his arm I saw this monstrous black shadow gliding in at the far end of the beach, just outside the line of gentle surf that a dozen campers were leaping about in, enjoying their mid-morning swim.

The shadow must have passed the swimmers no more than ten yards away. Even from a quarter of a mile off, we could tell they were totally oblivious to their danger. Nobody ran out of the waves, they just kept on diving and splashing and trying to catch the surf to the beach.

Then almost casually the shadow turned towards us and glided across the bay between Mt Matheson and the reef. It followed a course straight for the ball of rabbit guts we had dropped into the sea, as if guided by a deadly certainty, and as it passed directly below the ledge we were standing on it turned without stopping and took the whole bundle with a lazy sideways nudge.

No hurry, no bother. It just coasted up, and the guts were gone. Then it curved away in a slow arc and nosed along the reef before turning back the way it had come, right alongside the unsuspecting swimmers, then out past the far end of the beach that marked the harbour entrance.

Later, we both reckoned it must have been a good fifty feet long – which would make it an impossible fifteen-metre monster by today's calculations – though I now have no doubt in my mind that it was at least four metres from nose to tail. But one thing is sure, it was the biggest goddamn shark I've ever seen before or since – a huge white pointer.

That's all that happened. It just came and went, and Nathan and I were the only ones who ever knew. But I've always thought of it as a symbol of all that is treacherous out there, just beyond the place you think is safe, just beyond the glittering jewel-line of the surf.

It's the silent menacing all-devouring shadow that you never know about till you're standing out on the reef, looking back with the benefit of hindsight to the shore. The place you get to look from if you're lucky and others are standing there in danger – or, as Ralph would have put it, right up to their garters in it.

I thought about that shark as I sat there, watching Ralph sleep off the whisky. I went over and over the scene in my mind. I could see the giant efficient shape of death cruising just beneath my feet. One step outwards from the ledge and I would meet it eye to eye.

Then it was ten o'clock. Time to leave my secret memories and the life I had made secure because at the age of fourteen or fifteen I had become aware of its worst dangers. Time to go back to that other world of lives I knew nothing about. Ralph and Deenie's world.

A place of darkness in which I was helpless. A place of peril my children had chosen to make for themselves.

13

Ralph woke the same way that he did as a little child. He stretched out, pushing his arms down his sides and thrusting his neck right up from his shoulders, as if bursting out of the sea after a deep dive. Then he smiled, and of course he pushed his hands back through his curls.

Damn. It was actually a pleasure to watch him, because he so enjoyed his male glamour. It was the secure part of him, the part he had always been able to rely on. It was like sharing a private thought, just observing him rising from sleep, new and refreshed, yet yawny, chubby and slightly bruised-looking.

'It's ten,' I said, angry with myself for giving way to my memories yet again.

'Ten?' he asked, looking around bewildered. 'Night or day?'

'Ten at night. You told me to wake you. When did you last go to bed?'

Ralph grunted quietly, rubbed his eyes slowly and gently with his knuckles, then lay there and looked up at me, smiling. It was years since I had shared this kind of human intimacy, so I was caught off-guard.

'You went out like a light, son,' I said, because there was nothing else to say. And I couldn't just go on standing there, staring at him. 'You just lay down and switched off.'

This time he yawned as well as stretched. 'It's being back in the bosom of the family,' he croaked. 'It's so loving and peaceful. So trusting and restful.'

'The whisky, more like it. And I suppose you'd like a coffee now. You look as if you could do with a straightener.'

'Coffee would hit the button,' he said, trying to clear his throat.

'And there's still no smoking,' I reminded him, just in case he thought he might get away with it.

'I'll go outside,' he conceded with a very long yawn, then got off the sofa. 'The system always cries out for a quick-start or it won't function properly.'

The system, as he calls it, is half-shot, I thought to myself and made the coffee. It was only then that I noticed the cheap brandy I keep on the shelf above the dishrack was missing.

I leave a bottle there for the very odd occasion when I feel a cold or a sniffle coming on. A couple of tablespoons of brandy, the juice of one lemon and a big teaspoon of organic honey in a tumbler filled to the top with boiling water will scour all the germs in the world out of your throat. There's no medicine for colds to touch brandy.

And now it had gone. The whole bottle. Yet I wasn't surprised so much by the fact that it was missing – what really astonished me was how he'd managed to slip around me, lift the bottle and get away with it. I remembered him stretching, then yawning, then getting up, moving past me and going outside, but that's all. He was like an eel when it came to pinching things. In and out like a gliding shadow – like a bloody white pointer, come to think of it – then off. It was a special gift, if you considered it just in terms of physical ability, and it was one he could have done great things with.

I'm positive Ralph could have made the All Blacks if he'd been able to set his mind to it. He was a cert. Just think of it – second five-eighths or centre. The glory that would have brought the Granseys. And I'm not exaggerating – Ralph was strong and deep-chested, yet never bulky, and he was quick off the mark. But more than that, he was liquid. It's a quality of manly grace that few have. You're either born with it or you're not. But of course he could never have stood the drill, the training, the team work, the application. All that beautiful wasted talent. It had dissipated into a slippery skill. A genius for snaffling a bottle of his father's brandy.

I passed him his coffee outside and didn't say a word about the bottle. The stuff inside it was cheap enough, and if he wanted to rot his liver, that was up to him. I was only interested in one thing. A phone call.

But it was a long wait. I went back to my den and played a couple of discs from the shows, *Oklahoma* and *South Pacific*, then some Mantovani – I like the thought as well as the sound of strings swooping about in the dark. I listen and imagine owls gliding down from the trees. There's a superb phantom grace about all those Mantovani violins, and there's something menacing, something lethal about them, too. It's as if they're winging out of the darkness to tear out my living heart.

I also played a tape of Bing Crosby songs, from which I'd deleted 'I'm Dreaming of a White Christmas'. It's the only one of Bing's songs that gives me a pain in the rectum, because I've never seen a white Christmas and never want to. Christmas means beaches and swimming and heatwaves. Snow and Christmas are an absurdity that I just can't take.

In every other respect, however, Bing was the undisputed heavyweight crooning champion of the world when I grew up. But there's more than just strength in his voice. There's all that power, yet there are no hard edges, no raspings or rough bits, and provided he's played no louder than the sound a wind-up gramophone record aimed for, I find Bing and a few of the others, like Al Bowly and early Frank Sinatra, help me get by late at night when I'm feeling tired and sleepless or on edge.

Then at last the telephone rang.

Ralph had come back inside an hour or so earlier, and he was flicking through my old copies of the *National Geographic*, which for all I knew may have been the first time he'd had reading matter in his hands since he'd left school, if you don't count a regular copy of *Best Bets*. The clock said seventeen minutes past twelve.

'I'll take it,' he said, picking up the phone and waving for me to sit down.

'Yeah,' he said after a few seconds. 'He's here with me.'

Then there was a long pause while he listened, gazing up at the ceiling. 'Yeah, yeah,' was all that came out of him for a while. Then he said, 'No, it was all a coincidence. He only knows what the heelers told him. They told him the corpse went through the mincer. All messed up so no one would recognise – No, not the sheilas. I said the heelers with a haitch. The Bill. The fuzz. The bloody cops.'

I had to snort quietly. Ralph keeping up to date with what even someone like myself, who scarcely ever watched the box, could recognise as television slang made him sound such a half-grown-up schoolboy. It was pathetic.

Then I sat upright.

'No,' Ralph said. 'She hasn't checked in here yet . . .' Obviously they were now talking about Deenie. 'Yeah, it's bloody odd. She always does . . . No, I've been here since late

68

afternoon . . . No calls at all from that quarter . . . Yeah, I know it's serious . . . I told you, I appreciate that . . . Yeah . . . Yeah . . .'

Ralph did a lot more listening. Obviously the person on the other end was very stewed up, because Ralph frowned and nodded his head seriously from time to time, as if he thought he might be being watched down the phone line and was trying to demonstrate his loyalty. Then he said, 'Yeah, I'll be here. No, I won't go out even for fags. No, I'll take charge of it . . . Yeah, I've got that . . . Yeah . . . No problem . . . No problem.'

It was sickening to watch a son of mine perform so spinelessly. After all I'd achieved in life and the example I'd set, here was my boy Ralph behaving like a flunky.

I felt like saying to him that I'd seen and heard a few disgusting things in my life, and this had to rank with the worst of them. But what would've been the use? Ralph had almost reached his half-century. The way I looked at it, he was a lost cause, a lost soul. So when he finally hung up and stared at me in silence for a few seconds I simply said, 'Well, I think I got the gist of that. And the big question still is, where's Deenie — is that right?'

'She's missing and she's being bloody stupid,' he said. 'She's got the information about Tuggy that everyone needs to know, and she's gone into hiding. She's getting everyone in the shit. That's what our dear little Deenie's doing for us. And I need a drink.'

'You need a month's drying out,' I couldn't help saying, but Ralph ignored me while he fetched the brandy bottle from where he'd taken it outside.

At the time I could hardly be blamed for believing that a few more hours of Ralph and everything would resolve itself. I imagined that already we must be over the worst of it. Soon, there'd be answers and my life would go back to normal. Despite the corpse on the beach, this was Mt Matheson, not Chicago.

I decided there and then that, since he seemed to know so

much more than I did, it would be okay for Ralph to stay under my roof for the rest of the night. And in the meantime all I had to do was just keep on reciting one thing to myself over and over again – my dearest Deenie is out there somewhere, and she needs my help, and soon she'll be safe.

14

Ralph stayed the night on the downstairs spare bed, in the sewing room. It may have been a fact of circumstance that because of Deenie I couldn't get rid of him, but I certainly wasn't having him upstairs.

Funnily enough, I slept again like a babe. No dreams, no nagging prostate, and although on past form I must have got up a couple of times in the night for a pee, I swear the bed looked as though I had woken up in the same position I went to sleep in. I couldn't remember a night's solid rest like it in the past ten or dozen years – well, certainly in the five years since Grace had ventured on her last journey. The single blanket I slept under in summer didn't have a wrinkle. I had been totally wiped out by a deep overwhelming oblivious darkness.

But, as soon as I awoke, it was as if I'd opened a crammed cupboard door. In a matter of seconds, all the memories of the previous day burst out and came tumbling down on me. The body, the police, Nathan's visit, Belle, Deenie, Ralph, the late-night phone call, the lot . . .

It was merely a crushing, suffocating mental experience at first, one of those nasty black moments of despair, but it soon developed into the real thing – a full-blown physical attack. These little visitations hit me quickly out of nowhere and they're very unpleasant when they do come along. The only thing you can say for them – afterwards – is that they certainly clear the mind. They stop you thinking about anything else. You surrender to them totally.

I'm not sure how long I must have lain there trying to breathe properly, sweating with sickening pain and the terror that my heart would stop beating – but if past experience was anything to go by it would have been a very long ten or twenty minutes.

I have what Fraser-Lang, my doctor, tells me is a 'chronic heart condition'. Angina, hypertension, perished blood vessels, clapped-out valves, high cholesterol, the whole works – which is as much, technically, as I want to know about it. If Ralph had only bothered to ask me the night before, instead of trying all the time to make a drunken joke of it, I would have explained to him that this was the reason why Grace had put me onto a health-food diet, and why I more or less stuck to it. A turn like the one I suffered when I woke up that morning is enough to cure any lust you may once have felt for roast lamb or pavlova.

Sudden excitement or mental agitation often brings it on, though funnily enough, it's not over-exertion or annoyance that seem to be the main factors. Just lying or sitting about and remembering some chance event can trigger the damned thing, and the next moment I'm totally flattened by an attack of palpitations, sweats and flutterings.

Which is why, as I write my story, I feel so much better than I've been in years. It's the first time I haven't felt all knotted up inside or so full of pressure that I could have choked on sheer tension. I've never before been confident enough to sit down and relax, and trust myself to look back, outface my secrets and dismiss the demons of the past. I want to record everything exactly as it felt at the time, not because I'm looking for favours from anyone, but so that I can come to terms with what happened and explain it all to myself.

You see, everything that occurred to me from the moment I found that body lying there in the sand seemed to provide powder for a fuse that smouldered its way into the past where my whole existence – the sum of what I thought I knew about myself – was primed and set to explode into a cloud of dust. All that I thought was solid and substantial around me was about to puff away into nothingness.

Anyway, I managed to control my agitation and eventually reached out and grabbed one of Fraser-Lang's little white pills. It's extraordinary when you think how such an insignificant-looking wad of chemical compounds is the key to your continued existence. They work on me like magic, and in less than half an hour I was interested enough again in the world around me to be able to reach out and switch on the wireless for the local news.

A man in far worse condition than me – in fact, he seemed to be suffering from terminal hysteria – immediately screamed out that he was eager to supply me with a brand-new muffler and shock absorbers at today only's bargain discount price, if I hurried on down to Harry's Auto Shop in Q Street.

Christ, I told myself, that's probably the very thing I needed. A replacement set of shock absorbers.

Then the news came on, and I heard my name read out. 'Police sources have now revealed that Arthur Gransey, a Mt Matheson pensioner, is the man who claims to have found the body on the beach that featured in our news bulletins last night and this morning. Arthur, a former prominent local businessman, has so far declined to comment to the media on his discovery, but we understand that the badly mutilated corpse of a male is now undergoing further examination by police pathologists. Rownley police chief, Superintendent Rupert Myrtles, told Radio R that he has received several valuable leads from members of the public, and further investigations are proceeding to establish the dead man's identity.'

'Piss off,' I said out loud as I switched it off and got up a little gingerly to take a shower. The phone rang, but I ignored it. The only person it could be was Belle, of course. The timing was a give-away. She'd probably heard my name on the wireless and she would have wet herself racing for the torture machine so she could cackle down the tubes at me about how I had suddenly been elevated to the ranks of media personalities.

Belle was incapable of picking up the depressing hidden message of that bulletin. What it was all about was that I'd become some sort of unreliable and perhaps even disreputable witness, who only 'claims' he finds the odd body on beaches. And, more sinisterly, when you fitted all the descriptions together, I was now to be described vaguely as a former prominent local businessman. Former prominent? Local? Christ, the shadow I cast around here would once have reached up and down the coast for a hundred miles or more. Maybe I wasn't as powerful as some of those Auckland tycoons were reckoned to be, but I was Mister Big in this place – I was the pillar of this community. I propped this whole place up. Rownley and Mt Matheson rested on my shoulders.

Suddenly I could no longer avoid the stark truth of what had been happening gradually for years without my ever wanting to sit up and take notice: I had become a nobody who could be referred to over the air waves with impunity as 'Arthur' – as if I would ever have allowed some pimply young runt of a microphone attendant to be on first-name terms with me. It was just another variation of the humiliating way that only yesterday the police had felt it within their jurisdiction to refer to me as Fred.

The world was getting at Mister Arthur Gransey. There was no doubt about that. The whole bloody lunatic asylum out there was trying to rattle me. This so-called Mt Matheson pensioner was actually the same man they'd have bowed and scraped to a few years ago. Head of Rotary, Chamber of Commerce, local National Party Chairman, board of this, committee for that – once upon a time the whole lot of them would have got down on their knees and been honoured to lick my boots. In fact, I wouldn't even have had to ask nicely if I'd invited them to kiss my arse. They'd have been overjoyed not to have washed their mouths out for weeks.

So, had I become a different person? Had I been swapped

in the night with someone else, like some kind of ancient changeling? Once upon a time, in a far-off land, long, long ago, I was Mister Arthur Gransey MBE. I could even have expected to become an OBE or CBE or – why not admit it here and now? – a knight of the realm. There was no reason for not thinking so. At one time I could have just about banked on it, if there hadn't been a poisonous whispering campaign against me. But now, all of a sudden, I had become a nonentity called Fred or Arthur, a dimwit who 'claims' to find bodies on Ocean Beach, a poor old dribbling derelict who is capable only of stumbling across 'discoveries'.

I gave myself a good scrubbing with a loofah and a long-handled brush, then dried myself on a rough towel in front of the mirror. I felt surprisingly fit for a man who'd just had what Fraser-Lang calls 'a small incident'. Wiping the steam off the glass and measuring myself up front-on and sideways, I found that, no matter what anyone else thought, it wasn't as if I was bent, slumped or totally jiggered out, as the radio bulletin had more or less painted me for the whole of Rownley and Mt Matheson to chortle over.

I had hardly any pot, just a bit of what I'd describe as a proud sag in the belly department. Certainly, there were a couple of smallish folds of flab across my chest that made my tits baggy and perhaps just a bit womanly, yet they weren't what you'd describe as floppy and gross. I was not so much bald as distinguished by what looked like a priestly tonsure, and my body hair was still wiry and very springy and curly, even if it was entirely grey. My cock hung down like an old bat tucked up comfortably in the wrinkled folds of the little wings that bunched behind it – sleeping off its past follies, no doubt. But my legs were still unbowed and sturdy. There was nothing wrong with me. No matter what Belle said, I was no fat old film comedian.

In fact, if I breathed in deeply and thrust my chest out, I still cut a pretty good figure for a man of my age. It is a matter of considerable pride to me that Fraser-Lang said a few months ago, when I went in for my usual check-up, that I had the physique of a man ten years younger. And he is probably the top medical practitioner in the whole of Rownley.

Even allowing for the fact that I was a regular customer – and therefore fools who don't know me may think that I was paying Fraser-Lang to exaggerate to please me – there was still more than a word of truth in what he said.

Then an unwelcome voice broke into my thoughts.

'What the hell do you think you're playing at, dad?' Ralph asked.

If there's one thing I've always hated it's having children walk in on me, and even though Ralph, at fifty, was more or less what you'd call grown-up, he was breaking one of the strictest rules of this house.

'Get downstairs,' I yelled at him. 'You know you're not to walk in on people like that. I was having my morning shower . . . Doing my exercises . . . It's disgraceful.'

Ralph grinned with the unpleasant sneer he can put on when he wants to wound someone, and he said, 'Yeah, disgraceful, dad. That's exactly what I think about it, too. Flashing at yourself in the mirror . . . At your age. Just as well I'm family – if anyone else had caught you at it, they would've reported you straight to the authorities.'

'This is my house . . .' I began to shout, but he cut me off.

'The telephone, dad,' he said. 'Deenie just called.'

'Deenie?'

'Yeah. Silly bloody Deenie. Still her own worst enemy. Wouldn't speak to me. Just hung up before I could talk sense into her.'

I must have looked damned silly standing there with nothing on, clutching a towel in front me, but suddenly I didn't care. I strode across the bedroom and picked up the phone, as if Ralph hadn't told me she'd hung up on him and as if I really still expected to hear her voice.

Of course, all I got was the dial tone.

'What did she say, boy? What were her exact words?'

'Boy? Exact words? *Boy*?' Ralph repeated, still wearing that stupid grin.

'Tell me,' I shouted.

'Well, what she said was, "Hello daddy," and I said, "Hello Deenie – long time no speak," and she said, "Where's daddy?" and I said "Deenie, hold it a minute. I've got to tell you something really important," and she said two words beginning with F and O, which I wouldn't care to repeat to a decent and respectable old-fashioned Christian gentleman like you. Then she hung up. And that was our entire conversation, beginning to end – *daddy*.'

I sat on the bed, stunned.

'Come down and have some breakfast,' Ralph said. 'I wandered along to the dairy for some real milk, real instant coffee, real bacon and eggs, and some real white bread you can actually put under the grill and toast, and spread real butter and strawberry jam on.'

'I told you, I don't eat that muck,' I replied dully.

'Look,' he said, quite softly, and a lot more gently than I was willing to admit at the time, 'Just tell yourself that I went and got the grub for myself, but since there's plenty of it, you can then say you may as well have a gnaw at it. I really think it'll do you a power of good, dad. It's the kind of fuel an old man needs, and it's all been provided by Mother Nature – and she went to a lot of trouble to make it out of super-quality ingredients.'

'For God's sake, let me spell it out to you once and for all, I'm not interested,' I said in despair.

'And I got a copy of the *Echo*.'

'Not interested in that either,' I repeated.

'You will be when you see it. For a start, you'll be pleased to know you're famous again. Just like the old days. You're right in the middle of the front page, with a mugshot that can't have been taken any more than twenty years ago, when you used to imagine you were real big-time around the neighbourhood and you used to tell me how you cast a big black shadow from here to Rownley, and up and down the coast – and possibly to hell and back.'

How your own favourite words and thoughts can come

back to haunt you . . . I just stared straight ahead for a minute or two before I had the strength to get dressed. I had entirely forgotten I'd had a nasty little seizure that very morning. All I could now focus on was Deenie, and the way I'd let her down when she was in trouble and needed me most.

15

In daylight the view across my front lawn to the street was no longer menacing. The mysterious white van had gone, to be replaced by a green car and a red van with side windows you could see right through. It was empty. Ralph's car looked no more than what it was: an advertisement for scrap metal. It was impossible to reconcile the pleasant picture that greeted me with the uncomfortable feeling I'd experienced only the night before that someone could be out there spying on me. There was no way I could connect the bright world I gazed on with the dark and tangled web Deenie had got herself into or the even worse condition in which Ralph thought her boyfriend may have ended up. How could anyone look out at this perfect world and believe in mutilated corpses and vicious sickening evil?

It was a glorious Mt Matheson morning, cloudless, parched and with not even the whisper of a seabreeze. There wasn't enough lift in the air to support thistledown. The birds had more sense than to waste their breath on a whistle. The only sounds came from cars in the distance and the everlasting racket of the cicadas – as both worked themselves into a metallic frenzy.

I sat outside on the patio, under a sun umbrella, to eat my muesli, leaving Ralph to stink out the kitchen with his vile bacon and eggs – though there was once a time when I would have said that nothing in the world smelled so inviting or tasted more delicious.

Over half a century ago, when Nathan and I were young, the place where I was now sitting, taking my low-fat high-fibre breakfast, would have been within a yard or two of one of our favourite campsites. I had had my patio deliberately designed so that the outside eating area would be more or less plumb on the patch where we used to cook, just at the back of what once was a sheltered stretch of Smoyle's farm.

We liked being close to the dunes and the reef, within easy reach of the little general store, yet far enough away from the camping grounds to be out of range of their night-time sing-songs and the rasping of their wind-up gramophones. Being totally independent from the holiday-fun crowd gave us a tremendous sense superiority. But it was the meals that really made the place memorable. In fact, they focused such magnetic energy on this spot that eventually the memory of them drew me back here to live. Those meals were mighty and magnificent – and we paid for them entirely out of our own hard-earned pocket-money.

We would throw six or eight eggs, a pound of bacon and a great lump of salty farm butter into our huge blackened frying pan and watch it all spit and splutter over an open fire. In those days the eggs went a heavy clotted orange colour in the pan, and you often got double-yolkers, and the bacon wasn't this evil slimy skimpy stinking plastic-packeted stuff you see in the supermarkets. You bought it from the butcher who home-cured it, and he sliced off the rashers with a knife, dry and fresh from the back or shoulder, and you made a gap between your forefinger and thumb to show him how thick you wanted them.

As I closed my eyes I could actually taste the delicate tang of woodsmoke that would soak through those miraculous breakfasts, and I could still remember how we'd always argue about who had the right to mop the pan out with a hunk of bread, the one who cooked the grub or the one who skinned the rabbits.

But the memory was a brief one. The phone was now my obsession. I had taken it out of its holder in the kitchen and placed it on the table in front of me. It was one of those cordless gadgets that are a nuisance to older people like me, because we put the damned things down then never know where to find them again, and we have to stumble around after them like bloody old fools, following their beacon signals. But now it would stay where I put it, for I wasn't going to let it out of my sight again.

James and Bruce had bought it for me a couple of Christmases previously, arguing that if I was walking around the garden I should keep it in a pocket, then if I fell over, I could ring for help. Another one of their stupid interfering ideas, but I'd had the good sense to let them install it, just to stop them carrying on about looking after me while they were actually driving me mad fussing about and giving me a hard time.

However, over breakfast there were only two calls from what I'd call intimates – from Belle and Nathan – and a whole lot of nuisance calls from the *Echo*, Radio Rownley and a clutch of busybody ex-businessmen, golf buddies I'd once thought of as friends, who rang me without exception to say they'd read about me in the paper and thought they'd brighten my day with a selection of badly told, unfunny, so-called jokes about cadavers. One spun me a yarn of such plain filth that I told him to get off the line and go and see a psychiatrist.

Belle's call was to tell me she'd missed hearing about my adventures on the wireless because she'd been busy getting herself organised for a major expedition to leave the house and have her hair set. So help me God, she made it sound like General Eisenhower had called her in and asked her to slap her curlers on and lead the D-Day landings. However, she was now able to report that she was free of all prior commitments and she'd be listening all day to every news bulletin. Which reminded her – why hadn't I come clean and told her yesterday that I was going to be talked about on the radio? She wouldn't have known a thing about me being a famous news personality if a neighbour hadn't told her.

Holy hell, I had to remind myself, this was the woman I'd worshipped and confessed my love to. The woman I'd lain beside for years in the same bed, talked to tenderly on our pillows, and made pregnant with two children. The woman I'd nearly killed for. And now she wants to hear the mickey taken out of me on the air waves!

'You should have warned me, Arthur,' she protested. 'Think of the disaster if I'd gone into Rownley, with everyone looking at me, and me not knowing you'd been on the air, and my hair not set properly. It was only a fluke I decided this morning, etcetera, etcetera . . .'

I shut her up by saying I was the prime suspect, according to the Mt Matheson police, and she'd better start reminding her neighbours and anyone else she met in Rownley that she and I had been divorced for more than forty years, and she'd always been of the opinion that I'd end my life swinging on the end of a rope or cracking rocks on a National Park chain gang.

I had no sooner got rid of her, to clear the line for Deenie, than Nathan rang to say he'd heard the news report and picked up all the innuendoes about me being a prominent pensioner and how quickly and scandalously we'd become Yesterday's Men. But before he could get going, I told him he'd be welcome if he came over, but I was waiting for an urgent call and couldn't talk.

I was getting jumpy, so I tried to contemplate the ridiculous photograph in the *Echo* that Ralph had warned me about and study the report, compiled by two illiterates who managed to twice refer to me as a 'former leading businessman'.

Former leading? Who were these little twerps of newshounds who thought they could defame me like that? Why, I bloody well ran Rownley and Mt Matheson. This was my private empire, and I was king pin. I'm neither exaggerating nor am I being in the slightest bit conceited when I say that no man dared breathe the good air around here unless I first told him he could lift his snout to the breeze and sniff. It was Arthur Gransey who as good as chose the member of parliament and selected the mayor – none of those cocky little timeservers would've had the chance of a run with the ball unless they'd first got the nod from me; they'd never even have made it to the changing room to lace their boots up – and they all knew it, and not one of them ever tried to have me on and do a damned thing about it.

I had the power to make or break any man in town, and that goes for the women as well. No one was beyond my reach. If they crossed me, and if they made me mad enough, I could have had them tipped out in the street any time I chose – and I did, more than once, which is probably one of the grudges that lay behind that wicked whispering campaign, the one that cost me my knighthood.

So I ought to also make it clear that there was another, completely different, side to the story. It was equally true – and I'm proud of it – that if people played open and honest with me, I could always be depended on to shift heaven and earth to reward them. There are a number of contented men around this district who can thank me eternally (not that they ever seem to these days) for their nice cushy little business ventures or the sinecures they won from the council or the government, not to mention the rich gravy stains running down their waistcoats.

The whole of Rownley used to hum along sweetly because I took the trouble to grease the bearings. Cast your eyes around and wherever you look you'll find dozens of well-placed families who owe everything they've achieved in life to me.

I was thinking this with a certain amount of irony and a good deal of bile when Ralph came out at last for a cigarette. He'd shoved the dishes he'd used in the dishwasher – another useless machine I hate, though I had the damned thing installed to please Grace – and set it swishing away, for the first time in years, instead of using a fraction of the water and electricity by washing up in the sink. It took me a minute or two to figure out, on the positive side, that at least he was making a gesture of cleaning up after himself.

'Still no Deenie?' he said.

'You frightened her off,' I said bitterly. 'You should have called me when I was having a shower. What's wrong with you? Where are your brains? She rang here to speak to her father, not her useless gormless brainless brother.'

'Listen, daddy-o. You may have once had a small kink for making money, but when it comes to your brains and mine, let me tell you that if all the grey matter you've got inside your skull was Brilliantine you wouldn't have enough to comb through the hairs in your ears. So bloody move off the grass, will you? What you've got to say to her is neither here nor there. What matters is that I've got something to tell her she really needs to know.'

'Don't talk baloney, Ralph. And stop calling me daddy-o. It's profoundly irritating. And it's not only disrespectful and impertinent, it's . . . well, it's not decent. I shouldn't have to remind you that you're fifty or thereabouts. You're a middle-aged man. You'll soon be a senior citizen, like me.'

'But I can't help it, can I? I'll always think of you as my dear old dad. It's the way you brought me up, with all that soppy loving care and attention, when I was a tiny little toddler and I needed you to wipe my arse,' he said, with an expression I can only describe as something like a cross between a sly smirk and a sneer.

Whatever it was, he certainly wouldn't have got away with it forty years ago. I was never a violent man, but there are two things I have always refused to stand for, and they are a boy giving me lip, or answering me back with an obvious scrawl of dumb insolence all over his face. That's when I used to really see red. I couldn't help myself.

James, Bruce and even the one I got used to referring to as that stinking little scumbag, never got whacked regularly, because they never pushed the limits, but whenever Ralph stayed under the same roof he was always testing and probing and provoking me, to see how far he could go. I'll never be able to work out why he did it. All I know is that he could drive me so crazy I had to more than just hit him, he forced me to take my belt off to him more than once. And now, for the second or third time since he'd turned up only yesterday, I could feel inside me again the same old itch to teach the boy a few good manners.

I had always tried, within the limits of what was physically and emotionally possible in very difficult circumstances, to be a good father to him and to point him in the correct directions. I had really adored him as a little boy. But right there and then I would have loved to have broken a thick stick over his back.

What made the feeling worse was that I knew – and I knew that Ralph knew – there was nothing I could do about it.

16

Nathan arrived soon after this exasperating run-in, so my ill temper had time to settle down a bit while I bustled about making coffee, which we took outside. Immediately, of course, Ralph took his cue to get in a dig at Nathan. He'd had his little go at me, so he was obviously feeling lucky.

'How's dear old Daphers?' he asked.

The story of Ralph's first deep involvement with Daphne was something I didn't know about till years after it was over. Apparently, they'd been going at it like rutting animals, in secret and right under Belle's nose. What shocked me, when I found out, was that they were still schoolkids. In fact, I may as well be honest and say they started going the whole hog when Ralph was only sixteen and Daphne was a full year younger. She was below the legal age. She was borstal-bait.

For years it made me sweat just to think of the monstrous trouble they could have got themselves into – so, as it turned out, I did them both a service in more ways than one when I packed Ralph off to Queensland.

The pity was that they got together again in their mid-twenties, a year or two after Ralph came back from Australia. One way and another, they were both running right off the rails at the time and the whole thing would certainly have ended in absolute disaster, but fortunately, when they decided they were going to get married, they had the foresight to announce the glad tidings to Nathan – not to me. I would have more than just banged their heads together. I would have bloody well decapitated the pair of them.

Nathan – as I'm only too willing to acknowledge – took a far more clever and correct approach. He was brilliant. The tactics he used were to be very calm and civilised about the whole thing, and he actually thanked them for trusting him with the news.

Then he simply applied the old-fashioned time-tested remedy: he took Ralph aside and asked him how much he'd take to bugger off. Perhaps he didn't express it in quite those words, but that's what the guts of his proposal amounted to. And, after a few drinks and a long talk and a bit of encouragement, Ralph was only too happy to name a price.

When Nathan told me what he'd done, I called him all the fools in creation, for Ralph was smart enough to take the cash *and* Daphne. But Nathan had covered that option, too. He merely winked and explained, 'No chance, Arthur. You know very well I don't have that kind of money to throw away, so I got in first and told Daphne I'd put her future husband to the test by making a certain financial proposition to him, then I told her gently what he thought her market value was – the price she had fetched in the saleyard of his mind . . . Her value on the hoof, or between the sheets, so to speak . . .'

I had to laugh as I told him he was almost as big a scheming bastard as I was popularly reckoned to be, and he admitted that, naturally, Daphne's first reaction had been rather along that line, too – though she hadn't laughed when she told him so. In fact, she had cut up rough to start with and screamed that her father was an unscrupulous devious little bastard, and so on. But the ultimate outcome was that when she thought about it, she couldn't help seeing my son in an even poorer light.

As Nathan put it to me at the time, 'Ralph seems to have been born one move behind, if you don't mind me putting it that way Arthur, and I'm afraid he doesn't seem able to catch up. That's why he's doomed always to lose every dirty little game he sets up.'

So, when the boy now asked with all the impudence in the world how 'dear old Daphers' was, Nathan simply gave him a shrewd look as if lining him up in his sights and said, 'Never better, Ralph. She's discovered a real point in life. You'll be aware there are the three children for a start, of course. But, on top of that, she's now doing an extramural degree at Massey University. Daphers has actually got a fine brain – just like you, dear boy – so she's simply flying through the course . . .'

He paused slightly, than added, 'So let me ask you a question, Ralph. Why don't you do something like that, too? A bit of academic discipline with all that natural talent of yours and you may well surprise yourself with what you could still achieve in life.'

It was a beautifully calculated mix of cruel praise and pleasant insult, delivered in Nathan's deadliest manner, and I don't think I've ever seen Ralph more knocked back and embarrassed. It was a pleasure to watch. For a moment it almost looked as though he was going to blush. He'd gone a mile beyond the limits by raising the subject of Daphne and he'd been put down by an expert.

Being a moral lightweight, naturally Ralph filled in a bad moment by pulling out a packet of tobacco and elaborately rolling then slowly lighting a cigarette. I sat there and watched, my stomach heaving with silent laughter, as Ralph twiddled with his cigarette, blew one of his silly smoke rings, then made an excuse that he had to check out a sound that was worrying him in the entrails of the Falcon.

'Sorry for that, Arthur,' Nathan said as soon as Ralph had moved away.

But I wasn't interested in Ralph any more – the boy had asked for a roughing up and the treatment he'd got had been far more polite than he'd deserved. I leaned across the table and came straight to the real point. 'Any more sightings of Deenie?'

Nathan looked around slowly and carefully, then said, 'Deenie's lying low.'

'I know that. She rang here this morning, and like a bloody fool I wasn't organised. I was under the shower, and Ralph took the call. Of course, he frightened her off . . . The thing is, she's in some kind of trouble. There's something going on that I'm too bloody old and frightened to think about. And I don't seem to be able to . . .'

How could I suddenly drop the habits of a lifetime and speak the truth, and admit I was talking not just about my only daughter, but the one and only ideal secret love of my whole existence – the perfect idiot of a woman who yet again seemed to be deliberately destroying her life, the incomparable beauty who took up with human garbage and got serviced by slime from the gutter?

For a while Nathan gazed at me thoughtfully, but said nothing, then he looked around again and whispered. 'Before I tell you, you must promise me one thing – not a word to anyone. Is that clear?'

I could quite literally have fallen off my chair with shock. Nathan knew something about Deenie that I didn't know? He had news?

'Of course,' I said, without trying to conceal my excitement. 'I wouldn't breathe a syllable.'

'I can't tell you how serious this is, Arthur. So not even a whisper to Ralph. Promise?'

'For God's sake, Nathan. Tell me what's happened to Deenie.'

'Deenie has been in touch with me.'

'Of course she has,' I prompted him, almost laughing at

the simplicity of the scenario I imagined. 'That's Deenie all over. She's bright. When she found Ralph was here with me, she rang you straight away, so you could pass on a message. I can see her doing it.'

'She's in a pickle.'

'Ralph says she's in it right up . . .' I began. Then I realised I was a long way ahead of myself. 'Look, I really desperately want to know what's going on. I've got to help her. What kind of a pickle?'

'Well, you'd better hold your breath, Arthur. It's supposed to involve a lot of money. There seems to be some sort of mix-up about who owes who and how much. She told me that she's heard the figure of a whole million dollars being bandied about – though she claims that's not true. She said there's probably about ten or twenty thousand at stake, but she says everything suddenly seems to have got out of hand and a whole lot of people are prepared to believe anything, so long as it's lurid and terrible and silly enough. And the worst thing is she's frightened. This body on the beach business is only part of it.'

'Of course it's not a million. Come off it,' I babbled, as if I was trying to will it not to be true. 'Not Deenie. Like I said, she's bright, but she wouldn't have the . . . You know what I'm getting at. Deenie wouldn't know the ropes well enough to get herself in . . . A million bloody dollars? For Christ's sake, Nathan, it's bloodywell impossible. It's loony. What I need to do is to get her here and protect her until all these stupid dangerous rumours quieten down.'

'Well, if I could give you some advice, old friend, perhaps that's something you should ask Ralph about. When she discovered that Ralph was answering your phone, Deenie couldn't help thinking that people may be what is called "leaning" on him to find her and get their non-existent money back.'

'And Deenie? How is she – apart from being worried? I mean, what else did she say? Did she say anything about me – and coming back here?'

'I'm afraid not. Deenie gave me to believe that her boyfriend's inconveniently gone missing. In fact, she was pretty incoherent on that score. I couldn't quite understand what she was saying, but apparently he's called Sullivan. And he's the one who's supposed to have pinched the money somehow. Or lost it. A couple of days ago she got so worried that she decided to go into hiding. She wouldn't answer all my questions. It's very confusing.'

'Christ, it's getting complicated all right. Ralph told me that some people – and God only knows who they are – believe the man I found on the beach is this Sullivan person.'

'Deenie gave me that impression, too. But then again, she could have been saying something quite different. She was quite equivocal. And she hung up before I could ask her to slow down and speak clearly. She certainly gave me to understand that she knows more than she's letting on. That's probably why she's worried.'

'The money's gone? Sullivan's gone? And now they're all looking for her? And she hasn't got the money, because the money isn't there and never was? Am I beginning to get it right?'

Nathan nodded and said in his most meticulous civil service manner, 'She claims she neither has the money, nor knows where it may be found. And the last she saw of Sullivan someone was threatening to kill him. But then again . . .'

I banged my fist on the table. 'No buts, Nathan. If she says that's the truth, then she's bloody well not telling lies,' I shouted. 'If Deenie says something, I believe her. She may be a bloody fool with men, but you know perfectly well she's not a liar.'

'Oh dear, oh dear, Arthur. I'm afraid you've just about as good as broken your promise,' Nathan said quietly. 'I asked you to keep strict silence, and now all that shouting about Deenie seems to have attracted the attention of Son Number One.'

I looked over at the car, which had been moved down the

drive in front of the garage, and saw Ralph lowering the lid. Then he sauntered over towards us, wiping his hands on a cloth. His face was twisted into a cheeky expression of enquiry that meant trouble.

However, just at that moment the phone rang and a harsh voice asked for Ralph Gransey, so I handed over the phone and beckoned Nathan inside, shutting the kitchen door behind me.

'Okay, what does she want me to do?' I asked.

'You haven't got a million handy, I suppose?' Nathan replied, raising his eyebrows and pulling his lips into a comic grimace. It wasn't funny.

'Of course not,' I said. 'You know I'm not the sort to leave that kind of money lying around under a mattress or even in a bank account. It's all tied up in this and that, and most of it's in trust anyway. It can't be got at. Frank Pelley did it for me. Only a financial idiot . . .'

'I just thought I'd ask. It helps clear one's thoughts.'

'So?' I asked.

'So, I think we ought to concentrate exclusively on what's possible. For instance, perhaps – if Deenie rings again – we should suggest that we shift her out of wherever she is at the moment. Spirit her away, so to speak. I'm giving it a lot of thought.'

'I could hop in the car and drive her back to Wellington any time,' I said excitedly. 'Or up to Auckland. Or wherever.'

'That won't do, I'm afraid,' Nathan said, shaking his head slowly. 'There's only one road out of Mt Matheson and three roads out of Rownley. If anyone she knows drives out of here right now they may as well advertise she's a passenger. She says she thinks there's all sorts of people starting to watch out for her if she makes a move, including the police. I would suggest that secrecy is of the essence.'

'They can't be watching every . . .'

'But who can be sure? That's the important question, Arthur.'

'Air,' I said.

'What do you mean, air?'

'Air as in aeroplane,' I said, lowering my voice this time. 'It's simple. I get James or Bruce – it doesn't matter which – to land at Rownley, where whoever it is can pick up a Cessna, fly it over to the Mt Matheson Flying Club, then take Deenie up to, say, Ardmore. Then whoever it is – James or Bruce – goes back to Rownley, where he changes back to the plane he came on and flies home, while the other one picks her up, drives her on to Auckland or flies her down to Christchurch, it doesn't matter which, and gets her straight on a plane to Sydney, Los Angeles, Singapore – anywhere, as long as it's away to hell out of it. And we'll have left a lot of false trails that no one can pick their way through. The boys are always flying themselves all around the country. It's brilliant. It'll work.'

It was only a spur-of-the-moment thought, but its clarity and ingeniousness seemed unassailable, until Nathan said, 'If you involve James or Bruce and everything works out as you say, you do realise you widen the circle of those in the know and you may even involve them in some degree of danger. They could come in for quite serious retribution.'

'Retribution?'

The word was one I couldn't remember hearing on human lips for decades. It was a Sunday word, one you used to hear only in church. It was one of those black and white verbal signposts that pointed grimly in one downhill direction, while casting a nasty black shadow of Old Testament finality behind it.

'I don't think you've thought seriously about the precarious situation Deenie appears to be in,' Nathan went on, 'Or the way the danger that surrounds her resembles a condition of madness. It's like a disease – it's the kind of lunatic danger that spreads contagiously.'

Suddenly I understood what he was getting at. The appalling truth had to be that everyone who came near me was getting tainted by the mystery that gripped Deenie. 'Not you too, Nathan?' I asked. 'Oh God, of course . . . Look, how can I tell you this? I've been a selfish bloody fool. I don't want to get anyone else in trouble. I don't want you involved . . .'

Nathan nodded, but said nothing.

'Stay clear of me, that's the only safe thing to do,' I said. 'You mustn't come around for a while. I can't thank you enough for all the help you've given, but you've done more than your share . . .'

Nathan nodded again, then gave me a wry smile. 'Just one more promise, Arthur – that's all I ask.'

'Yes, of course.'

'Talk to Ralph. You get the boy's back up too readily. Ease up on him a bit. Your best line is the simplest one: try to find out what's what and who's who. I wouldn't expect Ralph to know all the answers, he's too unimportant, but he's still there at the edges of whatever's going on. And, just look at the way he tried to needle me. There's very definitely something on his mind, something that's eating him. I've a feeling he may unburden into a sympathetic ear. It may be useful for us to know what he knows. It may even be very important. Try a lubricant.'

'A lubricant? My God, he's already drunk a whole bottle of my best malt, plus half a bottle of brandy.'

'And a sympathetic ear, remember.'

Nathan wished me well, then went. From the door I watched him pass Ralph with a murmured goodbye – though he may as well have saved his breath. Ralph just sat at the table with the phone in front of him. He didn't move or even bother to answer. He looked sick.

Yet how could I feel sympathy for my son? How could I think anything other than that his futile pointless life was of his own making?

It was well past time for my morning walk along the beach, and since Deenie was now making contact through Nathan, it was probably all right for me to put on my hat and go. I tried not to imagine what might have been brought in on the morning's tide, and I had already decided to aim directly for the lower part of the beach. No fossicking around this time.

91

17

'Who rang?' I asked when I got back from walking a good two kilometres along the beach – during which time Ralph had managed to move all the way from outside the house to the kitchen, where he sat at the table, with a half-empty bottle of the agreeable white wine I always kept in the fridge, by habit, though I seldom drank it.

He ignored me, not that I really cared. I'd had a pleasant outing by the edge of the sea, and I'd had an opportunity to think in private of lines I might follow to discover where Deenie was and how I might even try to make sense of what was going on.

During the walk, I had an impression that several people were staring at me, so I must have earned some social standing as a temporary item of news, but to my mild surprise only one person actually came up to me, face to face, to talk about the body. An elderly woman – possibly a good ten or so years older than me, and going a bit doolally – bailed me up and asked if in future I'd give her first look at all the bodies I found. She'd lost her husband and she felt certain he would be tossed up on the beach any day now. All the others left me alone.

So I was in a good enough mood to ignore Ralph's brush-off. Instead, I went to the sink and made a bit of lunch. Some lettuce, tomatoes, red onions and health-shop sourdough bread. Then I remembered Nathan's advice and decided I'd open a tin of sardines. As a boy Ralph used to dote on them.

To my astonishment, the sardines still worked on him at fifty. Ralph followed me out to the sun sofa, leaned forward across the patio table, sniffed almost fastidiously, then picked up the tin and scooped three fish onto a slice of bread which he had plastered with a heavy golden coating of the 'genuine-article cow's butter' he'd bought that morning. He covered the sardines with slices of onion, shook pepper and squeezed lemon juice over them and gobbled the whole lot down with a churning, open-mouthed sound, like a mincing machine.

'Eat them all,' I said. 'I seldom touch oily food. I got them out for you.'

Without so much as a thank you, he scoffed the rest the same way, then wiped his hands on the teatowel I had laid out as an excuse for a tablecloth and lit a cigarette. I stuck to Nathan's recommendation, counted up to ten and refused to let myself get angry.

'You probably noticed there's another bottle of white wine in the fridge,' I said. 'Or scotch on the sideboard.'

Ralph gave me an especially mean look, then cocked his head on one side and laughed coarsely and disagreeably. 'Change of policy? Something on your mind? Want answers to a few questions – eh, father?' he asked, letting go a belch, which I also chose to ignore. Then he laughed again, got up and went to the kitchen.

A couple of minutes later – time enough, I imagined, to have first helped himself to a long gulp of scotch straight from the decanter – he reappeared with a half-empty bottle of sauvignon blanc, a full bottle of chardonnay, a corkscrew and two glasses.

When he had settled and was pouring the wine, I said, 'No, it's not a bribe, Ralph. Just a kind of peace offering. We may have a few more hours of this new togetherness to go through, before our ways part again, so we may as well try to avoid friction. For one thing, it exhausts me.'

'Oh yeah? Try pulling the other one. You're the most frictional . . .'

'You mean abrasive?' I corrected.

'Good word,' he agreed. 'You always fancied yourself with words, didn't you? Do you still keep a diary?'

'Yes.'

'And I suppose you've written up a bit of what happened yesterday?'

'I don't write things up, as you call it. Quite the opposite. I jot events down, plus a few things people said, with a few comments and phrases – all in a kind of private shorthand I've invented, just to catch the mood of the day. So, if you think there's anything I haven't told you . . .'

Ralph went back to the sun sofa, eased himself into it gently, stretched out, then set it swinging slowly. 'Come on, dad, enough of this bullshit,' he said. 'What do you want to know that I'm not going to tell you anyway?'

I was suddenly grateful for having Nathan as a friend. He was shrewd all right. Ralph was back on form again. He thought he'd sprung the trap I'd set for him, so he felt on top, and that meant he would almost certainly give me the opening I was looking for.

'I realise there's no point in asking you to tell me the truth about what's going on, because you wouldn't feel free to confide in me,' I began, 'but there is one simple little explanation I would like, if it wouldn't be breaking a confidence. You see, I don't know anything about the things you've been telling me, and it's something you said yesterday connected with this chap Sullivan that has puzzled me ever since. When I asked about drugs, you said something to the effect that I wasn't on the right track. Sullivan was also somehow involved in money. I can't work that one out. What did you mean by it?'

'Tut, tut. That really would be breaking a confidence,' Ralph said. 'What do you mean, telling me all you want is an explanation? Wipe the dribble off your chin, will you? What kind of a plonker do you take me for? I've known you far too long to let you come the puke-coloured prawn on me.'

He smirked triumphantly. But that was the trick; I'd snared him in his own self-esteem. He was so pleased to think he'd caught me out that he tossed off a whole glass of wine in one swallow, poured himself a refill and began to talk.

'Drugs are for growers and dealers,' he explained smugly. 'After all that Mister Asia business, and some pretty rich people getting very frightened indeed, the big boys don't directly involve themselves any more with shit and all that stuff. They often leave the organisation to the gangs.'

'Like Sullivan?' I asked innocently.

'Naw,' Ralph said, shaking his head as if he couldn't believe my imbecility. 'He's in between. He's the laundryman. And even you have to know what that means. It's totally different from being an out-and-out dealer. See what I mean?'

I shrugged to indicate it made no sense.

Ralph sighed. 'God, you don't try hard, do you?' he said. 'Put it this way. Tuggy Sullivan is the paymaster. He carries the bag. Which means he's top trusty, okay? Below him are the people who set up the deals and all that. The gangs do a lot of the bits and pieces these days. They organise the distribution. Sometimes they handle the whole operation. But there's a loose sort of business set-up behind the scenes, especially when there's such things as a large shipment to be paid for and moved. That's when Tuggy comes into his own. He produces the really big money and handles the cash and does the bookwork and – well, of course, he distributes the profits.'

'You mean he goes around collecting from those who do the purchasing . . .?'

'Christ no. That's what the dealers do. It's all very – discreet, you'd call it. Tuggy picks up the whole sum. He holds the bank. He's a kind of filter. They bring what's owing to him and deposit it with him and he puts it in a safe place for the shareholders, so they don't ever have anything to do with the filth. They don't want to be tainted by crime on the one hand or the Inland Revenue on the other. The shareholders are respectable people. They don't live in ostentatious wealth in resorts like Russell any more.'

'Why?'

'That lifestyle stuff makes them too alternative to be true. Makes them stick out, doesn't it? No, they live with the other rich pricks in Remuera and Khandallah. Probably Rownley too. Who would know? There's no list of names in the Yellow Pages.'

I poured a little chardonnay into the second glass, the one that Ralph had left empty without thinking to ask me if I felt like a drink of my own wine. Allowing myself no more than a passing regret, I also topped up Ralph's glass with the last of the sauvignon.

'I think I'm getting the picture,' I said. 'The top people are the investors. The shareholders, as you incorrectly label them. Then there's Tuggy. He's the so-called banker. The dealers, pushers, growers and so on do the production and distribution bit. And the public does the consuming?'

'Spoken like a true believer,' Ralph said. 'Though it's not all that well organised, despite the fact it's called *organised* crime in the newspapers, but you've got the general idea. It's actually a bloody shambles most of the time, and it needs a hard man with a steady nerve to sort out some of the tangles. It even gets dangerous occasionally, when the bonds of trust start slipping. But that's just old-fashioned capitalism in miniature, isn't it? That's free enterprise for you. In the long run it's in everyone's interest to make it work.'

'It sounds quite the opposite to me,' I said. 'It couldn't be further from my definition of free enterprise. It's far from open and free. In fact, the whole thing carries a nasty taint of monopolies and compulsion and enforcement of various kinds.'

'Well, you've got a point there, dad. But look at it in this light – it's the only way the world goes round, isn't it? And nothing that that smartarse Nathan stands for, with all his crap about devoting his life to the service of the public interest, could make it go any better. In fact, Nathan's is the sure way to bugger up the world and tip it off its axis. I grew up when this country thought it could keep all its citizens on the tit for life. But look at what's happened. It hasn't worked out the way the theorists said. The best kind of society operates the same way as crime does. You have your investors and your commercial people and those who demand your services . . .'

'I never thought I'd live to hear you talk like that,' I said truthfully.

Ralph raised his glass to that one and took a long slurp. 'It's unfortunate it never worked out the other way,' he said. 'It was a beautiful dream. All that stuff about looking after people from the cradle to the grave. But no one's giving me handouts, are they? Where's my payoff? The government's given up on me, hasn't it? Theorists like Nathan don't ring true any more. They talk out of holes in their arses.'

'You've never liked him, have you, Ralph?'

'That's one way of putting it, I suppose. But I wouldn't have expressed it as mildly as that.'

'Because of Daphne?'

'Because of her and a lot of other things. Including Deenie.'

'Deenie?'

'Yeah. He's bloody creepy is our Nathan.'

'What do you mean by that? I'd say that creepy was just about the last thing you could ever say about him.'

'It means as far as I'm concerned he's like a burst condom. He comes at you in his linen suits and striped shirts and smarm and service of mankind bullshit. And underneath he's just a prick with an itch looking for an opportunity to . . .'

'Watch it Ralph,' I said furiously. 'He's my friend. And I've known him slightly longer than you – for more than sixty years in fact.'

'Well, don't blame me if one day he stabs you in the back and wipes the blade on your best hanky.'

I took a steady sip of wine then cleared my throat to test it before speaking. Keeping absolute self-control, with my temper reined in tightly, I said, 'You can take my personal assurance on that – I won't blame you. All right?'

Ralph merely shrugged. 'I'm just telling you, that's all.'

'Well,' I said, 'You can't claim not to be prejudiced, can you?'

The truth as I interpreted it was that Ralph couldn't stand those who had tried to help him most. He was so hell-bent on self-destruction that he saw people like Nathan, who had glimpsed his better qualities and who had tried to straighten him out for his own good, as the enemy.

'Yeah,' he answered, after a while. 'I'm prejudiced. But I've been up against him, haven't I? So I'm the one who knows.'

'He's always gone out of his way to help you.'

'He's like a burst boil. He keeps the pus hidden under cottonwool.'

Bastard, I said to myself. You rotten little sneak-bastard.

Ralph knew nothing about the world that Nathan and I

97

had grown up in. Nothing about the horror of the Depression, the rise of Hitler, our fear of Communism, the guilt of what happened in the war, the atomic bomb . . . Let alone the little matter of what took place around the very spot he now sat on – the heroic battle there was to turn this country into a paradise – the long huge struggles that people such as Nathan and I had been tested by and had triumphed over.

Just as Ralph would never know how we were young once, too, and went through things he could never even guess at, such as the way we could have killed each other over his mother, or the deep trust and understanding that comes with age and wisdom. He didn't have the imagination or the human sympathy.

All my son knew about the world and its complexities could be bought for a can of sardines and a few glasses of white wine.

18

I got a terrific shock when Frank Pelley walked down the drive. I'd completely forgotten that sometime yesterday, after getting back from the Mt Matheson police station, I'd got in touch with him. But when had it been? In a sudden jumbled rush of recollection I could now vaguely remember talking to him on the phone, but I was damned if I could recollect exactly when or about what. These days I was becoming increasingly aware of what Fraser-Lang called my short-term memory loss, but I had no idea it was so far advanced. Perhaps I'd rung him when I had all that early afternoon wine inside me, just after Nathan had gone and before I went upstairs to lie down and crash out.

But I'd no sooner worked out that probability than I noticed the table in front of me. There was simply no denying that it looked as though I must have spent all afternoon on the piss. There were two bottles standing there, one empty and the other less than half full. But there was now only one glass. I must have nodded off for a moment, because Ralph had gone missing, probably to sleep off his lunch, and his glass had gone with him.

The picture I must have made – an old man having a private midday guzzle – must have put me in a pretty poor light, in front of Frank, who was dressed up in his lawyer's best, in a very good suit, shoes you could see your reflection in, a blue-striped shirt and a buttonhole carnation.

'Nice lunch, Arthur?' were the first words he said. He has a reputation for coming straight to the point and not bothering too much about the niceties.

I shrugged. There was no point in offering excuses, for they could only make the whole picture seem worse than it was. 'Would you care for a glass of wine?' I responded. 'There's still a chill on the chardonnay, but I can fetch another sauvignon if you'd rather . . . I can't promise it'll be cold enough.'

Frank raised his eyebrows and pursed his lips, but restrained himself from making some obvious remark about my thirst. Instead, he said, 'No thanks. I've only got a few minutes, then I've got to go back to Rownley. Sorry I couldn't make it yesterday or this morning. As I explained, I had to hop over to Hamilton. Everything all right now?'

'Oh that,' I answered, buying a bit of time while I tried to remember what I must have told him. 'I think so. Yes, in a general sort of way, so to speak. But the important thing is, what's your impression of it all?'

'All what?'

'What I told you.'

Frank looked at me with a puzzled expression, then he gazed thoughtfully at the bottles. How was he to know that I'd only had a couple of half-glasses of the stuff, and that despite appearances I was actually the very model of sobriety?

'You sounded more than a bit exasperated,' he offered. 'I

hope you didn't take it any further. It's always best to look at a problem in the light of a new day.'

'Good advice,' I said quickly. At last the shape of a memory was returning, though it was still tantalisingly out of reach, behind a shifting mist of thoughts and words. 'That's what I did. I let it rest overnight.'

'Excellent. The police often get a bit prickly when they've got an unidentified corpse on their hands. Especially when it seems to have been murdered quite brutally. You can understand their feelings. It's a great nuisance for them. It's very untidy. They tend to drop all the usual courtesies and just plunge on with the investigation.'

Yes, I'd got it now. I must have given Frank an earful about the man who'd called me Fred, and about the young girl munching chewing-gum in the car that brought me home.

'I accept that,' I said. 'But the thing that got me was they were more than just bloody rude, they were belligerent. And . . . well, it's hard to explain . . . they were sort of suspicious.'

'Suspicious of what?'

'Just suspicious. It was as though they thought I'd been up to no good – as if they were trying to make me feel guilty. It was bloody embarrassing.'

Frank gave me a hard disbelieving look, then he rubbed his chin. 'Okay then,' he said. 'Let me ask this, right out – had you been on the juice?'

'The juice? Drinking?'

'Boozing.'

'Me? Boozing? Of course not.' I waved at the bottles and my glass. 'Don't believe appearances, Frank. Whatever you think, I haven't put away all that plonk in front of me. Christ, I'd be on my ear.'

Frank merely nodded politely.

'No,' I went on. 'They were suspicious in a very peculiar sort of way. They kept sizing me up from a distance, sneaking little looks at me. And they didn't seem to know who I was.'

'How do you mean, they didn't know who you were? You told them your name, surely?'

'That's what I'm getting at. I told them, but it didn't seem to mean anything to them. It didn't register.'

'I don't quite see what you're complaining about, Arthur,' he said. 'Why should it mean anything in particular?'

'Good God,' I replied, in considerable surprise. 'They didn't know I was king pin around here. You remember the joke, surely. "King Arthur of the Rownley table." It was as though my life counted for nothing. They treated me like some kind of daft old nobody . . .'

Later that day, I made notes of our conversation up to this point, so I've got that just about word for word, but I didn't bother to take notes on anything from here on because I became too bloody angry. However, for the record, what next happened, as I remember it in general terms, was that Frank sat down beside me and took me by the wrist. He gripped me lightly, and started talking, and he didn't let go till he'd finished.

The gist of what he tried to tell me was that I ought to face up to the fact that indeed I was an old man, and pulling my head in a bit might be a good idea. I got an impression that I may have barked at him when I'd phoned the day before, and he was pretty alarmed by what I'd said.

He also remarked that, though it was perfectly true that I had spent my life playing a part in the commercial action around here, I had no right as such to expect special treatment. And when I insisted that I'd done more than 'play a part' – that it was a fact of history that I'd been the uncrowned king of Rownley – he said something to the effect that I was free to go around thinking that as much as I liked, but I shouldn't expect others to share the notion.

As I remember it, he maintained that Rownley had had several prominent mayors and members of parliament, including cabinet ministers, plus a couple of knights of the realm and a solid proportion of nationally famous people in business and sport. So there was quite a team of uncrowned kings, when you thought about it.

And, since I want this record to include everything that

101

happened, I may as well add that Frank alluded to a few other things he thought I ought to take account of, mainly to do with a series of nasty and entirely unfounded rumours put about by my enemies in the commercial world, besides some family gossip that seemed to have got around town about my children clearing off when they grew up, to put as much distance as they could between themselves and me for the rest of their lives. He even tried to soil Deenie's name by talking bluntly about some scandals she was supposed to have left at my doorstep – which did him no good at all, because I just switched off and let him ramble on.

Things had come to a pretty poor pass when the man you'd been instrumental in elevating to pre-eminence as one of Rownley's top lawyers could try to fill your earhole with a lot of stinking old garbage which took no account of the truth. It was nothing less than a gross travesty of the facts, not to mention a betrayal.

But let me point out, since I don't have the slightest patience with reticence or false modesty, that when he said it was time to go I stood up, looked him straight in the eye and shook his hand.

That's the way I've always conducted my business affairs. I've never been a cry-baby or a quitter, like some I've known who've crumpled and collapsed when confronted by adversity, and whose bones I'd had no option but to use as stepping stones to get to the top. I could face up to whatever the world threw at me and never flinch, while all the time I kept my secret feelings sealed off where no one could get at them.

Whatever had happened to change Frank Pelley from being one of my faithful followers was a mystery that I wouldn't waste my time trying to solve. So far as I was concerned, the important thing was that I still had my own pride, integrity and human dignity. I wasn't going to show him that he'd got hold of the wrong end of the story, that he had broken his sacred duty before the law to uphold the truth.

He even had the gall, as he left, to nod towards the bottles and tell me that I ought to see a doctor.

19

The police came back in the late afternoon. My third lot of visitors. It was beginning to get just like the old days again. I was once more becoming the man everyone needed to see.

I'd only just arrived downstairs a matter of minutes after taking a nice long nap to recover from the shock that Frank Pelley's extraordinary carry-on had given me. And the miracle was that yet again I'd had a long and luxurious sleep. Almost two hours of bliss. How was it possible, with all hell breaking loose around me, that I should suddenly be able to curl up like this, for the first time in years, and switch off like a babe? I was buoyant.

'That your Falcon in the drive, sir?' a young man in uniform asked.

Well, that was a breakthrough. A policeman had at last called me sir.

'You'll find it belongs to Mister Gransey. That's my name,' I replied, without actually telling an out-and-out lie.

Over the policeman's shoulder I noticed two more men in plainclothes had just climbed out of a big white police car in the street – where all my neighbours couldn't help noticing it – and were now walking down the driveway towards me. I guessed they'd hung back to get in touch with the Wanganui computer to look up the Falcon's registration.

The uniformed policeman turned around to the others and announced, as if he'd just made a breakthrough in the investigation, 'He says he's Gransey all right. That sorts that out.'

'Funny car for around here,' one of the plainclothes men commented. It was the short and bristly one with the Che Guevarra moustache I'd encountered the day before. The one who'd called me Fred.

'Takes all sorts,' his companion said. He was as tall as the other was short.

I could only suppose that it was some kind of talk they thought was the nearest thing to repartee. They sounded just like kids.

'We called to see if you could think of anything else to tell us about yesterday,' said the short one. 'Something you might've forgotten in all the excitement.'

'You know,' the tall one added. 'After a good night's sleep you wake up and your brain cells come up with something that could help us.'

'No,' I said. 'If I'd thought of anything else, I would have rung you.'

'That's good,' the short one said, leaning his head back, yawning and giving me a perfect view of the amalgam fillings in his back teeth. Then he looked around with a pleased expression, as though surprised by his own generosity, and commented, 'Nice garden.'

'Yes,' I said. 'I'm rather proud of it.'

'I've always liked gardens,' he went on. 'Would you believe, I've located two murder victims, both buried in flowerbeds. Never in the vegetable patch. Always the flowers. Funny that.'

'It makes sense when you think about,' the tall one said. 'Flowerbeds are for decoration, but you eat what comes out of the vege garden. You'd feel like a cannibal every time you tucked into your parsnips, wouldn't you?'

'I use quite a bit a blood and bone,' I conceded with a smile. 'But I get it from the garden centre, not the cemetery.'

'You trying to take the mickey, Mister Gransey?' the short one snapped.

'We don't like that,' said his companion.

'Anyone who smartarses us gets extra.'

'There's some misunderstanding,' I protested. Everything I did and said – even a harmless little joke – seemed to be landing me in deeper trouble, whereas the last thing on earth I wanted was to keep on mysteriously antagonising the police – as well as all the phantom lunatics surrounding Deenie and Ralph.

'I've tried to help right from the very beginning,' I told them. 'And I've done my duty conscientiously. I've always been completely and absolutely on the side of the police when it comes to this sort of thing. It's just that you've used up all my patience. I'm now becoming extremely exasperated. You two started all this nonsense about bodies in the flowerbeds.'

The pair of them had the cheek to stand there for about half a minute, just staring at me and saying nothing, as if they were trying to unnerve me, while all the time the uniformed man smirked as if he found them funny, instead of just plain unimaginative.

'Let me remind you this is a murder investigation,' the tall one said eventually.

'Oh, come on,' the short one announced. 'Let's leave him to sweat it out.'

The tall one took his time to consider the suggestion, then added in exaggerated tones of reluctance, 'See you sooner than you expect.' And away they went.

It took several minutes before Ralph at last felt brave enough to venture out from the garage, where he'd managed to hide himself away. He must have got down on my duplicate keys.

'Christ, dad, that was something. I never thought you had it in you. You've gone right up in my book for the first time ever.'

'Shut up, Ralph,' I grumbled. 'You talk too much. This whole stupid business is getting on top of me. Do you know, the police seem to have it in their heads that I've got bodies in the garden?'

'Bullshit, dad. I heard what they said – all that bodies shit was a put-on. They're not that dumb. They're out to wind you up so you'll drop your guard. They act the maggot like that just to get you off balance. It's a put-on.'

'It was bloody unpleasant. I suddenly feel very shaky.'

'Don't let it worry you. I've seen them do it over and over again. It's just a routine. And you did exactly the right thing – you handled them straight. Punch for punch, joke for joke.'

'Do you really think so?' I asked in genuine surprise. I wasn't used to praise from Ralph.

'You did bloody beaut.'

'Beaut? I haven't heard that word in years. Did you really think my joke about the blood and bone was one up to the Granseys?'

'It wasn't the joke, popsie, it was the way you said it and the way you followed it up. All innocent mischief. I had to bury my face in a snotrag to strangle the laughter.'

'Well, I'm not at all sure I ought to be too thrilled by that little revelation.'

'Well you bloody should. You made your son laugh for the first time in your life. From now on, it's the only way to go, dad. I've had a lovely little power-snooze and all I need is more battery acid. Let's have a drink and celebrate.'

'You mean *another* drink,' I said, not too certain that I wasn't being conned, and led the way back inside.

20

I got out a bottle of Chivas Regal. It must have been sitting in the drinks cabinet in the den for the past ten years, along with a whole lot of high-priced whiskies, brandies and liqueurs, and it had never been opened. If it wasn't for Ralph's visit, the whole lot would have been gathering dust there till the day I died.

My short-term memory may have become wonky but it wasn't entirely fuddled, because I clearly remembered Nathan's earlier advice again, and put it to good effect again by pouring out a stiff measure. It worked brilliantly. Two sips into his first 'real' drink of the day – he insisted that the wine he'd had with his lunch didn't really count as booze, for all it amounted to was 'a bit of a mouth-rinse to gargle the food down with' – and Ralph began to open up about the phone call he'd had a few hours previously, the one that had stunned him so that he wouldn't talk about it.

In fact, his mood had swung around completely and he now needed no prompting. He raised the subject himself.

'If you're still interested, that call I had when Nathan was here was from a prick called Tommy Farr,' he announced.

'Just like the boxer,' I said before I could stop myself.

'What boxer?'

'He fought Joe Louis, the Brown Bomber. But that was long ago and I guess it wouldn't mean anything to you.'

'Well, that may be, but the only thing I know about this Farr is he isn't far enough away for my liking . . .' He stopped and screwed up his face in an expression of distaste. There was real fear in his eyes. 'I'm telling you this for your own good, daddy-o. But afterwards you've got to forget I ever mentioned the name, okay?'

'Why's that?'

'Why's that?' he repeated, with an abrupt half-laugh. 'Well, the Tommy Farr I was talking to is the kind of joker you don't make fun of. And he's been sent to locate Deenie. You might find this very hard to believe, and it doesn't really matter whether you do or not, or even if it happens to be true or false, but it's being said that Deenie and Tuggy skipped off with a suitcase full of used banknotes. My Auckland connections asked me if I knew anything about a million bucks. A whole bloody million. You wouldn't read about it, would you? Our Deenie? A whole bloody million . . .'

I tried to look surprised.

'Anyway. This Tommy bastard kills people.'

'We should tell the police,' I said.

'Are you crazy?' Ralph asked. His mouth hung open. 'Everyone knows he's the prick who stopped that couple down in Christchurch two years ago.'

'Stopped?'

'Zapped. Injected with lead. Gunned down. Shot.'

'Well, I didn't,' I said. 'I've never heard of anyone being shot down there.'

'Man and woman. Right in front of their four-year-old daughter. It was an execution. He used a handgun. Gave it to

107

them close up. He must have been looking them in the eye when he did it.'

I vaguely remembered reading something a long time ago about a shooting in front of a little girl. Very gruesome – but just another horror of the day. There was so much of it. Wars everywhere. Starvation. Cruelty. That's why I seldom watched the television news any more. Endless bloodshed in full colour. What was the point of it?

'All the more reason to get in touch with the police,' I said.

'Not if you want to live, it isn't.'

'Look, Ralph,' I said. 'This whole thing is far too big and too serious for you and me. If what you're saying is true – and I can promise you I've got no reason to disbelieve you, have I? – we've got to tell the police that this fellow Farr is coming here and what he's already done.'

'And Deenie? What about her? If you push Farr and he finds her, she's dead.'

That was preposterous. It couldn't be true. No one would want to kill Deenie. She was beautiful and breathlessly wonderful and clever. And she was mine. No one would want to hurt her.

'That's stupid,' I said.

Ralph pulled a face that proved me right. 'A million dollars, a million reasons,' he replied.

'Well, before anyone starts making helpful suggestions, I've got to make one fact clear to you. I can't repay that million, even supposing it ever existed,' I said. 'I'm not so silly that I can't work out that certain parties could've very well hinted to you that I may consider helping to straighten their cash books. But the fact of the matter is I haven't got the readies. I can certainly raise the wherewithal to buy a cruise or a car, if I wanted one, but that's all. I've never had access to big money. Despite your naïve model of the way the system works, proper legitimate business doesn't operate like that. It may surprise you to learn that I've always lived on income, the same as everyone. I've never been able to get hold of my capital, just like that. It's always been tied up. And now it's complicated by being salted away in trust. Do you know, I'd have a job even selling this house to raise cash? It's something I'd have to get Frank Pelley to work on, and it wouldn't be easy. Just about every cent I've earned has been stashed away safely for future generations of Granseys . . .'

'Oh yeah? Including me, father?'

I looked at Ralph and last of my anger ebbed away. Poor Ralph. One of the Ruined Boys. The charm, the looks, the body, the brains – year by year they had been burning down to their last ashes in front of me.

'No,' I said quietly, 'You've had your chances, Ralph, and you've called on all the credit you ever had with me. In fact, you're overdrawn when it comes to that. But if you have children, which at your age is probably very unlikely, I'd say, well . . . Let me put it this way, there are provisions for the trust to look after them. Don't ask me to explain it – it's all there, locked up tight in fine print. And no one can prise it open.'

'Thanks dad. Thanks a heap,' he murmured.

For about fifteen minutes I sat there and watched him drink two large whiskies. Then I said quietly, 'Listen, Ralph. Hasn't it struck you that we're only going to fight our way out of this one by solving the mystery and finding out who the players are? If we knew who was in it, and who was looking for what, we might find an answer to Deenie's difficulties.'

The thought didn't seem to impress him. He just sat there, drinking and glaring out across the lawn to the street.

Nevertheless, I went on. 'For a start, we've got Tuggy and Deenie. She's in with him, and he's the banker for someone we'll call Mister X – and Mister X represents some sort of loose organisation of shareholders. He also employs someone called Tommy Farr. Then there's the gangs. They probably come into it somehow. Plus, there's your side. You're representing in a small way a man we'll call . . .'

'You've got it all wrong. What makes you think it isn't all the same organisation, the same company?'

At least I'd started him up again.

'Okay,' I said. 'But why would that company send you here to keep an eye on me? They don't need to do that. If there's only one player, then Mister X has got the whole scene tied up, hasn't he?'

Ralph shook his head, but said nothing, so I went on, 'You're here on some kind of scouting mission, or watching brief, or whatever you call it, because everyone's confused, there's a corpse floating about, and nobody has quite worked out what anybody else is up to. And we have to have at least two interested parties, because I've got a distinct feeling that one lot's watching every move the other lot makes, and the one to make the next move could start a war. Is that right?'

'I'm buggered if I can work it out,' said Ralph. He was leaning back in his chair, looking bloated, relaxed and a bit pathetic. I knew I'd got him. He was like a big lump of putty – I felt as if I could almost reach out and reshape him in my hand. 'I'm just watching this end of things. I'll tell you this, dad, in all honesty – I don't really have a clue who's up who. Nobody gives me names, and the numbers involved don't mean nothing. And who cares anyway? What counts is that enough of the crazy bastards have suddenly gone all twitchy. And – your guess is probably spot on – when they send Tommy in, it means they've decided to stop watching and waiting, and war's about to be declared. Money's missing. Someone's got killed. They want a result.'

'So you'd better tell me who sent you here.'

'You really want to know?'

'Yes.'

'It won't help you or anyone else.'

I waited.

'Jason Wakeworth is his moniker,' Ralph said quietly. 'And he's bad news, because he's a show-off – a Flash Harry from Auckland. He's probably not one of the principals, just an agent. And he's the one who thinks you hold the key, because you found the body, and because Deenie is bound to get in touch and try and come here sooner or later. They can't get it out of their minds that you're involved somehow, as well as

Deenie. Even though I keep telling them you're an old man and you drove off the road and over a cliff years ago.'

'And he pays you well?'

'Pays me?' Ralph gave a little snort and helped himself to an enormous whisky. 'That's a good one. I've got about one hundred and fifty bucks in my pocket, after which I'm going to have to think of something toot-bloody-sweet.'

He grinned at me stupidly, then lowered his voice and added: 'It happens that I owe a favour here and there. So I do all this for zilch. And I have to say I suppose I've suddenly found I'm partly doing it for you, too, though, God help me, I never thought the day would come . . .'

'For me?'

'I promise I didn't have any idea you'd gone so soft in the loaf. I didn't know you were living in dreamland, the way you are. You're rooted. You've fallen out of your pram. You need looking after.'

'Don't give me that bunk,' I said. 'You've got the hide to tell me you're doing this for my sake, when you know bloody well you're here to find out information about Deenie? When you're here to inform on your own sister?'

'It's not like that, dad,' Ralph tried to explain. 'You've got everything in a twist. It's not about loyalty to Deenie and all that. I don't want to see her go down in flames. You mightn't believe this – and I couldn't give a tinker's fart either way – but I keep trying to think of every possible wrinkle that could help her. But when it comes down to it, the only excuse I've got for being here is money. Not my money, but someone else's. Someone I've never met. It's all to do with company policy.'

'Bullshit,' I said. 'You weren't brought here by company policy. You were brought by crime.'

'Money,' Ralph repeated stubbornly. 'Once upon a time this was a land of milk and honey. Everyone looked after everyone else and it was a good place to be. Then the money-men took over and everything got a price tag. There's a ticket on the air you breathe. It all comes down to money. Nothing else. Deenie, you, me – we get born and we live and die. And in the end it doesn't matter.'

'And money? What happens to money?'

'You know the answer to that, dad. I learned it as a small boy, sitting on your knee. No man in this town knows better than you . . . Money goes on forever.'

21

Ralph and I shared a Deluxe American Special, delivered by bicycle from the Dial-a-pizza Palace in the Mt Matheson Mall. Then Ralph fell asleep on the sofa, just as he had done the previous evening. He'd had a huge amount of whisky.

To my surprise, I quite enjoyed the texture and flavour of the pizza. I'd never tried one before, and it tasted rather like heavy doughy bread with a thick vegetable spread, or at least mine did, for I picked off a lot of suspicious-looking sliced sausage bits I didn't fancy.

How extraordinary that you can just lift up the telephone and half an hour later someone arrives on your doorstep with cooked food. And this happens as though it's the most natural thing in the world, in a place where not so long ago there were cows, barbed-wire fences, huge macrocarpa trees and dusty metalled roads – in fact, when I first moved over here to the old farmhouse with Grace, the nearest stretch of tarsealed road was twelve miles away.

It was part of the treat of eating that pizza to think how far into the future people like me had dragged Mt Matheson, so I ate more than I usually do in the evening. Which I suppose was the reason why, after I'd filled a page of my diary, I also dozed off while I was sitting in a chair at the kitchen table.

I've no idea what woke me, but something must have startled me, because I was suddenly alert. The door from the kitchen to the patio was wide open and I hadn't yet turned on the lights. There was that strange grey illumination which sometimes seems to rise out of the ground just before total darkness.

In those few moments of weird shadow, I saw a man crossing the drive just behind Ralph's Falcon. I saw him look up at the garage and he must have noticed there was a double automatic light jutting above the door for he dodged backwards then cut at an angle across the lawn towards me. I leapt up and threw on every switch on the panel beside the back door. All the lawn, patio and kitchen spotlights came on in a sudden dazzling burst. I could see now that there were two intruders and for a second or two the lights seemed to have made no difference to them. They just kept on coming.

But then the man behind seemed to lurch and stumble – perhaps the lights had momentarily blinded him and he'd tripped – and immediately there was a strange and distinctive percussive sound, rather like a frog leaping into a pond. It was a kind of plopping noise, though a lot louder than one a frog would make – and immediately the front man spun around and fell over. The man behind him didn't say anything or even pause to look, but hurdled neatly over his companion, then dodged sideways and kept running, this time back to the street.

I couldn't move, but stood in the kitchen with my hand still on the panel of switches and watched as the man who had fallen now curled up, knee to chin, on the lawn. He clutched at his leg and held it just above the ankle. Then he rolled over, got up on his good leg and half-ran, half-limped, in the same direction taken by the man who'd jumped over him.

It was like watching a mime. No one had said a word. In fact, I must have gone on standing there, perhaps for another minute or two, in total silence. It was as though the clocks had stopped. Nothing moved, there were no sounds, apart from a couple of passing cars and the distant whisper of traffic on the Rownley Road. There was just a circle of intense light from the house, which reached halfway across the lawn and garden, where the diffused light of the streetlamps took over. And apart from a few moths, it was a world of emptiness.

I turned back to the kitchen and drank a small shot from the nearly empty whisky bottle, followed by a long draught of water from the tap. Then I woke Ralph and told him what had happened.

'Shit,' was all he said, before he staggered off to the down-stairs shower to wash his head.

He wasn't in much better shape when he came back, though he had made his curls look damp and glossy. My hero, I thought. I've just been witness to the most amazing drama I've ever seen in my life, someone gets shot right out-side my kitchen door, and my eldest son – who's been wished on me by some big-time Auckland criminal – picks himself up from the sofa and what's the first thing he does? Goes off to try to sober up under a shower, then looks at him-self in the mirror and combs his bloody hair.

I smiled at him. He was going to have a nasty little shock when the police arrived. I'd stopped to phone them just before I woke him. I'd had quite enough of this waiting around. If someone called Tommy Farr thought he was com-ing to Mt Matheson to make things happen, then he was going to find that Mt Matheson could also get off its arse and strike back.

As far as I was concerned, and even if I was now the last person to think so, I was still somebody in this town and I was buggered if I was going to have people shooting each other on my front lawn.

22

The expression on Ralph's face said it all when a police car pulled into the driveway with its lights flashing. Then four or five more cars stopped out on the road. The lights gave the whole place a festive look, like Christmas.

Ralph ducked down below the window so he wouldn't be seen and whispered hoarsely, 'For Christ's sake – it's the cops.'

'I know,' I replied. 'When people get shot, the police conduct an investigation. That's part of their job.'

'Oh God no,' he cried out in a very small and reedy voice that sounded just the way he used to wail when he was about ten years old. 'It wasn't you who called them, was it, dad?'

He looked absolutely terrified, but at least he managed to get his voice almost under control again. 'Christ, it can't be. I don't believe it,' he moaned. 'You crazy old bastard. This time you've fallen right off your fuckin' ladder.'

I simply shrugged and smiled, and went outside. I could still make decisions and take action, even if he couldn't.

The two detectives who'd come around earlier were the first to arrive. The tall one came straight up to me and said, 'I told you, didn't I – we'd see you sooner than you expected? I could tell there was going to be fun and games around here. You get a feeling for it.'

He asked me to point out the spot where I saw the man stumble, and the place where he fell. Then he got me to show him where I first saw the two intruders and the exact route they'd taken towards me and the direction in which they'd run away. More cars and a large van then arrived, probably from Rownley, and several policemen began hammering stakes into the lawn and garden and stringing rolls of tape between them.

The road was cordoned off. I recognised several of my neighbours gawking from the footpath and I enjoyed watching them being marched back out of sight.

Then arc lights went up and it became as bright as daylight outside, just like a carnival. However, the police weren't very jolly. There were about a dozen of them searching slowly and methodically across the property. I must say, they were a better organised and more business-like lot than I'd seen down on the beach. They were quite impressive.

Of course, I was asked to go inside and relate everything that had happened, then make a written statement – all under the eye of a man who was extremely well turned-out, right down to a pair of black gloves which he gripped tightly in one hand and slapped impatiently into the palm of the other with a rhythmic tap, tap, tap. It was gratifying finally to have the attention of someone with a bit of rank and style, though the glove-tapping business was the kind of self-important, irritating mannerism I'd soon have had him cured of, if I'd still been king of Rownley.

Several detectives came in from time to time to say how their search was going. One reported that there were no footprints – which any fool could have told him in the first place, to save him wasting his time. This part of Mt Matheson has fine sandy soil, which means that even when the lawns get water and fertiliser they always dry out by the end of summer and go as hard as concrete.

Then suddenly there was a shout of 'found it,' and we all traipsed out to see a detective leaning over a patch of lawn. A photographer stepped forward and shot off a dozen or so exposures from several angles. A tape-measure was produced and two policemen called out the numbers they read, taken from three or four points around the property. Then a small object was scooped into a plastic pouch. My eyesight was no longer good enough, even with glasses, to make out what it was. But the man seemed very pleased with himself and said, 'It looks like a thirty-eight shell. And in the very right spot, just by those gums.'

Gums? I don't have any gums. The idiot was pointing at my two specimens of old man saltbush, *Atriplex nummularia*, which stand out in lovely scaly grey in early summer against the lime and pale golden glow of my *Callistemon shiressii* bottlebrush. However, I thought it wise not to point out the mistake. I was learning slowly but surely that you could be too helpful for your own good. And, anyway, I doubted I'd be thanked for telling them.

A little later the search was abandoned, the lights were switched off and most of the stakes were pulled out.

The glove-slapper seemed very cheered up and pleased with himself, and he became almost affable. 'We're leaving two men here to keep an eye on things, Mister Gransey,' he said – and that simple little 'Mister Gransey' certainly went alongside the 'sir' I'd earned earlier in the day to mark yet another huge advance on 'Fred'. 'We'll need to have another sweep around in the morning, just in case. Will you be staying here? Or would you feel better . . .'

'Oh, I'm staying here all right,' I said. 'This is my house and no gangsters are going to make me leave it.'

'That's the spirit,' he said, a trifle condescendingly. 'My men will look after you. And we'll have another little chat in the morning and get you to look at some photographs.'

Then he went – in a surprisingly small and unimpressive car I'm sorry to say – and the tall detective came over and said, 'I've got two items of news for you, Mister Gransey – guess what?'

'Try to surprise me,' I said.

'Item number one is we know your son Ralph is living here with you, so he can walk in and out as he likes, if that's the way you want it.'

I gave a quick nod. What else could I do or say?

'And item number two concerns your recent visitors. Or one of them anyway. I've just had a call to say that a man fitting the description you gave is now in Rownley Hospital, under police surveillance. He has a nasty wound in his left leg where a bullet entered, clipped one of the bones, and lodged in the muscle tissue. God only knows how he managed to get up and run away. He must have done it on adrenalin.'

'But how did he get to Rownley? He couldn't have run all the way.'

'You can put a ring around that. His pal must have dumped him near the emergency entrance to the hospital. That's where he was found.'

'It looks like a proper balls-up all round, doesn't it?'

The detective looked at me sideways, with a squinted eye that was almost a wink. 'Just shows you,' he said. 'Guns are bloody dangerous things to play with, wouldn't you say?'

23

That night marked the occasion when Ralph achieved what I imagine was one of his life's ambitions. He had slipped upstairs when the police arrived and there was no way of getting him to go back down again so long as they were on or near the property. For the time being I saw no reason to tell him that the police had known he was here all along. That moment would come.

He took over the back bedroom, the one where you can glimpse the distant lights of Rownley across the harbour, and there he stayed put – with a bottle of my brandy, of course. Top of the roost at last.

It was also the night that Deenie rang. I must have just dropped off to sleep, only to plunge straight into a dream which was such an eerie distortion of the events of the past two days that I still remember every detail of it.

The dream opened with me running on sand. At first there was no resemblance to anywhere I had ever been. The whole landscape seemed to be endless desert. Then I realised I was actually on Ocean Beach. I asked myself why I was running, for there seemed no reason to be hurrying anywhere. It was all a mystery.

My legs found it hard going, but the exertion was exhilarating, and I could feel the wind coursing through my hair, and hear the pounding of the surf and the scrunch of sand below my feet. Then I began to feel cold. There was something near the end of the beach that began to chill me as I drew near it. I had a sudden premonition that a corpse lay there and I knew for an absolute certainty that I would recognise it and that it would stand up and say something to me.

With a huge terrified effort of will, I forced myself to turn away from the beach and run towards the dunes. Then I discovered I had managed to come out onto the old metalled road that used to meander for miles all the way around the head of the harbour towards Rownley. Something whacked me in the back of the leg and I looked down and realised my leg was broken. Someone was shooting at me from behind the shivering leaves of a long hedge of saltbushes.

I stumbled, but kept running, for I knew the unknown gunman would kill me if I stopped. Then I realised that all my efforts were useless. It had grown dark and in the light of the moon, on the curve of the road before me, I saw a huge shark lying in wait, opening its monstrous jaws like a tunnel. Its teeth sparkled as it willed me to enter and die. I pitched forward helplessly – then the phone woke me.

'Who's that?' a muffled voice said.

'What's happened?' was all I could think to say. My heart was thumping and I was soaked in sweat.

'Daddy?' said the voice. 'Daddy, what's wrong?'

'Deenie?' I asked. 'Thank God. Is that you, Deenie?'

The muffled sound vanished and I now heard her clearly. 'I've only got a couple of minutes. Your line's bugged, do you know that? Anyway, listen . . .'

'What do you mean, my line's bugged? It can't be. This isn't . . .'

'Stop it, daddy. I'm using a phone card. When Ralph answered I watched and the cops arrived in six minutes flat. Six minutes. So listen. I've been in touch already on the old one-two, okay? So that's how I'll make contact again in future. Got that?'

'What?'

'One-two. Oh for God's sake, you haven't forgotten have you, daddy? Look, I've got to go now. I've found a place to stay, but I'll have to move soon. Promise me you haven't for-gotten.'

'Deenie, where are you?'

'Don't be such a dope, daddy.'

'Why don't you move in here and stay? No one will touch you here. I'll look after you.'

'That's a good one. How many dead bodies do you want on your hands? Anyway, you know bloody well I can't stand all that Mantovani, late at night.'

'What Mantovani?'

Deenie broke into giggles then hung up.

I lay on my bed and struggled to picture my daughter and to think about her predicament and what she'd meant by the old one-two, but my mind kept returning to the dream. It simply wouldn't go away. In fact, it remained with me so clearly that surely it had to mean something. There had to be a message hidden inside it, but I was too exhausted to try to decipher what that could be.

I rolled over and went back to sleep, aware that I had been kidding myself for a lifetime. I was a useless old sod. What good could I possibly be to Deenie? I was no help to the world or anyone in it. Look at the way I kept on forgetting and get-ting flummoxed over stupid little things. I couldn't even think my way through a dream. I had failed myself and my children.

24

There is nothing that helps overcome a fit of anguish over the way you've made a mess of fulfilling your responsibilities to your children faster than to have them suddenly march in and start trying to reorganise your life for you.

As if I hadn't had a large enough dose of Ralph, what

happens the very next morning, but James turns up.

The first thing he came out with as he was crossing the threshold of the front door – no back door for him – was, 'I've heard enough about you on television, the radio and in the papers, and I've talked it over with Bruce. I'll jack up a doctor's certificate, so if the coroner or the police or anyone else wants you, they'll have to make an appointment. In the meantime, and right this minute, you're packing up and coming to stay with Joan and me. We'll get you into a home.'

'Thank you, but I'm not going,' I said firmly. 'I'm not leaving Mt Matheson.'

James looks very much as I used to. He's out of exactly the same mould as myself. Not tall, not broad, not handsome, not anything you could immediately put your finger on by way of positive physical description, except to say he's what's called solid and very average looking – yet he has this dynamic presence. It's an electric quality. As though he's been plugged into mains power.

Yes, that's how I would have described myself. In the old days I was restless and I wanted to get things done, and my whole being buzzed with energy. At times I could feel the force of it surging inside me. And James gives me that impression, too. Ever since he was a child he's been like that – a real human dynamo.

'Come on, I'll help you pack a few things,' he said.

'I'm staying here,' I replied stubbornly. 'There's no point in talking about it.'

James checked his watch. He looked very determined indeed. 'I've got the plane waiting in Rownley. We have to leave inside half an hour. That gives us ten minutes or so to grab a few things and lock up and hit the road. All we need is to chuck everything out of the fridge and grab some clothes. Joan and I can provide the rest.'

'No,' I said.

'Get cracking. Come on.'

Just then Ralph came down the stairs, pushing back his curls and grinning.

'Hullo brother James,' he said with a slight yawn. 'You aiming to kidnap my dear old dad?'

'What the hell are you doing here?' James asked, looking from Ralph to me, then back again.

'I'm the eldest son. Next in line to the throne. Remember? I'm keeping the cushions warm for when I take over . . .'

'He's here to help,' I broke in, before a stupid quarrel could start. 'He's keeping people away. And he's looking after me.'

How times change. Two days ago I would have got James to help me march his half-brother out to the street.

'Some help,' James said. 'You're hanging around, and a man gets shot here last night. So we can only come to the usual conclusion on that score, can't we Ralph? You make everyone's troubles worse, don't you?'

'Now, now, James,' I explained calmly. 'Whatever you may think, your brother really is here to look after me. And he's doing that extremely well.'

'Balls,' James said, looking at his watch again. 'You're on the national news. There were pictures of your front garden on TV this morning. There's a police car in your drive, another one in the street and I had to explain who I was before I could come in here. A policeman came right to the door with me – just in case you failed to notice. The family is not standing for this one single day longer. Joan's in a terrible state. She's nearly had a nervous breakdown, and the children are crying, and Bruce is steaming mad. I had to stop him from flying up from Christchurch to help sort things out. So, there's nothing further to discuss. We've got to get back to that plane – now.'

'I can't go and I'm not going,' I said. 'I'm not shifting from here.'

James hunched his shoulders and clenched his fists. I don't suppose people stood up to him too often like this. He resembled a small and extremely dangerous bull.

'That's not so, Arthur,' he said – Grace had trained her boys to call me by my first name, instead of father or dad; she thought it sounded so much more companionable – 'You're shifting from here for good and all – and that means till the cows come home, permanently, always and forever. Get it? Joan's been looking at retirement homes near us. And we think we've found one in Remuera that will suit nicely. We can wangle things to get you in just about straight away. In fact, she'll take you there to check it out this afternoon. You'll like it.'

'What did I tell you?' Ralph put in. 'It's a kidnap job all right. He wants to haul you off to an old people's home. Then he's going to lock you in and throw the key away. Just like prison.'

'Trunk out, blubberguts,' James said. Then he turned to me and told me, 'Quick. Grab whatever you need. You're coming with me – now.'

'That's if I let you, shitlegs,' Ralph said, leaning against the kitchen sink, grinning at James, daring him to make a move.

'Don't be a moron all your life,' James shouted, and he gave Ralph a look as if to say he was only just willing to concede that he may not have heard him properly. 'Look at the mess Arthur's got himself in. Living alone like this, in a huge empty house. Mutilated bodies lying all over the beach, men shooting each other on the lawn, police crawling all over the place, neighbours rubber-necking down the drive and the whole country talking about it. Joan and I – and that goes for Bruce and Jeannine, too – are not going to stand to one side and watch our father humiliate us all in public.'

'There's the business image to think of, isn't there? You've got to think of the firm, don't you? Well, that doesn't wash with me. So why don't you just do up your laces and piss off?' Ralph replied, with a very unpleasant edge of personal threat. Then he hitched his thumbs in the belt of his trousers and pushed his hips forward, gunfighter-style. Ralph had always been a boy who didn't go looking for a confrontation, but he had also been too well-built and slippery and quick to chance your luck with. I had the impression that even in middle age it would be a mistake to corner him and push too hard. He was capable of a violent flash of temper, and you could never predict what would happen to him then. Ralph was not worth testing.

There was a tense silence for a few moments, then you could sense James giving in even before he spoke. 'I'm not picking you up on any of those idiotic remarks,' he said. 'For the last time today, I'm telling you to come home with me, Arthur.'

'Thank you James,' I said. 'But my home will always be here.'

'Come on. I've got a plane waiting.'

'My mind's made up. Tell Joan not to waste her time and energy.'

'You're really not coming?'

'Never.'

James looked from me to Ralph, then he shrugged, looked at his watch and said, 'Don't be so damned sure about that. We'll talk about "never" when I've got more time.'

'Goodbye,' I said.

'Goodbye – for now,' he replied, this time without looking at anyone in particular. Then he simply turned and strode away, just as I would have done years ago, if I'd been caught in the same circumstances. Never hang about a scene of defeat.

'Goodbye brother James, don't forget to change into clean nappies when you get home,' Ralph called after him.

It was the first time in Ralph's life I could ever remember him winning a confrontation with any of his half-brothers. I looked at him and thought how sad that he had triumphed so late and in a cause I had won hands down so many times before. But though I tried not to give him too many credit points for his little victory, I couldn't help an uncomfortable feeling that without him for an ally I might just possibly at that very moment have been sitting in the back seat of a flash limousine taking my last look at Mt Matheson as I headed to the Rownley airport.

25

Visitors, visitors, visitors – the place had never seen such an interminable tumble of unexpected faces. It was like running a party, night and day. I had been called on by old friends like Nathan, my lawyer, two of my sons and a horde of strangers, including the police, reporters, neighbours, TV crews, two grim intruders with a hand gun, and a stream of local lookers-on who gawked across the lawn and down the drive. I was almost a public benefactor. After all, I'd found a dead body for everyone to talk about and I'd put Mt Matheson on the map for a few days of matchless notoriety.

I began to hope that perhaps people, including Frank Pelley, might be jolted into remembering who I once was and the power and influence I used to exert around here. More than anything else – except my goal of finding Deenie and helping her – that's what I hoped for.

Then my two favourite detectives dropped in again to see me. Naturally, Ralph found it necessary to scuttle off silently once more and hide away upstairs – so much for his victory over James.

I could see from the way the detectives bustled aggressively towards me that they had something to surprise me with, so I got in first by telling them something I should have thought of right at the very beginning: 'Look, I'm sorry, but we seem to be seeing quite a lot of each other these days, so I thought we ought to have proper introductions. As you must be aware by now, I'm Arthur Gransey – and you would be . . .?'

The tall one hunched his shoulders forward, as if considering whether he should bother to take an old goat like me seriously or give me a head-butt, then he lied to me, 'You must've forgotten, Mister Gransey. We always say who we are. I'm Inspector Hapwidd and this is Detective-Sergeant Brown.'

He nodded towards the short man with the comic-book moustache. Hapwidd & Brown. Sounded like a furniture shop.

'I'm pleased to meet you properly,' I said, with what I hoped sounded like heavy politeness, 'Because I've got a complaint. I've been told that my telephone has been bugged.'

Brown and Hapwidd exchanged oh-no-not-again glances, then Brown said with exaggerated patience: 'That's a good one. Would you trust me when I tell you that at least three-quarters of the population of this country share exactly the same belief?'

Hapwidd shook his head in agreement and added, 'It's like an article of faith, Mister Gransey. There's a national fixation about bugged phones. It makes people think they've been singled out and they're important. They never stop and think there wouldn't be enough policemen in the country to listen to even one percent of the calls.'

I wasn't going to take that for an answer. 'That's not the point. What I want to know is, are you bugging mine?' I asked.

'We can't just tap into people's phones,' Brown went on. 'We've got to have serious grounds for believing . . .'

'There's a whole legal rigmarole to go through. And anyway, there wouldn't be sufficient reason for us to intercept your calls, Mister Gransey, would there?' Hapwidd cut in. Which was also merely a way of turning the question around without giving me a proper answer.

'No,' I said, and I was just going to point out the defect in both their replies when he changed the subject.

'We've actually come about a new development,' he said. 'One that's involved us in a great deal of trouble and makes us believe that someone may be making a sustained attempt to set back the course of our inquiries.'

'We thought we'd tell you before any rumours start doing the rounds,' Brown added. They were just like a couple of stage comedians, the way they kept their patter going – except they weren't trying to be funny.

'There seems to have been an expectancy in certain quarters,' Hapwidd went on, 'to the effect that the body you discovered on the beach was that of a Mister Sullivan. A Mister Rolland Percival Sullivan.'

'Great name,' said Brown. 'Rolland – it was his mother's surname. It seems the Irish do that sometimes. His mother comes from Belfast.'

'Which is how he comes to be better known as Tuggy,' Hapwidd went on. 'It's something to do with tugboats. He's supposed to have worked on one. Though it was a long time ago, and when you think of it, there's no accounting for names, is there? You might have expected the Rolland to be shortened to Rollo, mightn't you?'

'We don't know whether you've heard that name in any connection recently, Mister Gransey, but it wouldn't surprise us if you had. He's well known. He's a man with a reputation. And he's got some odd connections.'

'And we can tell you categorically that Mister Sullivan and the body you discovered are not one and the same person,' Hapwidd announced, clenching his right fist and thumping it down in thin air. Then he stared at me angrily, for no reason I could think of.

'It's not Tuggy,' Brown said gently, as if translating. 'It's someone else.'

'Sullivan broke his left forearm in a so-called accident a year ago,' Hapwidd went on, as though he approved of the fact. 'And he had a metal pin inserted to hold the break together. We've discovered that from his hospital records in Wellington.'

'And the corpse doesn't even have a safety-pin in his left forearm,' Brown chipped in.

'So, we're particularly anxious to find this person Sullivan.'

'Particularly anxious,' Brown echoed softly.

'And therefore,' Hapwidd said, looking at me severely, 'We'd like to speak to your daughter Geraldine, if you would care to arrange a meeting.'

'Like – urgently,' Brown said in a whisper.

'We believe she may be able to assist us with our inquiries.'

Brown raised his voice again, 'She's a close pal of Tuggy's. And you know it.'

'An intimate friend,' Hapwidd agreed, now taking a cue to

lower his voice. 'We've known this right from the beginning. The Gransey connection is something we've had to take into consideration all along. Right from day one. The Wellington police know an awful lot about your daughter and her friend.'

'We're talking serious crime here,' said Brown.

'Mutilated corpses,' Hapwidd added, talking now in a stage whisper. 'They always point in one direction. Drugs.'

'Drugs. You can guarantee it,' Brown chimed in.

'Now wait on,' I said. 'This is ridiculous . . .'

'It's more than ridiculous,' said Brown, building up steam. 'It's bloody outrageous. This Tuggy bastard is a very naughty boy indeed. We know a lot about him and the substances he deals in, and he's a piece of filth. He's as bad as they get. Your daughter doesn't know the half of it. But we're ready to help her. We can offer her protection. She's got herself mixed up in bad company.'

'And that's putting it mildly,' Hapwidd said, changing his tone and increasing the volume. 'We think that Geraldine is hiding out somewhere in Rownley or Mt Matheson and that she knows the whereabouts of Tuggy Sullivan.'

'And she may even know who the man on the beach is.'

'And the man who shot Darryl Johnstone on your front lawn.'

'Who?' I asked.

'Never mind,' said Hapwidd.

'We've noticed that all roads lead through your property, Mister Gransey,' Brown said, twitching his silly moustache like a ferret. 'And they all head in the same direction – towards your daughter Geraldine.'

'She's in serious trouble,' Hapwidd repeated.

'And we think, Mister Gransey,' – now that Brown had started calling me Mister Gransey I wasn't too sure that I wouldn't have preferred to have kept my distance and remained plain Fred – 'that you haven't been fully co-operative with us. We'll bring your daughter in eventually. It's only a matter of time. After all, this is a small country. So don't try to bugger us about. Don't even think about it. Sooner or later we get to talk to her.'

'Unless something happens to her,' said Hapwidd. 'And we'd do anything we could to avoid that, wouldn't we, Mister Gransey?'

They both looked at me sharply.

'What do you want me to do?' I asked.

'If she rings, try a bit harder to get her address or tell her to meet you in secret,' said Hapwidd.

'The old one-two, Mister Gransey,' Brown added. 'Make an appointment.'

'It's for her sake. She's in very serious trouble. And we're the only people who can get her out of it.'

The old one-two? That was what Deenie had said over the phone. So, she was right – they were listening to my telephone calls.

One-two stood for number twelve. We had used Nathan's house as a place to meet.

26

When Ralph emerged downstairs again I asked him where he had been hiding – up in the ceiling or under the bed? Put that way, I admit I was administering a bit of a kick in the pants, but there was no real call for the way he turned on me and snapped, 'Deenie and I learned a valuable survival technique when you could be bothered having us around, dad – whenever there's big trouble, dive for cover. Why do you think Deenie's so good at pulling her head in? How do you think she's dodged everyone? No, don't answer that, I'll tell you – it's because of the stinking sneaky way you used to arrange secret meetings at Nathan's after school.'

'That's not true,' I protested. The last thing I wanted was to start Ralph remembering anything to do with number twelve. 'That's not the way it was.'

But I'd wound him up and he wasn't going to let me off. 'You trained her to be the way she is,' he said. 'And I learned a thing or two about secrets as well. Don't think you got away with a single slimy trick. You never realised, but when we were little, Deenie and I always used to compare notes. And just remember, you'll never know how much you really owe me. I never split on you, though any time I liked I could've dropped you right in deep shit with my mother and the law. I knew all about those private little arrangements at Nathan's.'

'Well, forget them, will you,' I said in a panic. 'You must never mention them again.'

Ralph laughed with that sneering tone that so irritated me. 'Climb down off the wall, will you, dad. Belle and the whole German army have surrendered. The war's over. What are you worried about? Think your ex-wife is going to take a court order out against you?'

I hated that kind of talk, and Ralph was a specialist at it. It made him sound like nothing more than a big spoilt brat. I had come to recognise his outbreaks of petulant bluster and I could see only too well what brought them on. From the furtive, nervy way he was looking around, I could easily recognise that what was making him so liverish was his anxiety about when the next drink was going to be delivered to top up the poisons already swilling around his system.

In the past two days my booze bill must have gone up by several hundred bucks. I wasn't too sure what current prices were like, but I did know one thing: I was beginning to feel as though I was throwing a free-for-all in a brewery. So far as I was concerned, Ralph could wait till Christmas.

'Anyway,' he went on. 'You haven't filled me in on the latest bulletin. What did the dicks want this time?'

'Oh,' I said. 'They had a few things to say about that Sullivan chap.'

For the first time, I had information that Ralph didn't. It amused me to know that he was now falling behind the play. Cooped up in his little back room upstairs, totally dependent on a bugged telephone, he wasn't in it any more, except as some kind of unreliable bodyguard. He still wasn't aware that Hapwidd and Brown had been aware he was somewhere in the house all the time he'd been trying to hide from them. The joke was on him.

'What about Tuggy?' he demanded.

'Tuggy? Tuggy?' I asked, pretending with a long yawn to be struggling to remember. 'Oh, him? Tuggy Sullivan? That Tuggy? Well, I can tell you something interesting about him. It turns out his first name's Rolland. What do you think of that?'

Ralph gave me a shrewd look. He knew very well I was toying with him. 'Okay, so his name's Rolland. I'd have to suppose it'll look impressive in letters of gold on his tombstone, wouldn't I?' he drawled.

'Oh, and there was something else.'

'I'm not a complete retard. I can tell that, daddy-o. So, come on, spit it out.'

'I'm doing my best, Ralph. I'm trying to remember. Except you haven't helped by not quite managing to stop yourself calling me daddy-o, which always makes me so angry I get completely flustered. And that encourages me to forget the important things I was just about to tell you. See how it goes?'

'Stop acting the mad fart.'

'No more daddy-os?'

'Okay. I'll give it a go.'

'Well that's a start. I think I can now remember what I was going to say. Oh yes, I've got it. It turns out he isn't dead. Or, at least, that wasn't his corpse on the beach.'

'Who?'

'Sullivan – everyone thought it was him, but it's someone else.'

'You're telling me Tuggy's alive?' Ralph really was shocked. He leaned against the kitchen table and stared at me with his mouth hanging open in a flabby gormless expression.

'No, I specifically didn't say that. What I said was the body isn't his.'

Ralph ignored my logic, as usual, and said. 'Shit. That's

going to insert more faecal matter into the fan. There's going to be bloody hell to pay. Tuggy could have got away to hell out of here over the last couple of days. He could've shot through already to Oz or Spain or America. This'll make everyone believe for certain he's ripped them off for a million bucks, while Deenie's been playing the bloody decoy. They'll kill her.'

I hadn't thought of that. I went into the den and fetched a bottle of whisky. Suddenly I began shaking badly, and I tried to hide it by clutching both hands around the bottle as I poured two drinks. I took mine without water, then sat down.

'I'm going to meet Deenie and turn her in,' I said slowly, concentrating on getting each word out steadily.

'Don't be a fuckwit.'

'I'm her father and I know what's best for her.'

'No you don't,' Ralph said. 'All you know is the sure way to sign her death certificate. They'll just sit about, picking their noses, while the cops pump her for whatever she knows, then they'll come around and collect her and kill her.'

'Well, why don't you tell me who "they" are and I'll stop them.'

'I only know that Jason bastard. I don't know the ones he's in with. There's probably all sorts of networks. Gangs, shareholders – you'd run around in circles and up your . . .'

'Well, let's flush them out and discover who they are.'

Ralph poured himself another drink. 'Bloody simple,' he said. 'We pull a chain and flush them out. Just like that . . . You really have fallen off the high wire.'

'No,' I said. 'I don't intend to do the job alone. For a start, we put the problem to Nathan. He has a mind like a rat-trap. He'll set something up for us.'

Ralph stared at me blankly for a moment, then he rolled his eyes upwards till I could see only their bloodshot whites. It was a disgusting childish trick that has always made me shudder.

'Nathan? You're not serious? You're actually so gone in the loaf you think a dithering old bastard – a one-armed civil service bicycle bandit like him – could help get you out of this one?'

'I may be an old bastard, too,' I told Ralph. 'But I'm not a ditherer. Never. And neither is Nathan.'

'The Golden Oldies ride again,' he jeered. 'Pump up your tyres and watch out for whistling wheelchairs.'

'Pathetic,' I said.

'Well, one thing I'll give you,' he conceded. 'You've been bloody clever at covering up the state you're in. The whole family thinks you've only gone a bit gaga, and not one of them has woken up to the fact you've joined up with the aliens from another planet. Christ, if James had got his timing right and he'd strolled in here right now, he wouldn't have let you cock your leg and take a second shot at the Christmas fairy. There's nothing I could've done to stop him. You'd have been certified on the spot and dragged out of here screaming in a straitjacket.'

'Help yourself to the whisky,' I replied. 'I'm also going to have another. Then lunch. Then a nice little sleep.'

My whole mood had changed. I didn't have to listen to him. I was steady again. Ralph's protests and, I suppose, the very small whisky I'd shared with him had stepped up my excitement level. At last something decisive was going to happen – I would force events instead of being their victim.

It was simple. I'd speak to Nathan. Then I'd get Deenie to meet me at his place. And we'd find out what had happened to Tuggy. Plus who the bastard was who thought he could send out people to shoot each other on my front lawn. And we'd attach a name to the body on the beach. And perhaps we'd even find out who'd mutilated it. Then we'd bring in the police, and Deenie would explain everything to them and the whole mystery would be solved firmly and decisively.

Yes, we'd flush out some human filth all right, and yes, we'd sluice it down the sewers of Mt Matheson. And, yes, people would once again recognise me for the man I was.

27

A pity a mood like that doesn't last as it used to in the old days. As soon as the whisky wore off I realised I'd forgotten to take my walk – the first I'd missed in as long as I could remember – and for the whole of the afternoon I mooched about, dozing on and off beside the telephone, or I got up and wandered around clutching hold of it like a toy.

I wasn't exactly depressed, but I definitely felt tired and frustrated. The orderly pattern of my life had been thrown into turmoil. My whole routine had been turned upside down. And here I was, all primed up to act decisively at last, but I couldn't do a damned thing till I'd heard from Deenie.

There was no way I could explain her call to Nathan over the phone. That would have been stupid, so the only method I could use to let him know what she had suggested was to invite him around for dinner – with a warning that he'd have to experience a police escort down the drive to the door.

When Nathan accepted he knew only too well that I was using the word 'dinner' only in the restricted sense of eating, not cooking. In his advancing years Nathan still had a hankering for the pleasures of the table, but my palate seemed to have corroded, so why pretend? Gourmet food was wasted on me and I certainly couldn't be bothered at this late stage in life to go to the trouble of learning to cook just to please others. I only had to ask myself how often anyone came here to eat anyway? And the answer to that one was: maybe once or twice in a very pale blue moon.

Wine was hardly a different matter. My cellar was laid down when Grace and I used to do a considerable amount of socialising and entertaining, and I haven't added to it in years. As I've indicated already, I'm not confident of what I'm drinking any more, unless I consult the label – and, since I'd paid for them, I knew their distinctions only too well – and about the best I could manage in a blind test would be to tell the difference between a big plummy Aussie shiraz and one of those shrinking Chilean cabernets. But I'm certainly not complaining. I don't feel I need to know more than that to impress anyone ever again. So, why bother?

Yet, as a concession to Ralph, though God only knows why, I dug deep in the freezer and got out three meals with meat in them for the microwave. Their use-by date was only a couple of months over the limit, because the last time Bruce and Jeannine visited me they'd cleared the freezer of all the packets they described as 'historically interesting' and replaced them with a whole lot of other stuff that included meat meals I've no use for. I'm not a vegetarian on principle, it's just that Grace didn't have much trouble converting me to plain and simple health food, mainly because, along with a lot of other base appetites, I'd lost the lust I used to have for flesh and I seldom felt a hankering for it in all its once-tempting varieties, shapes and presentations.

Anyway, I could at least claim that the meal I served had a fairly inoffensive smell, the taste was bland enough, and I felt confident that the information on the packets was correct and that we were eating Boeuf Stroganoff on some sort of rice base – in fact, the one thing I could be absolutely certain of was the rice. And to satisfy the last remaining cravings of my tastebuds, I did go to the extra trouble of chopping up a substantial green pepper, onion and tomato salad, all gathered from my own garden.

I made a much bigger effort with the wine, especially since Nathan had pointed out only a couple of days previously that I ought not to be hoarding the stuff. We had a nice robust burgundy with the meal, followed by a big solid raisiny Santo Sofia Amarone, which even I thought was pretty good. Then we had some coffee and armagnac – though once I produced the bottle and Ralph got his hooks into it I knew I would be kissing it goodbye. More expense.

Talk over dinner mainly centred on Ralph's culinary prejudices. Nathan on the other hand was far too polite to say anything about my choice of packet food, even if he did pick about at his plate without attempting to make a false display of appetite – let alone relish.

Ralph led the way by doing his hand-knitted beans and milkless-milk jokes to death. He must have got into my whisky in quite a big way before we ate, because by the time we got to the armagnac he was already well pissed and very repellent.

The only good thing about the state he was in was that he took his second glass of armagnac outside to have with a cigarette and at last I was able to tell Nathan about the visit I'd had from Hapwidd and Brown, then about Deenie's telephone message.

The last item of news produced just the effect I thought it would have. I hadn't seen Nathan so bright and bucked up in years. Even as a boy he could nearly always mask the quickness of his mind behind a deceptively lethargic exterior. He seemed to move and talk in such a relaxed manner that it was always surprising when he suddenly moved quickly or struck out with a sharp comment. Hunting rabbits, he used to slouch along as if he'd gone all dreamy. You wouldn't think he was paying attention, then in one sudden movement he'd whip the rifle up to his shoulder, fire, reload and take another bead. Then bang, again – and he'd drop another bunny before you'd noticed it was there.

When I used to question him about the relaxed way he handled a rifle, he always said that if he looked a million miles away he supposed it was really because he had succeeded in clearing his mind to allow it to concentrate on only two things: the hunt and the kill.

So it was a young Nathan I saw making this sudden jump from lethargy into excitement. 'She sounded so muddled up and confused when she rang me. It was Ralph who upset the apple cart,' he said. 'But this is great. She's about to do something decisive. I just know it.'

'Me too,' I said.

'And she told you she'd get in touch tomorrow?' he asked.

'Yes. And since that was some time during the night, I expect she means today,' I pointed out, in what I thought were excusable tones of triumph.

There was a silence in which Nathan leaned forwards and looked at me as if – well, as if I'd lost my full faculties. 'You mean tonight. Do you hear that? *Tonight,*' he corrected, getting very flushed in the face. In fact, his whole mood had suddenly moved up a full notch from excitement to anger. For some reason he had quite suddenly become very very mad at me. 'You damned idiot, do I have to remind you we've just had dinner. And it's bloody well dark.'

I was speechless.

'Deenie hasn't been in touch at all, so far, today. Do you hear that? I've only had the one call all day,' he snapped. Then he put his armagnac down beside a half-finished cup of coffee and got up from his chair. He was now trembling with rage.

'You should have told me this earlier, Arthur. You halfwit. You could have messed things up completely. Can't you see, she could be trying at this very moment to get in touch with me?'

'But I couldn't tell you any of this over the phone. It's bugged.'

'Don't be so bloody absurd. You didn't need to go through the ritual agony of clogging my innards with that excrement you've just served up to me. You could have told me about Deenie straight away. Christ, that hideous meal is the last I'm ever going to eat in this house. Your food isn't fit to feed to swine. Those frozen dinners are worse than the tins of beans we used to eat over here when we were young. Out of my way. I've got to get going right now.'

I hadn't realised that I was blocking his exit. I stepped aside.

'We ate bacon and eggs by the panful,' I said in some shock, pulling at his sleeve urgently, while he pushed past me.

Nathan had no right to lash out in a sudden fit of bad temper and try to demolish our past like that. It was callous. In fact, it was cruel. My whole existence was built on the foundations of my boyhood memories. They fired my secret dreams and ambitions. How otherwise did I come to be king of this place? How otherwise did I come to build my palace on the exact spot we were standing on?

'Nathan,' I yelled, so loudly that I forced him to pause and look at me. 'You've got it all wrong. We only kept beans for emergencies. We always ate huge feasts of bacon and eggs. Sometimes we'd scoff the best part of a dozen eggs, a loaf of bread, a packet of crumpets, a pound of butter and a pound of bacon between us – remember how the butcher used to slice off thick home-cured rashers with his knife? We sold rabbits and fish and forgot the Depression. We escaped from all that misery in Rownley and we roamed around here like the lords of creation. We were free spirits. Masters of the universe. We rolled in luxury. We ate like lords. We were rich, for Christ's sake. Don't you remember?'

'I only remember the beans,' he snapped, brushing my hand off his sleeve and stomping out through the door. There was not the slightest shadow of doubt that he meant what he said. We were like the historians of opposing sides in a battle over the true facts. We believed two entirely different versions of the events we had lived through. I was absolutely thunderstruck.

Not since the days when Belle had set us at each other's throats had we parted like this. I stared at his back in disbelief. Where were the campfires? Where were those times when we had wrapped ourselves in our blankets or pollard bags, as we curled up for the night, talking quietly about life and making plans for the next day, reaching out occasionally to grab a stick and poke at the embers or just gazing up at the stars?

Where was the heavy happy smell of those magnificent meals that used to hang in the stillness of the Mt Matheson of my dreams? Had they ever existed? Had I imagined everything?

28

I think I've now come to a point when there's something I should explain, something I have never before hauled out of the secret lockers of the past to hold up to the light of day. Even as I write these words, I find there are little droplets of sweat forming where the hair on my temples merges into the bald spot above them. It's pathetic, it's stupid, but I can't help it.

The facts are briefly these: when James and Bruce followed each other from home to go to university in Wellington, the other one – the one I'd got used to calling their so-called brother – was still a schoolboy. Grace doted on that child, she worshipped him and indulged his least little whim, but there was something odd about him that I always responded to with an instinctive distrust.

He had never captured my love as Ralph had when he was a very little boy, and I never held him in the admiration and pride I felt for James and Bruce. The feeling I had wasn't something I can define even to this day, and at the time I was so pressured day and night with all my responsibilities in Rownley that I couldn't sacrifice the hours or the energy that would have been necessary to sit down and work the problem through. But the nearest I can come to a word that captures the response I felt is – unease.

The boy made me feel physically uneasy when I was alone with him, and I felt guilty because I was unable to do anything about it. The whole problem was shifted to the back of my mind while, I suppose, I must have secretly hoped that everything would be sorted out as he grew up. The same way that I now admit I allowed myself to put my doubts about Ralph to one side.

The night I found out what Ken was up to in his bedroom with that Watkins boy was the worst moment of my life – far more devastating than when I came back from the Auckland National Party conference a day early and walked in on Belle and Nathan coupling in the marital bed.

That time there had been one hell of a row between Belle,

Nathan and myself. We screamed and bellowed like lunatics – and someone easily could have got killed. But when I found Ken and the Watkins boy in bed together, I discovered there is a degree of rage that far surpasses what I would describe as mere murderous or hysterical anger. This time there was no bluster, no shouting, no fire. I turned to ice.

I felt like an executioner when I took Ken to the garage and locked him in. Then Grace and I went to the kitchen and looked at each other. We must have sat there without speaking for about half an hour. Neither of us moved, except occasionally to shiver.

Finally Grace said, 'That boy is no longer our son.'

It was as though she was speaking through my mind, for those were the exact words that I would have said if my tongue had not been frozen solid.

Without needing to speak further, we went upstairs where we had found the pair of them and threw everything that was Ken's out of the window, clothes, books, mattress, skis, record-player, the lot. Then I went down and gave the boy the belting of his life.

Dealing out the punishment I thought Ken deserved was made easier for me by Grace's total support at the time and afterwards. We were like that; we arrived at decisions without the usual discussions and arguments most couples find necessary. We were tuned into each other, almost like the male and female aspects of the same person. No one else has ever made me feel like that, or ever could again.

Later, I have reason to believe that Ken recovered at Nathan's place, though neither Nathan nor his wife, who was still alive at the time, ever told me so. It was a chance remark from Deenie that alerted me to the possibility that this is what happened, but I didn't question her to find out the exact truth of the matter. The boy no longer existed so far as Grace and I were concerned. We never mentioned him again. And no other child was allowed to breathe a single word about him. His absence was as if he had never even been born. We simply wiped his slate clean.

But events were now going to prove that no matter how you rub away at the language of truth or how hard you chip at the facts, you can't ever quite remove all trace of them. I have been forced to learn that there is always the ghost of a lost word waiting in the shadows to leap out and startle you or some small malignant particle of the past that works its way through the layers of suppressed memory to swell and burst and suppurate in the mind.

So, who should be surprised to hear that when I went to bed that night, after Nathan had stormed off and while I suppose Ralph still sat outside, smoking and guzzling my armagnac, I had a nightmare that was related to, but far more terrifying, than the one I'd had the night before, when the shark got me.

This time I knew immediately where I was – on Ocean Beach – and I realised instinctively that I was running towards the point where, in my previous dream, I had forced myself to turn away to cross the dunes and take the road towards sure death – the road on which I would be shot at from the saltbushes then devoured by the shark. However, I now knew better than to make the same choice. Instead, I continued along the beach, gradually slowing down to a steady walk as I approached the upper end of the reef. From the distance I could see a large crowd gathering. My neighbours were there, so were the police, and there were television cameras following behind me.

Where the beach ended and the reef began I could see, even from a considerable way off, a body lying half-buried in sand. I walked up to it, then gave it a hard kick.

'Get up,' I commanded it. 'Get up, Ken. And show the world what I did to you.'

And slowly, like a huge mottled grey and pale blue slug, the thing in the sand uncurled from the seaweed and rose before me. Blood and mucus were now pouring out of his nose and mouth, as they had the night of the beating, and there were terrible weeping weals across his arms and legs where I had thrashed him with the buckle-end of my belt.

'I am the son of man,' he burbled through the muck in his mouth.

Then I woke. The upper sheet was caught around my arms and throat, and I was choking. I had to struggle to free myself to breathe properly. My heart was beating so furiously I thought it would burst.

I was convinced at the time that I knew what the nightmare meant. I decided I had had another near-death experience. Like the shark dream, there was no escape. I had been dragged down into an everlasting darkness and I told myself when I woke, frightened and trembling, that I had only just made it back to the surface of life again. The way I thought of it at the time, wrongly as it turned out, Ken had come back to try to lure me to my extinction.

29

The following morning I got up at six, and as usual on the days when John and Elsie Luckham are coming, I began pottering around in the kitchen. It was still dark, so I turned on the lights and washed and put away the cups and glasses left from the night before, then moved on to straighten the towels in my bathroom and impose some order on the mess in the ones upstairs and down that Ralph had been using, and finally I went out into the garden to clean up where the police had been trampling and shoving in metal stakes.

It's an odd thing, but I always follow a similar basic routine – rising early and tidying up – before one of John and Elsie's visits. I don't know why I do it, since I pay them well, but I suppose it could be something to do with my puritan upbringing. My uncle and aunt, who raised me from birth after the death of my mother and my father's subsequent disappearing act – a double loss that I now put down simply for the record, although I have never allowed myself to dwell upon or wallow in the fact – trained me from an early age never to lower myself in the estimation of others.

John Luckham is a slow-moving man, almost the same age as myself, but he's a wonderful steady toiler around the garden. He can keep up the same pace all day, like a machine, with only a stop for a cup of tea and a sandwich. And, unlike most of those who profess to be gardeners – or landscape consultants as they like to advertise themselves on the cards they pop through the letterbox – he knows what he's doing.

Yet, even so, I was still fascinated to notice that he and his wife are so phlegmatic, so uncurious about the world, so entirely focused on their work and duties, that they weren't in the slightest bit fazed by the experience of being delivered to the door by a policeman. It was an amazing thing to watch. Elsie didn't ask a single question or even look right or left. She just went straight to the kitchen and started cleaning the surfaces I'd already cleaned, and John got out the mower and all the tools he'd need that day, checked them over methodically, and never said a word.

He had just started working his way slowly along the front garden when Nathan arrived from Rownley, passed police inspection, and told me the disappointing news that there had been no message from Deenie. But, more than that, he said he'd also come to apologise for allowing himself to become so annoyed after dinner last night – 'especially after those two bottles of very good wine'.

Nathan was back in his usual on-top-of-it-all mood. He was affable, pleased with himself and relaxed. Civilised, I suppose, would be the word for the way he projected himself. In his panama hat and linen suit, he cut quite a dapper figure. Not at all the image you'd have of a retired top civil servant. He sported a cravat, with a matching handkerchief popping out of the breast pocket of his jacket, and he even wore some sort of soft slipper-like footwear, instead of proper shoes or sandals. You'd have thought he'd had something to do with the stage or entertainment, a bit like a slightly smaller version of Noël Coward or Fred Astaire.

So it should have been easy for me to tell him that it was all over and forgotten so far as I was concerned. But, funnily enough, I was the one to feel uneasy and awkward. I went through the ritual words of forgiveness, but somehow I began to feel that it was me who was in the wrong. It was hard to work out why.

Yes, I confessed to him, I had kept him eating and drinking at the very time that Deenie could have been ringing and – yes again – he'd been the one to think clearly about Deenie's interests when I'd proved myself to be a doddering old simpleton.

The thing that really got to me, I suppose, was having to admit to myself that I was no longer as clear-headed as I had once pictured myself. Especially since all my life I'd never experienced a moment of real self-doubt or misgiving – not in a full and overpowering sense. I'd always pictured myself to be a control man. A decider and a doer. An achiever.

'Don't take it so hard, Arthur,' Nathan consoled me, interpreting the deeper implications of my fumbling remarks with his usual accuracy. 'We can't be expected to be as sharp as we were when we were hot shots around here. We've earned the right to an occasional miss. By which I also mean that the meal wasn't as bad as I said – it was perfectly harmless and edible – and I made a much worse fool of myself than you.'

'You know you didn't.'

'Come on now, I think we've arrived at an age where we ought to be able to make a few allowances for ourselves, don't you? We're entitled to a bit of understanding, after all we've achieved in life. And the important thing to remember is that Deenie is still out there about to get in touch with us.'

It wasn't all I wanted to hear – for he didn't take a word back about only remembering the beans and forgetting the great feasts we used to cook – but I was grateful for any kind of healing comment, so we shook hands like old friends, then away he went again to resume what he called his vigil, 'Sitting down beside the telephone and waiting' – just as I had done the day before.

It put me in a better mood than I would otherwise have been in when Ralph finally surfaced, looking as though his face had been boiled in the booze that was killing him day by day before my eyes.

30

Ralph drank three cups of coffee straight off, the last of which he took with his first cigarette of the day, outside on the patio. From where he sat, crumpled in the grip of a hangover, he had a box-seat view of John Luckham, who was twenty years his senior, doing a full day's work in the garden.

The whole scene, on yet another glorious Mt Matheson morning, made me feel ashamed not just for Ralph, but for myself, his father, so I went around to the potting shed to clean it up for next spring.

Nathan had promised to call me with a coded message if Deenie got in touch with him. The signal was going to be a simple conversational statement that he was coming around for a bottle of Penfolds Grange – which, in fact, I would have been perfectly happy to open to celebrate such wonderful news.

But it was Ralph who got the first call and, after he'd taken four Disprin tablets, yet another coffee and (I had no trouble guessing) his first straightener of the day, he came around to tell me he was going over to Rownley for a short while, 'to use a telephone that wasn't broadcasting direct to the CIA'.

It so happened that his employer, Jason Wakeworth, had had an unwelcome visit from some very unpleasant policemen not long after he'd last rung Ralph, so 'complicated rearrangements at both ends of the line' now had to be made.

Besides which, he said, an old-fashioned penny had finally dropped and he had to find out whether it had come down heads or tails – a stupid Ralphism that was no help towards an explanation of what he was thinking or doing.

'Aren't you frightened the police will simply watch you leave here, wonder who you are and what the hell you are up to, and follow you over to Rownley, then listen in to what you're saying there?' I asked through sheer politeness.

'Not the way I do things,' Ralph told me – a remark for which there was no answer, for I'd always thought if you wanted an arrangement completely mucked up Ralph would be the very man to do it for you.

So, apart from having a few brief words with John Luckham about changing the layout of the back garden next spring, I was left alone to get on with cleaning out the potting shed without further interruption all morning. I had the telephone beside me, but no one rang.

When Ralph returned he completely failed to register that the police took his presence so much for granted they simply glanced at him without bothering to check him out. He drove down the drive as though he was the Invisible Man.

He was clutching two pies, one an excellent dryish vegetarian effort and the other a squidgy steak and cheese pastry which reeked of the abattoir, and it was only then that I realised that I too wasn't fully taking in my surroundings. I'd forgotten it was lunchtime. Again, I'd missed my morning trip to the beach, which was getting more than just a bit worrying.

'So, how went the telephone talk?' I asked Ralph, as I sat outside eating the vegetarian pie and drinking orange juice (I had headed him off with a bottle of cooking wine – not that his head or palate would have been able to tell the difference that day).

Ralph munched at his appalling gut-rot lunch, swilling it down with gulps of rough wine, then as usual he wiped the back of his hand across his mouth and produced a cigarette. He belched twice, quietly but with satisfaction.

'Well, if you've done one thing, dad, you've buggered up

someone's plans for applying Tommy Farr to the problem,' he announced, after blowing a smoke ring into the cloudless faultless skies. 'The cops got into one hell of a twist when they overheard that Farr had been called in. Jason was very pissed off with you about that little intervention.'

That was too rich for me to pass over in silence. 'Intervention? You're forgetting – or he's forgetting – that I had nothing to do with it,' I told him testily. 'The police are tapping my phone. But that's not my fault, is it? If anyone's to blame it's your friend Jason. He shouldn't spill his secrets down other people's telephones, should he? I didn't ask him to blab about sending in Farr.'

'Right or wrong, that's not the way he sees it. He's upset that his special representative isn't going to be here on hand to look after his interests.'

'He's got you.'

Ralph wrinkled his forehead, pursed his lips and looked at me through slits. The sunlight was obviously getting to him. The gap between his lids was so narrow I couldn't see the reds of his eyes.

'I'm only here to look after you.'

'You mean you're here to make contact with Deenie – and you somehow have the bloody nerve to call that "looking after" me.'

Ralph did what he always did when he seemed to be getting nowhere. He shrugged his shoulders and poured another drink.

'Anyway, everyone's very agitated about the body not being Tuggy's, that's for sure,' he conceded.

'Great. So what's the new theory? Surely there must be a theory about what's going on . . .'

Ralph began a harsh little laugh that finished up as an even harsher smoker's cough. 'There's bound to be no end of theories, all right,' he said, patting his chest between painful-sounding barking fits. 'But one thing's got everyone guessing and that's the question of who'd do a thing like bashing a man's face in and removing his prints.'

'A psychopath would do it, Ralph.'

'Yeah. So that's a big help, isn't it?'

'All you've got to do is run down a list of known psychopaths, surely – and you've got your killer.'

'Pity they don't always advertise. You know, like in the personal columns of the newspapers – Psychopath available for mutilations. Got any other bright ideas?'

There was a silence between us while Ralph filled his glass yet again, then he went on quietly, 'Jason thinks Tuggy must've done it.'

'Tuggy? Why?'

'A cover up. You know, a decoy, a false trail. To give him time to get away.'

'Christ. A man like that . . . Friends with Deenie . . .'

'Sick, eh? Beauty and the Beast all over again.'

I stared at the table for a while, before I could trust myself to speak without choking. 'That still doesn't explain why Deenie's here. It doesn't make sense.'

'Maybe she was just hanging on his arm, the way couples tend to do. Tuggy came here – so she came too. Or maybe she's his bait. He's got her hanging out on a long line to hook in the big fish while he swims safely away.'

'She's not that stupid. Not Deenie.'

'She's got a diseased taste in ratshit men. If Tuggy told her to do something, she'd fall over herself to please him. How many days since you found that body? No, don't strain your poor old brain, I'll tell you. I've slept here three nights, so this is day four.'

I was surprised he could think back so far, but thought it better not to say so.

'And right now, Tuggy could be guzzling champagne and catching peanuts in his mouth in a bar in Mexico City. It all fits. Jason and a whole lot of other people have been conned. They're now saying that the million Tuggy was looking after is only the tip of it. He could've cleaned out the kitty.'

'What kitty?'

'God only knows what the arrangement is, it's all hearsay.

Tuggy's now rumoured to have ripped the arse right out of everything. He's fiddled the books. No one's sure how much he's lumbered. Two million maybe. Who knows? Personally, I think it's all bullshit. I've heard those kinds of figures being thrown up in the air for the last thirty years and I'd say it's an odds-on bet that someone's inventing a whole row of noughts so that everyone's fogged up and no one ever finds out what's really missing. You never believe any figures when it comes to drug money. It's all fantasy. Only the corpses are real. Tuggy's giving everyone the opportunity to do some really creative accounting, while they're settling a few old scores in the name of taking reprisals. God only knows how a brainless swede-gnawing little scumbag like Tuggy did it, but he's got all the patients in the nut-factory jumping out the windows and running all round the country with firecrackers up their arses.'

'Good,' I said with some satisfaction. It was pleasant to think of those people, whoever they were, getting a splattering of their own filth from one of their number.

'No,' said Ralph. 'Not at all good – not from our point of view. Deenie's still around, and you can bet your bottom dollar that once Tuggy's in the clear he won't lift a finger to get her out. He must have sold her a world of dreams to get her to come here and dress up and act stupid – if that's what's happened. And now she's dead meat, is Deenie.'

Quietly – much more quietly than I thought possible – I said to Ralph, 'How can you talk like that about your own sister? That's the second most depraved remark I've ever heard fall from your lips . . .'

But he cut me off. 'You're forgetting what I told you before. There's worse to think about.'

'Worse?'

'You found the body.'

'So what?'

'Don't you ever remember anything I explain to you? Everyone thinks you're involved. And even if they don't think it, they *want* to believe it, because that way they get to take their shitty livers out on you.'

'Meaning?'

'Meaning you're dead meat, too.'

'Me?'

'Jesus, how many times do I have to spell it out to you? Look dad, I'm right up Crapper's Creek with you, too. Guilt by association, I suppose you'd call it. Nothing actually has to be true about anything connected with drugs. That's why I haven't gone near them for years. I never touch powder. I don't even smoke shit any more. It's all too fuckin' hairy and paranoid. If these people believe they've lost what the rumours say, they won't be looking for justice, they won't be enquiring about rights and wrongs and facts and possibilities, they won't even want paybacks. They'll be sick in their heads. Try and get your thinking gear around that, will you? I'm talking about real frightening sick. Sick, as in wanting to wade up to their ankles through fuckin' rivers of blood . . .'

Ralph leaned back in his chair and grinned at me. Then he said, 'We're dead, daddy-o. But the funny thing is, for the first time in my life it's made me feel close to you. Life's a bloody mystery, even if death's a racing certainty. So, now we've sorted out the philosophy, why don't we enjoy a drink while we can?'

'Please, Ralph, stop calling me daddy-o, will you?' I implored my son, as I went off to fetch him a bottle.

31

The growing certainty that someone unknown to you may be plotting your death is one of those alarming bits of information that may be useful to be aware of, if you know who the enemy is, and when and where they're likely to strike.

It's possible that soldiers manage to cope with the prospect of being killed not just because they're well trained and they've acquired an inner discipline that allows them to be quite detached about their chances, but because they usually have a fair idea of the general identity of those they're fighting and where the front line is. Without that essential information, the news that someone may have plans to end your life can make you feel profoundly disturbed, and even physically ill.

I'd never experienced the situation before, but as I returned with a bottle the implications finally sank in and I felt distinctly unwell. It was a strange sensation, like a kind of bilious seizure, not localised in the stomach, but affecting every part of my body. Even my arms and legs and head felt afflicted; I could taste bile in my mouth.

Yet I knew at the time that this terrible fear wasn't just a consequence of the danger I seemed to be in. It also had an irrational aspect. The thing that kept coming back to me was the need to tidy up my papers.

That may seem to be a bit crazy, when it's put as baldly as that. But it's true. The only way I can explain it is to say they represent my life. It's all there in secret code – in the diaries and tables and figures. My records are myself, and I'm damned if I'm going to leave them in a muddle for James and Bruce to sort out when I depart to join Grace.

My hands were shaking so violently that I had to clasp them together between my thighs to try to hide my reaction from Ralph. Put it down to pride, or the way I'd been drilled by my uncle and aunt since I was a boy, or whatever, but I eventually managed to get control of myself. After a few minutes I even felt confident enough to stand up and make a curt remark to Ralph about how I hoped he would be able to manage the wine on his own without assistance. Then I said I had some urgent work to do and I stumbled off to my den without either bringing up or tripping over.

While I was still able to, I plunged right into my accounts. Most of them were already in pretty good order, but the odds and ends needed attention. I paid all outstanding bills, struck balances and made sure every detail was easily accessible for probate, then I packed all my old diaries into shopping bags and addressed them to the firm in Rownley that shreds documents. My current diary was the only one in which I had begun to record the plain truth, so I decided to hang on to that. The rest were full of details the world would be better off not knowing.

Something very odd was happening inside me, though I remember avoiding the full possibilities of the action I was taking by telling myself at the time that what I was doing was much the same as if I'd been a woman of my aunt's generation. In a crisis, she would have got on with the washing, darned the socks and stocked the baking tins. Same thing – just housekeeping, trying to steer my mind away from dwelling on my larger predicament.

I felt a lot better when I'd finished. The thought of putting anyone to personal trouble after I've departed this world, or leaving a needlessly bad impression – just supposing anyone could have really been bothered to break the codes I'd so carefully devised to conceal my diary jottings – had given me a sudden bad fit of the trembling dib-dabs.

But this wasn't the end of my strange experience. My next reaction caught me right off guard. It was quite different – not at all physical – and it gave me a hell of a turn.

As usual, I had looked through the news section of my morning copy of the *Echo* over breakfast. Then, afterwards, I had taken the business news pages with the share listings into the den, just in case I needed to check out some of the more interesting facts and figures. It's another of my little routines. But this time, when I had put the paper down, I'd accidentally left it folded, so that now when I finished tidying up my bills and dumping my diaries my eye happened to fall, quite by accident, on an advertisement.

It was one of those public appeals for cash that I never take notice of. I've always been too busy to pay attention to the needs of the halt, the lame or the starving. Which probably sounds callous, though I don't mean it that way.

The thing is, I've always shelled out for every good cause

going – but I've never actually thought about them. My attitude has been simple and practical: I'm not going to let the world's problems worry me into the grave while I've still got enough of my own to make sure I can get there under my own steam.

When I was in business I contributed to every charity that came to me with a begging bowl. My secretary sorted out the details, using a system I had devised, based on the simple principle of a sliding scale calibrated to geographical proximity. African appeals got the standard fifty bucks, Pacific-based charities got a hundred, New Zealand ones got up to five hundred, depending on whether they published the names of donors, and Rownley appeals got a thousand. In other words, the rate they got derived directly from the golden rule that charity begins at home.

I don't see any point in continuing to make a secret of the fact that over the years I earned a reputation for generosity and public spirit, when in truth it cost me bugger-all and earned the firm good publicity. But don't let's be cynical about this. It was a transaction in which everyone came out a winner. Let me make it absolutely plain that I think it was an honourable, worthwhile and effective policy.

But suddenly, looking down at the advertisement in the newspaper, which was for a community shelter for Rownley's mentally handicapped, I had one of those strange sensations of genuine spiritual vertigo that most of us experience perhaps only once in our lives. In fact, some may not even know what I'm talking about.

It's a feeling of total disintegration, as though all of your life certainties have suddenly collapsed inside you – a disastrous, desolate, falling-apart sensation, which comes from God knows where or why.

If I could liken it to anything, I'd say it's as if you're caught up in one of those old black-and-white courtroom movies, where someone is trapped in a trial for their life, for a murder they haven't committed.

I suddenly felt as if I hadn't put my affairs in order at all, as if I'd been paying my social dues like a kind of insurance policy. I had a sickening, hollow feeling that I'd somehow been in the wrong, that I hadn't been generous or public spirited, in the true definition of those words.

As I write now, with hindsight, I am sure I was being grossly unfair to myself. But at the time, the feeling was real enough. It was as though I was considering myself from a long way off, and I didn't come up to standard.

Rightly or wrongly, I knew myself to be a fraud and an impostor, and this secret knowledge shattered me. It was far worse than the feeling that someone might be out there planning to kill me.

I'd heard Ralph stumping off upstairs sometime before, probably to sleep off the daytime booze he'd just taken to cure the hangover he'd earned the night before, and I was still sitting there, staring at the advertisement and experiencing a gutted sensation of how a huge awareness of the world around me had entirely escaped me, when the front doorbell rang – which was a change from the way everyone, except the ever-reliable James, seemed to have been dropping in across the lawn, or down the drive and across the patio to the back door.

32

Standing at the door was a young policeman in a blue short-sleeved shirt, wearing a peaked cap that made him look as though he was some kind of junior officer on a merchant ship or perhaps a uniformed chauffeur. Absent-mindedly it occurred to me that no policeman I'd seen recently wore proper bobby-type helmets. It hadn't registered on me before. What had happened to them? Then, the next thing, I was tipped right over my beam end.

'There's a Kenneth Gransey wants to see you. Is that okay with you, sir?' he said.

'What?' was all I could think of saying.

'He said you'd be expecting him. Is that right?'

'No,' I blurted. 'It's not right.'

'He's waiting up the top of the drive. He wouldn't come to the door with me. He says he's your son.'

'My son? Ken says that?'

The policeman gave me a hard sideways glance and said, 'Whoever it is, you don't have to see him. No one comes in here without authorisation.'

'Then tell him to bugger off,' I said.

'Well, let's say I'll inform him that access is denied,' the policeman said, grinning. And he did a little skip down the front steps and went back up the drive.

I didn't bother to look further to see if the boy was standing there. My blood was boiling with rage. How dare he ask to come to see me? I strode through to the den and threw a long seat-cushion off the top of a fitted locker onto the floor, raised the lid and took out my old BSA single-shot twenty-two, the one I'd owned for over sixty years, and I said out loud to myself, 'If that bastard comes in here I'll shoot him.'

Then I lowered the rifle onto my lap and waited.

A minute or two must have gone by before I looked up and saw Ralph standing just outside the den in the hallway, yawning and stretching. 'Put the artillery away, you stupid old bugger,' he said, patting his lips with the back of one hand and suppressing a last yawn, 'or I'll take it outside and smash the bloody thing over the chopping block.'

I hadn't realised I had pointed the rifle towards the door and it was aimed directly at Ralph. Of course there was no bullet up the spout, but it must have looked as though I was waiting in ambush for him. It could hardly have been for one or both of the Luckhams. There was nothing else I could do but lower the rifle a bit sheepishly. I got up and took it back to the locker and hid it away again, then replaced the cushion.

'I'm sorry,' I said. 'I didn't mean to point it at you like that.'

'I should hope not, dad. It's right against the law for one thing. And it's a danger to life for another. Also, it's very bad manners. And I'll bet you didn't know that in some quarters it could even rate as a sure sign of mental instability. I thought you would have had enough of people pulling guns around here.'

'It was all to do with him. The bloody little scumbag who . . .'

'Oh Christ no, it was Ken.'

'Never mention that name around . . .'

'You fuckwit old fool. I asked him here.'

'You what? You dared . . .'

'Quick. Where'd he go? Did you see?'

'I didn't look. Deliberately.'

'Then come on, grab your keys and lock the back door. Jump in the bloody car. And don't ask questions,' Ralph shouted at me, and he half-dragged, half-pushed me out of the house.

33

I heard Ralph's words clearly, but I was so stunned by what had just happened with the rifle that when he let go of me, after manhandling me outside then rushing around to the far side of the Falcon, I just stood beside the passenger door in the driveway. I hadn't even looked at the rifle since the day I'd put it there when the house was built in 1963. I'd never taken it out before.

'Don't piss about,' he yelled. 'You're going to help me look for him. He'll give us the slip.'

Somehow, I compelled my legs to move and got in beside him. The force of the car's sudden acceleration as Ralph spun it around in the drive then shot into the road nearly threw me out again, before I slammed the car door. I just managed to take in the astonished expressions of the two policemen standing on my front lawn.

'What are you doing?' I bawled at him. 'You'll kill us both.'

'Hang on daddy-o,' he said. 'I think I've spotted our target.'

'Then slow down, for God's sake.'

Ralph actually did slow down, though I guessed it was only because we'd almost caught up with the car he was looking for. It was then that it dawned on me, at last, that this chase was totally crazy. I definitely didn't want to see Ken – in fact, more than that, I wanted positively and at all costs to avoid him. So what the hell was I doing here in Ralph's car?

'Turn around. I've decided I'd rather go back,' I protested.

Perhaps I sounded a bit feeble – remember, I was really frightened out of my wits by Ralph's driving – for all he did was laugh and say, 'Balls you're going back. You nearly buggered up a lot more hard thinking than you'd ever be capable of understanding.'

'I don't wish to follow that boy's car,' I said.

'Whose bloody car?' Ralph asked, and he sounded genuinely surprised.

'You know as well as I do,' was all I'd concede. I didn't want to hear my youngest son's name pass my lips.

'Bradley Brunning's?' Ralph surprised me by asking.

'Who?' I said.

'Shit, dad. You've got the wrong end of everything, haven't you? Ken's just the passenger. Or at least I hope he is.'

I said nothing. For once it seemed that Ralph had half a point. I certainly didn't have the faintest idea what was going on or why he was driving towards Rownley.

'If you really want to know, we're not following Ken as such. At the moment you and I are trying not to lose sight of that beaten-up old Skoda just in front,' he announced contemptuously, hawking out of the window. 'That yellow rust bucket three cars ahead, in case you can't tell. Typical bloody Brunning. Riding through Rownley behind the wheel of a clapped-out Skoda. He's just the type.'

I resisted the temptation to tell Ralph that he was also 'just the type' to drive through town in a battered Falcon with odd-coloured replacement doors he'd bought from the wreckers and splashes of undercoat testifying to his hoonish way of driving and the art of panelbeating.

'So, you'd better tell me why you got out the artillery, don't you think?' Ralph said, abruptly changing the subject.

'Well?' he demanded, when I didn't answer.

'Just take me home,' I insisted.

'Not till you tell me what the gun was all about.'

I didn't really believe he was making a bargain that he intended to keep, but everything was happening so fast that I thought I'd better answer truthfully and hope for the best. 'I can't explain it,' I said. 'It was something to do with . . . you know who I'm talking about . . . I suppose I panicked.' And I told him about the policeman asking me if Ken could come in to see me and how I'd said no, and how I must have got into a bit of a mad state when I'd gone into my den.

Ralph didn't see the sad and silly side of it all; instead, he found the whole thing quite hilarious – just as I expected he would.

He slapped the steering wheel, making the car wobble in a very dangerous way, and he shouted out, 'Shoot your own son, would you daddy-o? By Jesus, you're the wackiest old gunfighter in town. Just imagine that the cop had let Ken in after all, on his own say-so. With a shaky old bastard like you behind the trigger, anything could've happened. Just think if he'd walked in the door and you'd gut-shot him accidentally. You'd have spent your last years in the slammer . . . Christ Almighty, can you picture James and Bruce if they'd turned on their TVs and heard their dear old dad had plugged their queer baby brother. Talk about a riot in a fun-factory.'

Ralph spluttered so much at the thought that naturally he needed the comfort of a drink. He fumbled under the seat and found a bottle, which turned out to be empty. 'Shit, who drank that?' he yelled before slinging the bottle across the road where it bounced magically into the long grass without breaking.

'It wasn't loaded,' I said.

'Naw,' he said, with a little snigger. 'Empty as an old man's ballbag. Some bastard must've guzzled it.'

'I meant the rifle. It wasn't loaded. I popped the ammo into my pocket.'

This made Ralph break into raucous yelps of laughter and again he slapped his hands on the steering wheel. It was the first time I could ever remember being his passenger, but if this was the way he usually drove it was a miracle he'd lived so long.

'I don't believe it,' he said when he'd got his breath back. 'I walk in on a scene like the showdown at the OK Corral, my old man waving a bloody great howitzer at the doorway as if he's heard voices telling him he's Wyatt Earp, and how am I to guess it's not me he wants to splatter all over the wallpaper – and there's no bloody ammo. I tell you, daddy-o, you sure had me convinced. I thought, the way you were twitching the trigger, the bloody thing might go off any minute. Jesus, what a family. It's no wonder I'm the mess I am when I've got your blood pissing through my arteries.'

Ralph beamed away happily to himself, obviously enjoying a stupid little private movie in his head, while he rolled a cigarette with both hands, steering with his wrists and elbows, and somehow managing not to drive us straight off the road.

Eventually he seemed to return to some kind of semi-consciousness, for he waved an arm out of his open window and said, 'You wouldn't read about it, would you? After all that fuckin' drama, here we are, father and son, out for a quiet little family spin, following Bradley Brunning's boy-racer special into the metropolis of Rownley.'

He drew hard on his cigarette, hummed a few bars of a tune I couldn't recognise, then added cheerfully, 'If only the bastard's name wasn't Bradley, you'd almost think we were part of the normal world, wouldn't you?'

'What's wrong with "Bradley"?' I asked.

'Have you met the prick?'

'Not that I know of.'

'Well, I happened to go to school with him and I've bumped into him off and on ever since, so let me put it this way – I've got nothing at all against the name, but he's exactly the type you'd expect to be called Bradley.'

'Just like you're a Ralph?' I asked.

'Piss off, will you?' he said, shaking his head and laughing.

34

There was a peaceful silence between us as Ralph pulled in to the kerb. We were in the Underham area of Rownley, right at the harbour edge, next to the port. Nowadays it's a very seedy and decrepit district, but not so many years ago it was the heart of the town.

I remember a time when Underham was crawling with storemen, wharfies, seamen, businessmen, labourers, clerks, railwaymen, odd-jobbers, fishermen, bookies, drunks, thieves, whores – the lot. There were hand-barrows, horse-carts, vans and square-shaped lorries with wooden-spoked wheels everywhere, and there was the smell of fish and coal and horseshit in the air. You could close your eyes and listen to the traffic and the shouts, then take a sniff of the place where you were standing and you could just about tell which street you were in from its particular sound and stench.

In those days Underham was full of bustling warehouses, woolstores, coldstores, poky offices, railway sheds, small factories, merchants, coalyards, scrapyards and shops of all kinds – chandlers, ironmongers, Chinese and Indian importers, second-hand dealers, sly groggers, gambling dens – you name it, you'd find one. You could easily have believed it would go on like that forever. There seemed to be a need for all those people and the goods, services and vices they dealt in.

But the day the wharves moved over to containers

Underham curled up and died. It just took that one crucial change. Boards were nailed over the windows, chains and padlocks were fastened to the gates and doorways, and that was that. Finished.

Which was no great tragedy so far as I was concerned. It's my certain knowledge that in no more than five years' time, give or take a year or two, Underham will see a real bonanza by way of a waterfront redevelopment. It has just been lying there catching its breath and waiting to take off again. Wise people have been mopping up property here as a future investment. I know, because for the past seven years the Gransey Trust has been gradually acquiring a holding in prime Underham real estate. It has made up to some extent for the manner in which my old firm was outmanoeuvred by Trupper Enterprises when it moved in to rip the arse out of our holdings. We've put together a completely watertight little parcel of derelict land, plus a couple of fine old woolstores and a row of adjoining shops, all of which will turn out to be better than a goldmine for James and Bruce when I've moved on to the other side to join Grace.

I was enjoying the pleasure of this thought, when Ralph switched off the engine and began to get out of the car. Then I remembered Brunning and what we were supposed to be doing. I'd completely lost concentration. 'The Skoda,' I cried out in relief. 'Thank God we've lost it.'

The spell between us was broken. Ralph raised his eyebrows and looked up at the heavens. 'Hold on to the sides of your pram, will you,' he said. 'I spotted my old pal Bradley just back there, and it's quicker to walk straight through than try to dodge around the one-way system. He's right in front of the Globe Hotel. Which means he must know some real desperadoes. Even I wouldn't drink in a piss-pit like that. Now, listen carefully this time – what you do is sit tight here. You don't go anywhere. Have you got that? Understand? All you do is look up at the sky and count all the flying Skodas you see, and you tell me how many you saw when I come back, okay?'

I suppose he thought he was being funny, but I merely wanted to see him make a botch of things, as usual, then take us home, so I didn't pick him up on his manners or style, but just nodded and waved him away with a shooing gesture. Not putting the boy in his proper place was getting to be a new habit with me – something I should have spent more time thinking about, if I hadn't been so preoccupied.

Ralph was gone only a couple of minutes before he came back, hurled himself in the car, swore profusely and shouted at me to belt up double quick. I clipped the seatbelt on immediately, just as I'd been ordered. Another new habit I seemed to be acquiring.

It turned out that Ralph had indeed mucked things up, for Brunning must have just shot in and out of the pub briefly, and he'd gone. I was congratulating myself when Ralph let out a whoop and I looked up to see in the distance a battered yellow Skoda take a left hook into Main Road. Naturally, Ralph took off after it with screaming tyres – just like the great big kid he was – and a hundred yards or so along the road we caught up to within a couple of cars of it. We followed the Skoda, comparatively sedately, to the middle of town, until it pulled into the single empty parking bay in the street.

It was only then that we saw that the passenger seat was empty. Somewhere along the way he'd dropped Ken off, and we hadn't noticed. Ralph and I looked at each other and we could read our expressions without having to say a word: another fiasco.

'Well that definitely settles it,' I said thankfully. 'Can we go home now?'

'Okay, I give up,' Ralph conceded. Then he tapped for a few moments on the steering wheel, changed his mind and added, 'But while we're here why don't we just hang on a minute or two and see where the bastard goes, shall we?'

The way we were double parked and making a nuisance of ourselves to cars behind us reassured me that we wouldn't be able to stay where we were for long, so I was quite content to watch as Brunning got out.

Although he ignored the parking meter, he didn't immediately walk away, but stood on the footpath indecisively for a few moments, so I managed to get a good look at him. And I'm afraid that Bradley Brunning didn't cut an impressive figure. He was short, hollow-chested, pallid, and the long grey hair that straggled over his ears merely accentuated his bald patch. He was dressed in a T-shirt that bore an advertisement for tomato sauce, a baggy pair of trousers held up by a drawstring that made them look like pyjamas, and a pair of sandshoes with Nike emblazoned along them – the goddess of victory, no less. But as if that wasn't enough, he had enormous, dangling, paddle-sized hands which were out of all proportion to the rest of his body, and he wore powerful fishbowl spectacles that seemed to cover half his face.

We watched for a while, then just as Ralph reached out for the gearstick to leave, Brunning quite suddenly and with surprising agility dodged into the traffic and across the road. He looked furtively left and right, then darted into a small alley.

'Hold on, here we go again,' Ralph shouted and like a lunatic he spun the car right around, within inches of a vehicle coming the other way, and shot up the alley after Brunning. He stopped at the end and threw the car into another spin, then raced back down again, slamming the brakes on as we came to the street. You could smell the burning rubber.

'Stay there,' he shouted as he leapt out. 'I've got to find Ken.'

35

But that's not what happened. Ralph had been gone for no more than ten seconds when Brunning reappeared beside me, brushing up against the Falcon as he squeezed past where it blocked the entrance to the alley. Then he scuttled over to the yellow Skoda, climbed into the driver's seat and pulled out.

Without a moment's hesitation to consider what I was doing, I twisted myself across the front seat and got in behind the steering wheel. Since he only intended to be gone for a minute, Ralph had left the keys in the ignition, so I simply switched on and took off after Brunning on my own.

At my age, I make no false claims about my ability to cope with city traffic – I admit I've lost the technique – on top of which, even in my heyday, I'd never driven a car quite like Ralph's through the centre of Rownley. The big cars I owned had always had plenty of grunt, but they were aristocrats and more or less drove themselves, and the little Japanese machine I'd finished up with was like driving a pedal-car. You just aimed it down to the Mt Matheson supermarket, and it went there and back, easily and cheaply. This one was different. It demanded to be driven. It seemed to have a swing and throb of its own, and you had to curb it and work out your manoeuvres.

I knew I was making a hash of things, so it was hard to concentrate on chasing the Skoda – and the task wasn't made any easier by a couple of lunatics who almost swerved into me, then blasted their horns as if it was my fault.

In fact, I nearly lost Brunning twice, once at a set of traffic lights that I took a chance on and just squeezed through on red, and the second time when a delivery van cut in front of me and blocked my view, and it was only by pure fluke that I picked the Skoda up again several turnings later.

With some surprise I found the trail led straight back to Underham and the pub we'd called at – the Globe. I drove slowly past Brunning as he parked, then stopped a little way on and decided to wait. Ralph may have been able to stroll into a pub and not be noticed, but I had no doubts I'd attract the attention of the whole bar.

Brunning reappeared in a few minutes, accompanied by a stocky man wearing only shorts, a black singlet and work-boots, with an odd pair of football socks pulled up to his knees. He was a tough-looking customer, even though he was no taller than Brunning. They got into the Skoda and drove off.

This time, Brunning travelled past only a couple of street corners before he turned up a narrow road with a footpath running down just the one side, then pulled over in front of the junk-strewn yard of one of the derelict Underham warehouses that will go straight under a bulldozer the day the developers decide to make their first move.

I stopped a short way on and walked back to see Brunning and his companion disappearing up a set of sagging wooden steps. After watching and waiting for a minute or so, I decided to follow them. Not once did I reflect on what I was doing. My hair stood on end. It was as though I was compelled to follow them. There was no option; I had to know where they were going.

36

The steps didn't merely sag, they wobbled sideways as I climbed. The wooden runners were rotten and pulling away from the crumbling brick wall to which they had once been bolted. One day soon, if a bulldozer didn't manage to get there before the natural processes of time and decay took over, someone would get no more than halfway up, then take a nasty ride through the sky, outwards from the wall and down into the yard. The whole structure was a death trap.

Ordinarily, I would have turned back after the first few steps, but I watched Brunning and his companion make it right up to the top landing on the third floor, so I decided I also had a good chance of getting there, and I followed them carefully all the way.

At the top there was a half-open door hanging on broken hinges. The door frame had been splintered fairly recently where the lock had been forced. I entered cautiously and the first thing I noticed was a smell of ancient mould and filth.

Then, in the distance I could hear voices. I made my way as quietly as I could towards the sound, through a large storage area. There was no ceiling, just immense ceiling joists and long blackened rafters beneath a tin roof through which I could see patches of daylight.

The place was empty, apart from a few scattered boxes and crates. The floorboards were broken and rotten here and there, and made the going slow and dangerous, especially for someone of my age.

At the far side of this open space there was a long and narrow room, where the ceiling and floorboards seemed to be almost intact. At the end of this room I could clearly see, from where I stood in deep shadow, the two figures I had followed. They were bending over.

Suddenly one figure jerked upright and raced towards me. I thought I must have been seen, so I automatically put my arms up to defend myself. But the figure – I could now clearly see it was Brunning – stopped just as suddenly as it had started, leaned across the opening into the open space in which I stood, clutched at an old wooden box, and vomited.

'Try strangling it, there's enough of a pong in here without you chucking up, Brunning,' the man in the shorts and singlet complained. Looking past him, I saw what seemed to be a heap of sacking on the floor. I stepped forward a few paces, then the first faint stench of it hit me. It was a sweetish though vile smell, a bit like rotten bacon.

As if that wasn't enough, a few moments later I also caught the gut-wrenching stink of Brunning's sick, and I staggered back again. Brunning was coughing and spitting, and trying to wipe his mouth with a handkerchief. He looked up and saw me.

'Oh, no,' he moaned. 'That's all we need. Arthur-bloody-Gransey . . .'

At this, the man in the singlet looked around, cocked his head and squinted, then came towards me. 'Who's this prick, eh?' he demanded.

'He's all right. I can't explain,' Brunning blurted out.

166

Then he pulled himself upright, gave a couple of dry, painful-looking retches and gasped, 'Look, Bill, we've all got to get away the hell out of here, quick-fast.'

'What about him?' said Bill, indicating me. 'What do you mean, you can't explain? He doesn't look like anyone who ought to be here. He knows what we've found.'

'Well, he also knows what's good for him, so he doesn't know anything, okay?' Brunning insisted in between little gagging noises. 'He didn't notice a thing.'

'I don't fuckin' like it,' said Bill uncertainly, but Brunning turned to me and said, 'You didn't see a thing, did you? You've never even been here, have you?'

'No,' I said.

'Come on, then,' Brunning said, leading the way. 'Let's only hope to God no one saw us coming in. And watch where you put your feet. All we need now is for one of us to break a leg and we'll be in it like Rumpel-bloody-stiltskin.'

We made our way with dangerous speed across the rotten floor of the main space and down the steps, where Bill gave me one last threatening look and said, 'I hope you know what you're doing Brunning. I'm fuckin' off, and I'm telling you, I never bloody saw you, nor told you nothing, and I don't never want to bloody see you again. We could've been trapped up there.'

And with that he crossed the yard, slipped noiselessly over a rusty corrugated iron fence and disappeared, leaving Brunning and me to poke our heads out into the alleyway to make sure the coast was clear.

In the few seconds it took to do so, Brunning at last noticed the Falcon and said, 'You tailed me in that thing, didn't you?'

'With some difficulty,' I admitted.

'Well, wouldn't that root you? And to think I actually noticed it a couple of times, but it only half-registered.'

Then I said to him, as steadily as I could manage. 'That was a body in there, wasn't it? That thing you were standing over.'

'You don't have a clue how I know you, do you?' was all

he replied, ignoring my question. 'I recognised you straight away, back in there. I worked for you once, though you'd never remember the circumstances. But you're Ken's old man, which is the only reason why I didn't set Bill on you. He'd have thrown you out the window if I'd told him to. Christ only knows, I owed you.'

'So, what did I ever do to you?'

'Don't ever ask me again or, so help me, I'll call Bill back. You've just cashed in on the luck factor. Got it?'

Before I could take the matter further, the street suddenly became clear – there were no vehicles and no one else was in sight – so we both went for our cars. Of course, I was much slower than the agile Mister Brunning, and he was starting his engine as I passed.

I took my chance to lean in the window just as he'd lowered it to let air in. 'You'd better tell me. Who was it?' I asked again, struggling to suppress all thoughts of Deenie.

'Tuggy Sullivan – who else?' he said and took off.

37

If there's one thing I've learned in business it's never to trust what Brunning casually referred to as the luck factor. When most people get a deal, an investment or a policy right they congratulate themselves and put it all down correctly to skill and foresight. But when they come a cropper they more often than not put it down to chance factors. That's human nature. They look for someone or something outside their control to blame for the balls-ups caused by their own miscalculations or incompetence.

That's something I've never done. Experience has taught me that there's no such thing as good or bad fortune. There are two kinds of people in this world: winners and losers.

You're one or the other. And if you've got winner inscribed in letters of gold across your forehead, well, you may have your ups and downs, but whenever you get the basics right, you come up trumps, and that's all there is to it. If you're a born loser, well, the best thing your mother can drill into you is always brush your teeth and wipe your arse.

Except, this time I knew in my bones that I had been exceptionally lucky. Two nights ago, when that pair of heavies had been sent in to sort me out, there'd been the accidental shot that had winged the one the police had called Darryl Johnstone. Who could have counted on that – the bullet knocking him over like a skittle? Who could reckon the odds on that happening? The chances may have been one in a hundred – or more. The bullet could have gone anywhere. It could have hit me in the head or the heart and I'd have been a goner, or it could have spun on a trajectory a mile out to sea or drilled a rosebush. Strange, isn't it?

And now there was a question of a body in a warehouse. Whoever had passed on the word through Bill to Brunning that there was something interesting in the far corner of the third floor of an old and rickety warehouse, with a dangerous set of steps to climb and a rotten floor to walk across, must have had the whole scenario worked out in his or her mind, with everyone's entrances and exits allowed for so there'd be all the likelihood in the world that we'd become accomplices after the fact. It was too close a call to be a coincidence. The taint of the mystery of the body I had found on Ocean Beach was spreading to affect us all. Somehow, everyone who came near me became implicated in some sinister way. Deenie, Ralph, Brunning, and perhaps even Nathan and Ken. Not for the first time I felt as though I was the accidental agent of some terrible calamity.

And just imagine if the police had found me on the premises. I'd already come under suspicion and surveillance in the matter of the body on the beach. No one would have believed it to be a coincidence that I'd stumbled on another corpse. There aren't that many dead people scattered around the beaches and warehouses of Rownley and Mt Matheson. It would definitely be considered inexcusable in a community like ours to earn a reputation for finding corpses.

The whole way the warehouse was so difficult to get into – and even harder to get away from – made it a perfect trap, just as Bill had said. Someone must have known that Bill and Bradley Brunning could have easily been caught there, and it had probably worked out that way for Tuggy Sullivan in the first place. It was the perfect spot to snare someone in, then nail them. A certain amount of thought had obviously gone into its choice. But it was too much to hope that it would keep on working.

When you weighed it up, the whole set-up showed a limited imagination. There was something about it that was beginning to smack of improvisation and lack of attention – everything that was happening was being fluffed.

And I couldn't help thinking that somewhere in the background was a shadow, which I knew to be familiar. Every clue seemed to me to be pointing towards Ken – there was no way of avoiding it. But how had I allowed him to insinuate himself so cleverly and slyly? What was he up to? How did he fit in? How could I even begin to believe that he could be here to offer me favours? Surely he would be motivated by revenge against me?

All these speculations flashed through my mind as I went back to find Ralph. It was the first time in days that my brain seemed to be functioning properly and I was making connections that I couldn't quite explain but which still had the ring of probability to them. There seemed at last to be a pattern emerging to give shape to the mysteries that surrounded me. I could feel my heart banging away with excitement. I was worried – but suddenly I was also exhilarated.

38

Altogether, I suppose, my little excursion to Underham and back in Ralph's car would have taken no more than half an hour. But I was so out of practice and intimidated by the car's resistance to me that I could easily have got picked up anywhere along the road for a traffic infringement and I could well have ended up being booked and having the keys taken off me. Luck again, I had to suppose.

But, of course, Ralph was in no mood to be told that. He was almost off his head with rage when I drove up to find him stamping his feet up and down in a central Rownley phonebox, thumping its windows and shouting into the handset.

The moment he saw me, he simply dropped the phone, left it swinging backwards and forwards, and ran right across the road, weaving through the traffic and almost getting himself run over.

'I've spent twenty bucks on phonecards trying to trace you, you stupid old bastard,' were his first words as he threw himself in beside me, on the driver's side, and tried to push and bundle me back across the seat. 'I'm going to chain you up in a kennel like a fuckin' dog when we get back home.'

'So, it's "home" now, is it?' I asked, with a smile.

'I tell you,' he shouted. 'That's the last stroke you ever pull on me. You think I'm some kind of mug, don't you? Well, I'll chop your friggin' legs off if you ever try anything like this again. From now on you're in solitary confinement. You don't speak to anyone or go anywhere, not even a morning walk, ever again. I'm locking you up with a padlock the size of a friggin' lunchbox – you hear that?'

He chucked the motor into gear and took off with a graunch, a lurch and a roar that made at least four or five people turn around in their tracks and look at him. Big deal.

'Oh, I can hear all right,' I said mildly. 'For instance I can hear police sirens from down by the waterfront, can you?'

'There's been nothing but sirens blaring all over Rownley

since you buggered off with my wagon. I thought you must've ram-raided the central police station.'

'But can't you tell the difference?' I asked. 'All the noise is heading towards the waterfront. Underham direction, wouldn't you say?'

Ralph glared at me, but said nothing. He took the Rownley Road and it wasn't until we were halfway back to *my* home – not his – that he recovered from his evil temper sufficiently to demand, 'All right then, you old prick. You'd better tell me now. Where did you go?'

'Underham. Where all the sirens were coming from. Just there and back, that's all. The Gransey Trust has got a substantial property investment there, did you know that? A superb location and all very neatly dovetailed.'

'Huh,' was all he said. He was in a very black mood.

Altogether, another five minutes must have passed before he even looked at me again – and that was only a passing glance.

'Okay, what's got into you?' he asked at last, as we took the turn into my street. 'You're hiding something from me, aren't you?'

'No,' I said. 'I'm merely keeping something to myself. There's a vast difference, you know.'

'Stop fuckin' pissing me about, will you?'

'I'm not. It's called keeping one's own counsel. I absolutely refuse to talk to a boy who uses foul language to excess the way you do. The occasional swear word has its place now and again, and I sometimes use such expressions myself, but . . .'

Ralph spun into the drive and revved up as he charged the garage doors. Then he stood on the brakes and gripped the steering wheel. We stopped an inch or two short of disaster. Again, I could smell burning tyre rubber.

'Spill it,' he roared. 'Where the fuck did you go?'

I got out and stretched. 'I don't see why I should spill anything to an idle dissolute drunken foul-mouthed no-good son who's nearly killed his father in the worst exhibition of driving he's ever seen and who's been threatening him with abuse of several varieties, including the removal of his lower limbs. Do you know, Ralph – call me old-fashioned, but someone ought to rinse your mouth out with soap and water. I think you're a spoilt oafish bludging useless nobody. And I blame your mother.'

I couldn't help that last bit, though I immediately wished I hadn't said it. What was past between Belle and me should have been over and done with, not raised in such a petty way. It detracted from the truth of the rest of the message.

But I had more important things to dwell on. I opened the door and went through the kitchen to my den. Then I kicked off my shoes and lay down on the leather sofa, rather as Ralph sometimes did, and tried to think of what these latest events meant so far as Deenie was concerned.

I recognised that since I'd left the warehouse in Underham I had put off dealing with the implications of what I had just seen and experienced, as they affected her. I had managed to separate my own feelings of excitement, as I'd begun to gain a larger view of the confusions that surrounded me, from the desperate flounderings of my wretched efforts for my daughter. It was as though I could only look at problems with tunnel vision, one glimpse at a time. Perhaps this was an old man's failing. A condition I'd never before come up against in all my years of retirement. Perhaps also I really was losing my grip. Like forgetting I'd rung Frank Pelley. Perhaps it wasn't a failure of nerve, it was a condition of age.

Even though I knew there was a pattern out there ready to be recognised and interpreted, I simply could not focus on it any more – not in the way I once had when I was king of Rownley.

My feeling of exhilaration had long since ebbed away. For the first time it struck me that, without knowing when or how it had happened, I was becoming like that old mad King Lear in the play Grace had taken me to when we had gone to London so many years ago.

I was alone on a desolate stage peopled with liars and fools, stormed by nightmares and twisted memories. All I needed to complete the picture was a torn dressing-gown and a white beard.

39

I don't know what made me remember, but my mind drifted right back to the war years. Perhaps it was stress. All that anxiety about defending things dear to me and the worry about being killed – and my total ineptitude on top of everything. So I suppose I've got nothing to lose now when I reveal the embarrassing secret that neither Nathan nor I did a single thing to be proud of during that time.

The pair of us would have been among the fastest and most accurate snap-shots in Rownley, we were dependable in the outdoors, we were clever and we were destined to become leaders of men. But when it came to confronting the great evil of nazism and Japanese imperialism I admit that we pulled our heads in and made ourselves inconspicuous till the threat passed by.

The way we worked it, we wore the best camouflage for being entirely overlooked by the war machine: we concealed ourselves in military uniform. There were plenty of others like us. We went along with things and did exactly what we were obliged to do – and no more. By taking this line, I suppose you could say we ended up making ourselves useful to the war effort, but only just. I went into what the famous song of the time called the Quartermaster's Stores – equipment, supplies and the requisitions end of things, while Nathan had the utter bloody audacity to hide out as a clerk in recruitment, where he sometimes had to help chase up conscientious objectors and lazy young buggers who made themselves stupidly conspicuous by dragging their feet on the way to join up.

Both of us had the one absolute essential to get by – the

ability to work our way into the esteem of our senior officers, who were mostly decent old codgers who'd earned a stripe or two in the First World War. This meant that whenever it was touch or go whether we'd be sent overseas, we could always rely on them to get our postings deferred and keep wangling a place for us on their staff on the grounds of our vital contributions to the war effort. They liked us and protected us, purely because we unashamedly brown-nosed them.

The manner by which we saved our skins has always been a matter of private shame for me and I've often wished in my secret dreams that I'd gone overseas and risked my life. I know I'd have made a good soldier if I'd only had the commitment.

The way I explained it to Belle – for she and I got married before the war ended, so she was a wake-up to the fact that I was getting special privileges – was that, after the war was eventually won, I knew there would then be a glorious peace to be secured by freedom-lovers like myself, so there I was, fulfilling my obligations to the uniform I wore while at the same time saving up my supreme efforts to triumph in the era of reconstruction that would inevitably follow the fighting. She agreed with me that it was the right thing to do, for if I'd got myself killed, who then could the country turn to when it came to leading the way into the future?

Nathan's case was probably a bit different. I'm not at all sure that he saw himself in the same way that I did, with a heroic role to play in the processes of peace. When I finally got around to mentioning the subject, circumspectly, some years after the war was over, he asked me who the hell I thought I was kidding. So far as he was concerned he considered that the pair of us had very sensibly been looking after number one – which no sentient creature could be blamed for doing in the circumstances.

But Nathan's case was special. Perhaps because his father was a clerk in the railways, I'd now go so far as to say that there was always something a bit clerkish about the pair of them. Like father, like son – there was something in the genes;

it was inescapable. Whenever the boy had to go to see his old man, he'd find him behind the wire grille of the ticket office or out the back, among the shelves, pigeonholes, files, boxes and the mounds of paperwork. It had to have an influence.

I remember the old sod as a wizened dark homunculus, with a blueish five-o'clock shadow, a bit like a walnut to look at, with deep creases in his face and folds in the skin of his neck. Nathan had the same brown eyes and an identical problem with a heavy crop of facial hair, though his skin was fairer, and I remember several times over at Mt Matheson, when we were after rabbits, how he'd go to elaborate lengths to explain to me how his father looked different from the other dads in town because he came from the Greek community in Alexandria, in Egypt, and was therefore descended from an ancient line that included the great heroes of Greek mythology – who, in those far-off days, I'm glad to say, we still learned about in school.

Naturally, I believed him. Why shouldn't I have done so? Though I once heard one of the boys at school maintain that he had heard his father tell a friend that Nathan's old man was nothing but a greasy Levantine. It was an insult that you never hear now, and most people wouldn't know how damaging it was intended to be, for it didn't just describe a kind of sweaty Middle-eastern type, it carried all sorts of nasty un-Anglo-Saxon messages about being untrustworthy, mercenary, devious and cowardly.

Whatever the truth of his origins, however, the one remarkable thing I shall forever remember Nathan's old man for was the way you'd never see him in anything other than a waistcoat, and always with a steel-spring clip in the breast pocket, from which two indelible pencils obtruded. Whenever he opened his mouth to say something, you could see a poisonous-looking purple stain on his lips and tongue, which he got from licking the lead.

As I said earlier, Nathan had to leave high school when his father died, which meant he had to take his exams at night school. He became a cadet, in the Railways at first, of course, and he was bitter about it, even though in those days he'd managed to land what people thought of as a safe job, with prospects and security.

His bitterness was compounded by the fact that he and his mother, to whom he was utterly devoted, lost their home. Unknown to them, the old man had run an extraordinary double life. He'd had access to free train tickets to Auckland and back, which he managed to use mostly at the weekends, and he'd excuse his trips on the grounds of important railway business.

God only knows what tricks he got up to, for Nathan never explained the details to me, but the outcome was that he'd mortgaged the house to the hilt and run up a heap of strange debts. His wife had no idea what had been going on and she had no alternative but to give up and get out. Nathan and his mother moved into a cheap and squalid place at the Riverview end of town, and his mother had to look after an old couple who tyrannised her all day. Remember, we were just coming out of the Depression and things were pretty rough for a widow who found she'd been left destitute. What else could she turn her hand to, but housework? It was hell, and eventually she got some sort of rapid wasting sickness and was dead herself in less than two years.

I never went to the funeral, if there actually was one, and I never asked Nathan about it – he was as hostile and protective and vicious about the whole thing as a mad dog, so he wouldn't let me near him – but he once let drop a remark that he was never going to forgive any bastard for what had happened. In a way, I think Nathan must have always blamed both the system that allowed his mother to die homeless and no better off than a scullery maid, and the country that endorsed such a system. It explains a lot of things about him. It accounted for an ambition to get to the top and change things, and for his cranky life-long belief in social engineering. I'm also convinced it motivated his actions – or, rather, his lack of them – during the war. He wasn't going to risk his neck for a country that he felt had betrayed him.

177

Strange, the way the mind works. As I lay there, thinking about the past and recollecting so many details of the men I'd known who went away, never to come back, and those, like Nathan and me, who had a cushy time of it, swinging the lead, I could at last see only too well why I'd failed my daughter.

I'd also never been committed to anything or anyone, except those that had helped advance my own ambitions. I'd asked for sacrifices all round from everyone, but I'd never sacrificed my own interests, not even to my wives and children. How could I? Like I said earlier, my whole life seemed primed to blow away into nothingness; it was as though I'd never existed.

Somewhere, in some old battlefield of the past that I couldn't quite place, I'd gone missing in action. Nathan too. He'd been caught in some mysterious crossfire in the past and he was a casualty. The things that really mattered had also passed him by.

40

When Ralph came in with a glass of clear fluid I thought for a moment that he'd taken my criticisms to heart and gone on the wagon. Of course, I should have known better. He had merely widened his range of activity by helping himself to my vodka.

'Okay,' he said, seating himself right across the room from me. 'I've done some thinking and I've decided apologies are called for.'

'Good God, Ralph, have you? Really?' I couldn't help sounding absolutely stunned. When he was a boy I used to have to thrash an apology out of him. I looked at his face to see whether he was having me on.

'Maybe I went overboard,' he said, and there was no doubt he meant what he said. 'Maybe I did give you a mouthful.'

He paused, then added, 'But take a raincheck on what you pulled on me, will you? You pinched my car, didn't you? And in my book that has to rate as a number-one top offence.'

These are the words of a middle-aged man, I thought, whose first crime nearly forty years previously was stealing cars. I'd banished him to Queensland for it.

I suppose my jaw must have fallen open, because when he stopped to judge the effect his words were having on me, he felt the need to make his message even clearer, 'You never take a man's car. Never. Have you got that? Do you get the point I'm driving at? It was a bloody crazy thing for a doddering old fuckwit to do, wasn't it? What if you'd crashed the bloody thing? What if you'd killed someone? See what I mean?'

Ralph nodded his head slowly, as if endorsing the wisdom of his remarks. Then he rather spoiled the effect by slurping at his drink and having to wipe a glittering trickle of booze-dribble off his shirt before continuing in a pathetic fake-fatherly tone, 'However, I can't help being a fair and reasonable sort of bastard, so I've decided this time to overlook your behaviour. The way I see it, no decent person could blame me for blasting off at you, both ends of the shotgun, could they? But just the same, on this occasion only, I'm willing to let bygones be bygones. Okay?'

'Are you, indeed?' I said neutrally.

'Yes I am. Though it's a mystery to me how I've gone so soft on you. When I first came here I told myself I wasn't going to put up with any of your old bullshit and bullying. I've had enough of that for one lifetime. But the funny thing is I've learned to go easy on you. It's beyond all possible argument that you've given me sufficient cause for having you put away in a padded cell, but I've discovered I'm just not the type to see even a silly old bastard like you incarcerated for life. I believe in liberty. And, besides that, it's getting near your dinnertime – and mine – so in the interests of family harmony and the need to take a pit-stop, why don't we cool it? Sound reasonable?'

I felt too worn out to explain to him that in no way did these words amount to an apology. The boy was what he was and there was no hope of redemption. Just as well, I supposed, that I wasn't a priest. I'd have consigned his soul there and then to hellfire, with far less than a faint hope of a reprieve.

'I don't wish to pursue the matter,' I agreed wearily. 'You're a hopeless case, son, and I gave up on you long ago . . .'

I sighed, shook my head and looked at the beautiful ruin he was becoming, then couldn't help adding slowly, 'Even if I've also got to concede I'm amazed I've been able to share the same breathing space with you day and night all this time. Yes – really, deeply, profoundly, utterly amazed . . .'

'So, what happened?' he asked quickly, as though he couldn't bear to hear me out – as though he was embarrassed to allow me to develop my confession.

'What happened?' I had completely lost the drift of what he was going on about.

'Yeah. Something happened all right. Over at Underham, or wherever you went. And you haven't told me yet, have you?'

'Oh, that,' I said. 'You've got this way of changing the subject and it's very confusing.'

'Okay then. I've changed the subject. So what happened?'

'I had a very strange experience.'

'And . . .?'

'Would it surprise even a man of the world like you to know that I've seen the corpse of Tuggy Sullivan?'

Ralph took a long swig from the glass, leaned back in his chair, squinted at me out of one eye, then the other, before repeating slowly and softly, 'You've seen the corpse of Tuggy Sullivan?'

'Well, I didn't know it was him actually,' I admitted. 'I had the word of Bradley Brunning, who was with someone called Bill. They got quite a bit closer to the body and apparently they seemed to think it was Tuggy Sullivan.'

'Shit.'

'I thought you'd come out with a perceptive remark like that.'

Ralph pulled himself upright again and didn't look at all well – though not as bad as Brunning had been. 'Whereabouts?' he said, now beginning to raise his voice. 'Would you please tell me where you saw Tuggy?'

'On the third floor of a derelict warehouse, right in the middle of Underham, near the wharves. If you showed me a street map I could probably point out the street. I've completely forgotten what it's called, though once upon a time I could've recited the names of every little alleyway in the area. It's a very narrow one . . .'

'Stop shitting me, will you? Just tell me how he came to be there. In the bloody warehouse.'

'What makes you think I'd know the answer to that? I mean . . .'

'Well, how long had he been there?'

'All I know is he was ripe enough to make Brunning vomit, though the one called Bill didn't seem to be affected in any way – except he was worried about me having walked in on them . . . You see, while you were gone Brunning drove past, so there was nothing else I could do but follow him, was there? It was an impulse decision, but that's how I came to see . . .'

Ralph began to fire questions at me. In any other circumstance it would have amused me to see him suddenly so agitated on my behalf.

'Christ, don't you know what this means?' he shouted at me. 'Why didn't you tell me before? Why didn't you get out of there straight away? Can't you see it must've been a set-up? Are you a complete bloody cretin? Did anyone spot you coming or going?'

Finally, I just gave up and told him with a sigh, 'I was just going over all these questions myself, in my mind, before you came in just now. Do you know, I'm beginning to believe in the power of good fortune. I've been converted.'

'Give us a break, will you, dad . . .' Ralph complained, but I cut him off quickly.

'No, Ralph,' I said. 'I happen to be very serious indeed. I really think I had a lucky escape in there. Whoever it was who let Brunning and his friend Bill know they'd find something interesting in Underham must have got their timing wrong. The cops must have been just behind us. It stands to reason. I guess that was what all the sirens were about as we were leaving Rownley. Do you remember me drawing your attention to them?'

Ralph snorted. 'That kind of luck never seems to happen to me. I've always got caught.' Then he added gloomily, 'I expect I'd better get in touch with Auckland. I hope you know this changes everything.'

For a moment I did not want to utter the question that was on my lips. I didn't want to let the words out, then have to force myself to lower my feet to the floor, go to the kitchen, scratch up a meal and fill in time, haunted by the thought of what might even now be happening to Deenie. It was too terrible to contemplate.

But Ralph surprised me by showing a rare understanding. 'You're thinking of Deenie, aren't you?' he said softly.

'Yes,' I said. 'I am.'

'Well, don't think I don't feel sorry for you – and for her, of course. Best thing is not to dwell on it, dad. You won't help yourself – and you won't help Deenie either.'

'But I need to do something. What's the point . . .'

'The point is there never is any point,' he said. 'That's the one grim lesson I've managed to learn in one useless lifetime. What you do is sit tight and wait, and hope you're given half a chance before you hear the final whistle and it's all too late.'

'There's nothing else?'

'Well, you were talking about luck a little while ago.'

'I'm not sure that my faith stretches quite that far.'

'It's all you've got, dad. You hang about with your flags flying, your hopes high and your fingers crossed. In spite of everything. That's all there is.'

I got up and went to the freezer to select two dinners for the microwave when a strange thing happened. Ralph came up to me and put an arm over my shoulder.

'Bad days, eh?' he said almost in a whisper. 'Don't think I don't know, you silly old bugger.'

That's all that passed between us, but it was the closest we'd been in at least forty-five years – in fact, since he was a beautiful little Cupid of a boy; my handsome, perfect child. I couldn't help trembling.

Then I said I was going to the cellar to choose a good wine, and I went in and closed the door behind me, and leant over the first rack of bottles and wept long and inconsolably.

I wept for Ralph and for Deenie, and I wept for myself. But most of all I wept for all the years of life I'd lost and would never have again. I wept for all the secrets I'd bricked up in the cold recesses of my heart, secrets that amounted to nothing because they could never have mattered a damned thing to anyone, secrets that had withered without even leaving skeletons to crumble into dust. I wept for the meaningless messages I'd written in my diaries, thinking I was making sense of my life. I wept for the love I'd missed. I wept for my own mortality and for the way things fall. I wept for the end of the world.

41

Just after we'd eaten, Ralph took his car out and did not return for an hour. It was only when I looked at the clock that I made this discovery, for I must have nodded off at the table pretty well as soon as he left. It was getting to be a new habit, no doubt due to an unusual and regular dosage of wine, and there I was, opening my eyes again to find myself slumped forward, resting my head on my left arm, with Ralph shaking me and saying I ought to think about giving up the piss if I couldn't take it without disgracing myself. Our relationship was back to normal.

'How was your friend Jason?' I asked when I'd swallowed a glass of water.

'What do you mean?'

'Don't be tedious, Ralph. You told me you had to get in touch with Auckland – and even at the time I thought that was probably a slight exaggeration. I mean – making contact with a whole city. So far as I know there's only one person you'd run the police cordon outside to get in touch with. Your pathetic non-paying employer.'

Ralph stomped away grumpily and came back a few moments later with a bottle of rather good brandy. He ripped the top off, flipped the cork in the air, caught it with one hand while he poured a drink with the other, then he lifted his glass and took a good snort with his eyes closed. A single drink later and his whole expression was transformed as if by magic. I could actually observe the outward signs of a chemical change as it occurred inside him. It may have been over in a minute or two, but it was quite spectacular. He was suddenly cheerful and on top again.

'Listen, daddy-o,' he confided. 'When I say he was bloody well amazed to learn about Tuggy, you can take it I'm putting it mildly,' he declared. 'And, by the way, just in case you think the heat's off, it's back on again.'

'What heat?'

'The uniformed cops are still out there in front of the house, but this time there was a plainclothes dick sitting just over the road in a car and he took off after me and tailed me all around town. I had to park outside the Queen's Head, nip through the back and slip over a wall to shake him. And I used a number I hope the dicks haven't wised up to.'

'I'm impressed.'

'Like I said, Jason was amazed. He's coming down. Personally.'

'I expect there'll be a red carpet, a silver band, a big bouquet of flowers and a mayoral reception.'

Ralph didn't bother to answer me – unless a long loud yawn can be counted as a reply. He picked up his glass and my bottle of brandy, and went into the den, from where I soon heard him knocking balls around the billiard table – or 'snooker table' as he preferred to call it.

I had to follow him into the den to help myself to a small drink, but he still ignored me, so I took the bottle from him, without saying anything, and carried it back to the kitchen, where I sat down and tried to read the local advertising rag just to stop my mind from speculating on why Nathan hadn't rung with a Penfolds Grange message, and therefore, what might be happening to Deenie. My entire willpower was concentrated on blocking off my imagination. I had already broken down once in the cellar, a thing that had never happened in my whole life before. God only knew what I'd do if I was taken in the same way again.

It was only then that I noticed a slight tapping noise at the side window where the patio takes a narrow turning towards the back garden and the potting shed. I looked up and saw a face that froze my blood. I stood up, kicking back the chair, and lurched sideways to the sink. Then I looked again. It was unmistakably the face of the boy whose name was never mentioned. He was peering in at me. And standing next to him was a shorter man, unrecognisable and terrifying, because his face was pushed against the window and his nose was squashed flat.

My hand trembled and I spilled brandy down my shirt. I could smell the liquor and feel the dampness of it on my stomach. Then I gathered all my strength and went to the door and stepped outside.

'What do you want?' I croaked.

'I've got Ken,' the short man said. 'Ralph asked me to find him.'

The T-shirt, the pyjama pants and the sandshoes emerged from the shadows. 'Good God,' was all I could manage to say, 'It's Brunning . . .'

Then I turned and staggered back to find a chair. My heart

was beating so fast I thought I would faint. My throat was dry and I was short of air and I could not see properly. I tried to yell, 'Go away!' – but no sound came.

Finally, I clutched the bottle and tilted it into my glass, then took a short sip. At last I managed to get my throat working again. I could feel the muscles freeing up. But when I tried to speak, I slurred together all the words I was trying to say and the only sound I could make was a choking groan.

42

When I came to properly, it was to find that Ralph was undoing the buttons of my shirt. 'You mean you were looking at him through the back window?' I heard him asking. 'What the hell made you do that? You're lucky he seems to be coming round. The shock could've booted the poor old bastard right over the goalposts and into the next world.'

'But we saw a car parked out the front, and there's a guy in it pretending he's reading a copy of the *Echo* – under a bloody streetlight,' Brunning replied. 'It gave me the creeps. After the way your father managed to tag along behind me through the streets of Rownley this afternoon, I've suddenly got nervous about people hanging about in cars.'

'Well, he's looking a bit better,' Ralph decided, referring to me. 'I'd say all he needs is another shot of brandy to re-light his fuse, then we can see if we can make him go bang again.'

'It's the worst thing you could do,' said a voice I knew to be Ken's. 'It's a myth about brandy. It's the worst thing you can give someone in shock. You shouldn't even think . . .'

'Bollocks to that, sonny-boy,' said Ralph. 'The poor old prick's got his foot down on the accelerator of life, he's going flat out to hit eighty and all this excitement's burnt up the blood in his arteries, and he needs every drop of brandy we can pump into him.'

As I sipped at the glass Ralph forced between my lips, Brunning chimed in, 'If there's some of that to spare I wouldn't say no to one myself. After spotting that snoop in his car, I need a shot.'

'Rip into it,' Ralph answered generously. 'There's more piss around here than there is in Liquorland.'

I looked up for the first time and managed to wheeze, 'Who invited . . .?' before my voice gave out again. All three of them were now guzzling my expensive brandy – including that piece of human filth I'd thrashed within an inch of his life.

'So how did you get in here?' Ralph asked his half-brother.

'I told Bradley to drive around the block, then we parked over the back, at the Hetheringtons' . . . Well, it used to be the Hetheringtons' . . . And we came through the hedge, where I used to cut through to go to the harbour beach . . . You know . . .'

Ken's voice trailed off, and no wonder. The memories must have been flooding back as he looked around and took in his Lost Eden. I hoped his heart bled.

The Hetheringtons', as he called it, was where Robyn had lived until she married just before last Christmas. She and Ken had grown up together and Bert Hetherington and I, and our wives, Grace and Barbara, were best friends. We'd always just taken it for granted that Ken and Robyn would stay the way they had since they'd been little kids – playmates, best friends, then partners for life.

We never talked to Bert and Barbara, or Robyn, about the reason for Ken's sudden disappearance. We just dropped him as a subject for polite conversation. His name was never mentioned again. But I've always suspected they must have got wind of something, for they never pursued the matter with us, never asked a question. In a way, it was uncanny. We all just clammed up about him, and our two families almost immediately stopped dropping in on each other at any old time of the day or night, the way we used to, and we ceased to be close friends and became just good neighbours.

I saw very little of Robyn after that, especially when Grace passed over, but three or four months ago I noticed her photo in the *Echo*, in full bridal rig, in front of St Paul's in Rownley, hanging on to the arm of some rich dude from Hamilton. The camera caught her giving her husband a sly smug look that made me laugh at the time – the kind of look that said, I've got a grip on every one of this joker's strings, so just stand back and watch me make him jig.

'Are you all right, Mister Gransey?' a voice asked. Of course, it was that little paddle-handed busybody Brunning. 'Would you like some water – or some fresh air?'

'You sound like a petrol attendant,' Ralph shouted, slapping Brunning on the back. 'Forget the bloody water and free air. Fill his bloody fuel tank – and see to your own before all the turps in the bottle evaporates.'

The sound of Ralph playing mein host with a bottle of my Rémy Martin was all the medicine I needed. I managed to wriggle up onto one elbow, from where I was stretched out on the carpet, and I meant to give them all an earful – but, looking around me, I realised that somehow I must have lost consciousness for a while. My last definite memory was of looking out of the kitchen window and pouring a drink, but here I was in my den. They must have carried me through – which meant that Ken would probably have touched me . . .

I tried to yell at them, but all I made was a silly grunting noise. Then I must have flaked out completely, for I awoke in my bed. My clothes had been removed and I was dressed in my pyjamas.

They must have seen me in my nakedness. They must have handled my skin. How could they have dared do that to me?

43

I woke in the early morning feeling terrible, but I managed to haul myself out of bed and stumble through to the bathroom. I washed my face, enjoyed a long pee, took a little white pill and two Disprins with a glass of water, and cleaned my teeth, for my mouth tasted of sick though I couldn't remember bringing up. Then I went back to bed.

This time I must have slept well, for I woke feeling much better. I even practised whispering to test whether I'd lost all power of speech permanently, and I sang a few lines from 'God Defend New Zealand' – but very, very quietly – I certainly didn't want Ralph to hear me:

> God of Nations at thy feet,
> in the bonds of love we meet . . .

Even at the time it struck me as a very odd thing to sing. Perhaps it was something to do with all that corny 'bonds of love' business and the strange way my family had turned out. But at least I discovered that everything inside me was in working order again. I switched on the radio, and immediately caught a cowboy song I hadn't heard in years. It was one you seldom hear now, though for me it held the key to many special memories of my youth. Nathan and I used to sing it when we crossed over to Mt Matheson on the old harbour launch to go shooting or fishing. The chorus went:

> Oh, they're tough, mighty tough,
> in the West.
> You can tell it from the hair
> upon their chests.

Another strange song to start the day with, but there is no escaping the tortured rhymes that are drummed into you in childhood, and it carried me back into a film-show in the past, where Nathan and I walked along the edge of the dunes, picking off the bunnies in the first light of dawn.

I was so lost in the magic of nostalgia that I almost missed the news. The only bit I caught was, 'the police have identified the body as that of Rolland Percival Sullivan, aged fifty-four, a resident of Wellington. Next of kin have been notified.'

Fifty-four? That made the bastard how much older than Deenie? Well, not so very much, actually. But he certainly fitted the pattern. What could she have been thinking of? There was something drastically wrong with the girl – always had been, ever since she'd worn plaits. Older boys, older men, they had always formed a large part of what was wrong with her. They were like a disease.

Feeling angry, but a good deal better, I got up very carefully and showered, then went downstairs, sniffing as I went. Ralph must have used my absence to take the liberty of smoking indoors for the first time. I'm extra-sensitive to the smell of tobacco and I can pick it out anywhere. The vile stench of cigarettes permeated the whole house.

I opened the patio doors and all the windows on the lower floor to let fresh air in. Then, after I'd had fruit juice and muesli, and biffed out the completely empty brandy bottle into the recycling bin – the three of them had obviously thrown a nice little party for themselves to celebrate the return of the evil one – I went upstairs and opened several windows to create a through-draft to ventilate the whole house.

It was another gorgeous Mt Matheson morning, scented, dewy, utterly still and promising a day of sizzling late-summer sunshine.

Stopping outside Ralph's room, I wondered for a moment whether I really had the right to intrude and make sure his window was open, too. Then I thought how absurd it was to hesitate. The house was mine, after all. And Ralph was here only temporarily – and on sufferance. Besides, the way he had broken my express order not to smoke indoors entitled me to go in. Any argument and this time I really would order him out once and for all.

Imagine my surprise, therefore, when I threw the door open and found the bed more or less made and Ralph missing. Some of his clothes were strewn about the room.

I went downstairs and walked out onto the patio. The Falcon was still there . . . Then I remembered. Brunning and the other one had come through the hedge between my place and Bert Hetherington's and they'd probably gone off with Ralph by the same route.

The only thing to do was to get on with a bit of light gardening, at least until someone decided to come back and tell me what the hell was going on. But I no sooner had the wheelbarrow out than I had to sit down again. I was still very feeble from my experience of the night before, and I guessed I really ought to make an appointment with Fraser-Lang. Then, while I was sitting there in the sun, Hapwidd and Brown drove sedately down the drive.

44

I watched them get out and stretch. They were both pretty tired, I could see that straight away, and I had a rough idea that Rolland Percival Sullivan, aged fifty-four, a resident of Wellington, had had something to do with it.

'Good morning officers,' I said as they walked over. 'Looks like a day right out of the box, doesn't it? Makes one feel quite glad to be alive, don't you think?'

Brown turned away and yawned, but Hapwidd came straight to the point, 'Better than being in the state we found Tuggy Sullivan in, don't you think?'

'Yes,' I agreed. 'I heard about it on the wireless. Interesting to think he had next of kin you could notify, wasn't it?'

'What's that supposed to mean?' Brown snapped.

'Look,' I said, with some irritation. 'If you've come about this Sullivan person, I didn't know him, I've never met him, I haven't a clue about the hows and whys of the way he ended up as he did. In short, you're wasting your time discussing him with me.'

Hapwidd gave me an odd look. 'What do you mean by "the way he ended up as he did"?' he demanded. 'We haven't released any information to the media about the way he ended up.'

'Come on,' Brown added belligerently. 'What do you mean?'

This was a pretty close call and I knew instantly I'd just about dropped myself right in it. But I haven't survived having had many a carpet pulled out from under me in the top boardrooms of Rownley and elsewhere, without learning a trick or two.

'Why, ending up on the wireless in a pathetic little news bulletin, of course – what else did you think?' I said, with an air of mystified innocence.

'Oh yeah?' said Brown. 'So where were you yesterday between the hours of two and four?'

'We'd like a minute-by-minute account, if you don't mind,' Hapwidd added.

I scratched my head. 'I expect I was here,' I said. 'No, wait a minute, I went into Rownley to do some shopping.'

'What kind of shopping? Where?' asked Brown.

'Well, it was more in the nature of an expedition to view some properties I have,' I said. 'You'll be able to check that out. And we stopped somewhere to go into a pub to ask for directions, though I can't remember where it was.'

'Underham?' asked Hapwidd.

'That's right,' I conceded, scratching again. 'You can check everything out with my solicitor. I have a portfolio of properties there.'

'And you're telling us you had to ask for directions to find these properties?'

'Ever since this new one-way system came into operation, I keep on getting lost.'

'It's been in operation for at least five years,' Hapwidd observed.

'Ah, yes, young man,' I said, shaking my head sadly. 'But I've lived in Rownley and Mt Matheson all my life and it's easier for me to remember the way things were fifty years back down the track than it is to try and cope with what happened a mere five years ago. You'll find the same thing happens to you when you've achieved my seniority.'

'You were observed driving a Falcon, similar to the one now sitting in your drive, right through the middle of Rownley at approximately three-fifteen yesterday afternoon,' Hapwidd said, 'and we have received a description fitting the same car from the Underham area. It was observed parked in a street near the waterfront.'

'Simple,' I said. 'Two cars. This one and another like it. I've seen a lot of Falcons like this around town, haven't you?'

'Don't piss us about. It's your son's car, isn't it?' Brown asked.

'It belongs to one of my sons, actually,' I said. 'One of my sons drives a Saab. Do you know, it cost almost a hundred thousand dollars? And another son – that's Bruce, for the other one I mentioned, the one who drives the Saab, is James – drives a Porsche. That's a bit older, and he bought it second-hand, though you'd never know. But it cost a fortune, too. I'd never spend that kind of money on a toy. Total and complete waste, though in the old days I used to own . . .'

It was inevitable that one of them would cut me off, and it happened to be Hapwidd. 'You were driving that Falcon around Rownley yesterday afternoon? Right or wrong?'

'I own a Mazda actually. You'll see it in the garage, if you'd like me to show you. I've still got a licence, but I wouldn't consider driving a car over to Rownley these days. I use it strictly to pop down to the supermarket and the Mt Matheson health-food shop.'

'So, someone made a mistake?'

'They must have. Can you imagine me driving through Rownley traffic? In a strange car? That has to be a joke.'

'That's what we thought.'

'Well, why did you ask?'

'Because someone got their lines mixed up and reported that you were seen in the Underham area, driving a Falcon of that description, at about three-fifteen.'

I had a weird sensation rather like the one I'd had the previous day that I was riding along on the crest of a wave called luck. 'That's very odd,' I said. 'My son Ralph took me into Rownley yesterday in his Falcon. And round about that time we were looking for a place to park. Ask him.'

'Perhaps we will,' Hapwidd said. 'But what really interests us is why you might think it would occur to us that we ought to ask questions about you hovering around the neighbourhood of the place in which we found Tuggy Sullivan.'

'I've no idea. It's a mystery to me,' I replied.

'Try and concentrate,' Brown chipped in.

'You really think I've got some way of knowing how these corpses get strewn all around the district?' I asked mildly.

Both men looked at me steadily as if they were actually trying to read my mind. Then Hapwidd said, 'It just strikes us as a very odd thing that this car, or one very like it, was seen driving around town, then parked in Underham, at about a quarter past three. And the description of the driver more or less matches you. Now that's amazing, wouldn't you agree?'

'Very.'

'Well, try to come up with an explanation, will you? Because we can't think of one.'

'We don't like coincidences,' said Brown. 'They worry us.'

I looked up at the sky for a while, then I gazed from one to the other and said. 'I don't like coincidences either. There have been too many of them, and I'm beginning to feel they've been used, deliberately or just plain fortuitously, to set me up. That's the expression, isn't it?'

'And why would anyone want to set you up, eh?' asked Brown.

'Think,' added Hapwidd.

'Because they knew my daughter was associated with this Sullivan person, and they wanted to associate me with him as well, because that's the easiest . . . though I don't see how . . .'

Hapwidd butted in before I could waffle on any further. 'Exactly right, Mister Gransey,' he said. 'It strikes us that a whole lot of people have been getting the wrong end of everything and believing that you've been implicated.'

I said nothing, for I realised he wasn't just talking about a whole lot of nutters out there, but the police themselves, and I didn't want to create any more traps than the ones that were already set for me.

'There's just one thing we keep coming back to, though,' said Brown. 'It is rather funny that you actually were floating round Rownley at the time, wouldn't you say?'

'We know exactly when you left here, after all,' Hapwidd added. 'Our men outside here made a note of it. You didn't bother to tell them you were going.'

'I'm not exactly under house arrest, you know,' I protested as meekly as I could make my voice sound. 'I thought I was still free to come and go when and where I like.'

Hapwidd shook his head sadly and commented, 'We don't have to go into that question right now, Mister Gransey. But all I would say is it was bloody lucky for you about the car. Anyone can see you couldn't possibly drive a beast like that through Rownley.'

Privately, I couldn't have agreed more. It was out of the question.

45

When I entered in my diary the bare details of what had taken place in the twenty-four hours previous to my visit from the two great detectives, I couldn't help jotting down at the foot of the page – without bothering to use the code I'd invented – the comment that of all the peculiar things that have happened in the course of a long, often complicated and super-active life, these events had to be the most mysterious and weird. Underneath which, I also noted that this was to state the case mildly.

I still had no clear idea of what was going on, and neither, so it seemed, did anyone else. That some person or parties believed me to be enmeshed in some sort of conspiracy with my daughter was plain to see. But why? Because some drug baron or barons had lost a lot of money? Because my daughter chose to cohabit with someone who was now in the Rownley morgue with a tag tied to his toe? It was absurd.

How could I possibly have been drawn into it all? A huge monstrous destructive machine had been set in motion and it was heading inexorably towards me. But why? The question I had to keep asking myself was what had I ever done in life that marked me out in my old age for this kind of working over?

Certainly, I had once had a reputation for toughness – but not ruthlessness. There must have been plenty of occasions when I'd had to come down hard on someone who had broken the rules, but that was always in the interests of justice. I'd never damaged anyone just for the hell of it. Fairness has always been the star by which I've steered my career. It has never been in my nature to deliberately set my course at people to wreck their lives or destroy them.

I rang the only person I could turn to for help, and was relieved to find Nathan at home.

'Look, old pal,' I said. 'I've had some rather unpleasant experiences, yesterday and this morning, and I need someone to talk them through with me. I'm actually getting the shakes. I can't make sense of what's happening. Can you come over?'

'I'll avoid lunch, if you don't mind,' Nathan replied – which made me laugh and immediately feel as though the day was improving, 'but it looks like being rather a nice day for a glass of one of your best whites, before they all turn to vinegar in your cellar. How about two-ish?'

I told him I had gardening to get on with and my usual

walk to take, and two would do very nicely. And it occurred to me, not for the first time, that my life would have been pretty empty without a real friend to summon, even one who couldn't remember the difference between bacon and eggs and baked beans.

I then enjoyed the last hour or so of tranquillity I was to know throughout this whole strange business.

I returned to the garden, shifted a couple of wheelbarrow-loads of weeds and clippings to the compost bins, then set off to the beach.

The ocean was a glittering silver-blue, and as calm as I had seen it all summer. Yet even on a windless day, there is always a small but steady swell breaking right along the beach with a heavy rumble that enters the lives of those who are lucky enough to reside in Mt Matheson.

It's a bit like a heartbeat. It's there, even when you don't notice it. In fact, days can go by without your attention being drawn to the sound – then suddenly, perhaps when you're alone at night, listening in bed with your windows open to the stars and the sea, you become not just conscious of it, but part of it. You're inside the sound – it's as if your house has become some sort of cosmic listening device – and it's almost as though you've become tuned in to the universe.

Sometimes, also, when you just happen to be strolling along the beach, you hear it with a strange, drumming clarity. You catch the graunching of the shells as the sea sucks at the beach, then there's the crackle and fizz of a new wave curling towards you, and finally there's the whoosh and thud of the sea upon the sand.

It's in moments of perfect peace like those that I sometimes find myself communing with Grace. And this morning she got in touch with me again. It hadn't happened often before – just passing instants of pure harmony. And let me say quickly that there's nothing peculiar or spooky about the experience. Getting in touch with those on the other side is not a mystic or mysterious thing. You don't roll around on the sand in ecstasy or levitate over the dunes. It's absolutely natural. You walk along the beach, looking and acting perfectly normal, while the mind simply empties itself of all the day-to-day rubbish of existence and becomes a two-way transmitter for messages to and from the other side.

As I said, these moments only last for a very brief time, though the strange thing is the process can sometimes seem to have lasted for hours. It's just that afterwards, when you look at your watch, you always find it all took place – at least, in human, terrestrial terms – in a matter of minutes or sometimes seconds only. You may have had a conversation across infinity that took in huge areas of experience and an immeasurable quantity of thought and feeling, yet it comes compressed into a package of illuminating insight that flits by in a flash.

This time, the way it happened was that I absent-mindedly looked out to sea and was immediately distracted by a shadow. Suddenly, I heard the waves breaking all around me and the terrifying image of the shark Nathan and I had seen when we were boys returned to me. I must have stopped to stare, squinting my eyes against the blinding glare of the sea, but there was no fin and the little patch of shadow vanished as quickly as it had arrived. Perhaps all it had been was the cast of a little puff of cloud.

Then I heard Grace. She didn't actually talk as such, but I was aware of the message she was sending me. It's an odd experience – rather like a conversation without words.

I wasn't frightened. The whole thing seemed perfectly natural. She was there all right and what she seemed to be saying was that I had to forgive Ken.

I remember swallowing hard and replying, as gently as I could, that I didn't really think I could manage that. Then Grace told me that I could and I must, and that she was merely confirming what I already knew to be true in my heart. As simple as that.

I looked up from the sea into the sky and noticed there were actually no clouds to be seen. Even at the time that puzzled me, for what could possibly have created the shark-like shadow I had definitely seen? Then, the next thing I knew, I was talking to old Bert Matthews who had taken the shortcut over the dunes and had come up beside me. He was also staring upwards.

'Can you read what it says?' he asked.

'What?' I said, in some astonishment.

'The message in the sky up there.'

'Where?'

'It's the radio plane, isn't it?'

I looked at Bert, blinked hard, then gazed upwards again. Crawling across the sky was a small aeroplane, towing a long sign. For a while I couldn't make out the message, then I had to tell Bert he was right. The words read: Radio R. The Voice of the Skies.

46

I got back from my walk to find Mrs Luckham busy in the house and her husband John mowing the front lawn with the roller mower, turning it into a green and beige mottled billiard table. I'd forgotten they'd arranged to come in for a few hours that day to make up for some time they were going to take off the following week to attend a nationwide conference on the compulsory sterilisation of sex-offenders or solo-mothers or some such thing – and, of course, I'd also completely forgotten Ralph's instructions to close all the doors and windows when I'd gone down to the beach. The place had been left wide-open. If someone really was out to get at me, they wouldn't have had the slightest trouble walking in.

I went inside, but there was still no sign of Ralph, and Mrs Luckham told me she hadn't seen anyone since she and John had arrived. So, where had the boy gone and what was he up to?

It must have been well after twelve o'clock, I suppose, and I'd gone outside to help John in the garden, when the telephone rang. Of course, as usual, I hadn't bothered to take the damned thing with me, so I had to turn around and go back inside again when Mrs Luckham shouted through a kitchen window that I was wanted urgently.

It must have been something to do with the use of that word 'urgently' that warned me to be on my guard, for I took the call in the den, where I could shut the door and be alone.

The voice on the other end of the line made me almost choke and for a few moments I didn't trust myself to answer.

The voice said, 'Are you there? Hullo. Hullo . . .'

'Ken,' I said, after a while.

'That's right. I've got something to tell you.'

I will never know what made me interrupt and blurt out the next few words, but I couldn't help it. There was an irresistible force inside me that made me say, 'Son – I forgive you.'

There was a silence. Then Ken said quietly, 'I don't think you've got anything to forgive.'

In the circumstances, I thought that was a funny sort of answer. But I decided not to get angry, so I repeated plainly and firmly, 'I've a distinct impression that you don't fully comprehend what I just said, boy. Despite everything you did to your mother and me, I've just told you that you're forgiven – I forgive you.'

'I'm not going to argue about it,' he replied, still speaking quietly. 'But the question you should be asking is whether you can ever be forgiven by me.'

I removed the telephone from my ear and looked at it. A lump of green plastic, that's all it was. No more than an ossified slightly flattened green banana. A poisonous deformed vegetable growth with a long coiled tap-root buried into the wall. Slowly and deliberately I resisted the temptation to smash it across the room, and instead I lowered it gently into its cradle.

Then I steadied myself and remembered to do several

deep-breathing exercises that Fraser-Lang had advised me to perform whenever I lost my temper.

The telephone rang again, and I let it go for a bit, until I remembered Mrs Luckham. She would be sure to be bustling back to the kitchen or an upstairs room to answer it, and I didn't want her interfering.

I picked up the handset and this time it was Ralph.

'What's got into you, you crazy old fuckwit?' he shouted. 'Ken rings you up to tell you about bloody Deenie and you hang up on him. Now I'm telling you this, once and for all – you're a pain in the arse, you're off your bloody chump, you'd be certified in two minutes flat by any shrink the length and breadth of the country, so until the day we decide to call in the men in white coats and have you booked into a padded cell you're going to be pleased to speak in a proper civilised manner to your own son, and none of this bloody forgiveness bullshit. Have you got that . . .?'

I didn't answer.

'. . . Because,' he went on, 'if you're really lucky and you catch him in a good mood, one day he might even see his way towards wiping everything you did to him off the charge sheet – and you won't spend all eternity in hell, where you belong. Have you got that?'

I still didn't answer.

'Good. Well I'm handing him over – and you'd better listen, okay?'

'The phone's tapped,' I said.

'Just listen.'

My hand shook, but I managed to hang on to the damned thing. Ken's voice asked just the one question. 'Have you talked to Nathan?' it said.

'Yes,' I replied. 'He's coming over at two.'

'Good,' Ken said. 'Bradley and I will come over about then, as well. Ralph will follow.'

I waited, but he said nothing more. 'Is that all you wanted to say?' I asked.

'That's all for now,' Ken said.

'And Deenie?'

'Save it till we see you, okay?'

'But do you know anything about her? Where she's . . .'

'Wait, will you?' was all Ken said, then he hung up.

I couldn't believe it. The bunch of them had been off somewhere all night, leaving me alone and in danger. And now they were putting me through all this anxiety and argument – and what for? To tell me they were coming around at two? They could've turned up at any time without all this ceremony. What did they think they were they playing at?

I bumped into Mrs Luckham outside the door to the den. She had an armful of sheets and a couple of T-shirts she was taking to the washing machine.

'You ought to tell your house guest,' she said, referring obviously to Ralph, 'to change his shirts more often. You should see the collars and the stains. The grime of ages . . .'

I could have told her a lot more about Ralph and his habits, but I didn't.

47

I took an old *National Geographic* out to the patio and sat under a sun umbrella, while the Luckhams tidied up inside and outside. In spite of all those years of extra effort I'd always made when they came, and the habits I'd become accustomed to, I suddenly felt so washed out that I decided there and then to put my feet up and relax, as I was damned-well entitled to. I was paying them good money to do the work, so why shouldn't I rest up? For the first time in my life I didn't care whether I was making a big impression on anyone. Somehow or other the past few days had changed me. I was definitely modifying the conditioning of a lifetime.

The magazine had a long section on the Aztecs, with some

striking and imaginative coloured illustrations of a few of their bizarre rituals. Apparently they went in for human sacrifice in a big way. A thoroughly despicable civilisation. Ripping out hundreds of living, palpitating human hearts to appease their gods and their frightful bloodlust, and all the while dressed up in their best regalia. They made the Tuggy Sullivans of this world, and all the other assorted scum I'd recently been hearing about, look like proper little gentlemen. At least Sullivan and his associates killed and mutilated their victims one or two at a time, and they didn't try to make a religion out of it.

After a while I must have dozed off, for the next thing I remember is Mrs Luckham putting a lettuce and tomato sandwich and a glass of apple juice in front of me.

I blinked and thanked her, and realised I was giving yet more evidence of losing my grip. Not for the first time, I realised that everything the children – James and Bruce, and now Ralph – had been telling me was not far short of the mark. In the past few days I had definitely entered a new, perhaps last, phase of dissolution. I was in the first stages of becoming a dreamy old man.

It took me some time to take in my surroundings. The Luckhams were sitting together inside, at the kitchen table. As always, they weren't talking – in fact, they must have finished communicating whatever they'd had to say to each other decades ago – but just munched away at their sandwiches and drank their tea. For all the world, it seemed that they were the owners of the place, and I was just some passing tramp they'd decided to feed outside.

The lawn was beautifully mown. Not a blade out of place, rolled out in perfect lines. The sprinkler was whizzing around near the street, sending up a brilliant rainbow spray. The flowerbeds were perfection itself, not a weed to be seen. I guessed that the washing would be out on the line around at the back, and I supposed that John would start on the vegetable garden soon, not that it needed much attention at this time of year.

It was almost impossible to recall that in my own lifetime we'd come so far. I'd seen all this covered in grass that had to fight for survival against the encroachments of ragwort, gorse, blackberries and thistles. There were ragged hawthorn hedges here and there and little scattered dumps of old fencing and cast-out rubbish and busted rusting farm machinery. The main signs of life weren't human in those days, for the main population were hundreds of Jersey cows, Border Leicester–Romney cross sheep, rabbits, pigs, chooks, dozy half-draught farm horses and chained dogs you hoped never broke loose.

As usual, Mrs Luckham would soon be busy doing my ironing and cleaning out the kitchen and bathroom, washing down the walls, doing a lot of quite unnecessary hard work. Good God, who really needed to have their bathroom walls washed twice and sometimes three times a week? What was all this effort for? Cleaning, dusting, mopping, washing – on and on and on? There didn't seem much point to it all. I could have got rid of the Luckhams there and then, and let the cobwebs gather around me and the weeds sprout for a year before the place would have needed a good tidying up.

Funny when I thought about it – it was the Luckhams who seemed to benefit most from my arrangement with them. It filled their lives with order, ceremony and continuity, and I suppose it also helped pay for the groceries, but otherwise a lot of what they did suddenly seemed to me not to have very much real human purpose.

The Aztecs had been like that. Very orderly people. Splendidly clean and upright. They would organise a few thousand captives and rip their living hearts out in a tidy and systematic manner. No unseemliness, no stains on the walls, no cobwebs – and absolutely no point to their efforts.

I looked at my watch. Almost one o'clock. Just over an hour to go.

48

I got up to take a short stretch, after sitting down and reading for so long, then gazed around me and immediately realised that something was wrong. I couldn't figure out what it was at first, but something was definitely out of place or missing; something I'd failed to spot earlier that morning.

I walked about the front lawn, noticed nothing, then went to the top of the drive. And there it was – or, rather, there it wasn't. The police car had gone. I'd been left without protection – though, after Ken and Brunning's easy entrance of the night before, that was probably no longer the correct word for it.

I felt another buzz of excitement, even more intense than the one I'd experienced the day before when I had recognised the first signs of a pattern. At last – I was absolutely certain – everything was about to become clear. It was just an intuition, based on the one simple and apparently trivial fact that a police car wasn't where I'd expected it to be, but I knew it to be a definite and unmistakable sign.

At some time between the arrival of my son Ken last night and just after the visit of the two detectives this morning, something decisive had taken place. And where had I been while this had been happening? Taking a walk, pottering about the garden, then dozing off beneath a sun umbrella – an old fool of seventy-five, sleeping like a babe.

I don't know how I got through the short time till Nathan arrived. I felt elated, yet perplexed and frightened, and altogether dizzy and just about off my head, but the very first thing I realised as soon as I saw my old friend, just before two, was that I'd forgotten to put a bottle of white in the refrigerator.

Because I was trying hard to conceal the state I was in, my forgetfulness came in handy as a diversion from the tumult inside me. I took Nathan straight off to the cellar to choose a chardonnay. He homed in right away on a Cloudy Bay 1989, which he claimed was right at its elegant best and would taste just fine at cellar temperature. How he had got to know about these things, I've no idea. With all the time and energy he used to put into his job it stumps me how he'd had the opportunity to become a wine buff. And, although he had been on a pretty good salary, with no wife for the past ten years to spend his money on, and a grown-up daughter old enough to look after herself, I would not have thought his pension was sufficient to really let go and indulge a taste for expensive wines. When I retired I would have been earning possibly ten times more than he did, and I would have paid no more tax than him, even in a bad year. In terms of spending power the comparison was unreal.

The Cloudy Bay was among the last good wines I'd bought. In fact, as I've already said, I hadn't laid down anything much after '90, and most of my vintages would have been middle or late '80s. According to Nathan (who always enjoyed telling me such things), some of them had probably gone past what he called their use-by date, and even at the rate we were now whacking into them we weren't in the slightest danger of helping to solve any potential problems in that area.

'Look,' I said to Nathan as we were taking our first sip. 'Let me come straight to the point. I've had good reason to believe that some lunatic has been plotting to do me an immense harm – perhaps even to kill me. But, do you know, I have a hunch the danger's over at last. What do you reckon to that?'

As a conversation starter that's probably the very best I've ever come out with. Nathan raised his eyebrows and looked at me steadily. Then he sniffed his glass and held it up to the light. 'Remarkable wine,' he announced. 'Do you know that at this very minute we belong to a select though unofficial club whose members are able to raise a glass and tipple a white wine which would rank with the best in the world? It's a remarkable thought, when you put it that way, don't you agree?'

Then his voice became confidential, and he added slowly and carefully, 'Look Arthur, would you like to know something else? I'd be very careful who I was talking to before I came out with a line like that. For a start, when people begin imagining that someone out there has been actively plotting to do them in, it's considered by many to be a sure indication of paranoia.'

'Well, I thought I'd tell you, because it's not paranoia, it's a fact, though I've got a feeling that it hardly matters now. You see, I expect shortly to have news of Deenie at last . . .'

'Deenie? Do you?' Nathan said, not bothering to conceal his astonishment. 'Are you absolutely sure?'

'Oh, yes,' I went on confidently. I don't know why, but I felt a powerful surge of certainty, as though the pattern I had been seeking was making itself apparent to me as I spoke. 'Which reminds me, I forgot to ask whether she managed to get in touch with you.'

Nathan sipped the wine as though it now disagreed with him. He had a puzzled frown and he watched me intently. 'No,' he said after a while. 'No. She didn't get in touch. Quite honestly, Arthur, I don't think we should expect her to, after all this time. She's probably managed to slip out of town again.'

'That's not like you to be so negative. And you're quite wrong,' I insisted. 'Any moment now . . .'

I had no sooner uttered those words than – right on cue – I heard a voice call out, 'Where are they?'

In the distance, Mrs Luckham made some sort of answer that I didn't quite catch, but she must have said I was in the den, because a few seconds later Ken just burst in without knocking. How my stable rational world seemed suddenly to have been tipped off its axis.

'They're here,' he shouted over his shoulder, 'I've found them. Stay outside for a moment, will you Bradley. I'll deal with this. It's a family matter.' Then he closed the door behind him.

49

To say that Nathan was just about flattened would be the understatement of the last four days. He spilled his wine, grabbed the silk handkerchief from his top pocket to wipe it up, and spilled some more. He looked at me, red in the face, then said in a kind of strangled sigh, 'Good God. It's him . . . It's Ken.'

This must have been the only time in my life I'd ever seen Nathan at a complete loss for words. Even when we were just about ready to kill each other over Belle, he'd never been short of a comment, an accusation, a wounding insult or an outright explosion of violent hatred. He began to stand up, wobbled a bit, then sank back in his chair again.

Ken stood over him. A not very intimidating figure by some standards perhaps, but he'd toughened up quite a bit over the years – a fact that hadn't really registered on me till now. He was stringier and harder, and there was something cruder and coarser about his expression. The truth was he was an adult, and I suppose I'd still been thinking of him as an adolescent boy – the one I'd booted out of the house all those years ago. It had taken me a long time to grasp it, but Ken was now a man.

There was sweat on his brow and he was panting slightly. He looked at Nathan, then at me, then back at Nathan again. There was something very odd about his stance. He seemed to hunch his back slightly and glare – a bit like a cat. You could see his teeth.

'My dear old Uncle Nathan,' he said, as though spitting the words separately into Nathan's face. 'Looked after me and took me in, didn't you? Just like you did with Ralph and Deenie and my mother. Anything to get back at your best friend, eh?'

'What are you taking about?' I asked. 'Where's Deenie?'

'Deenie's safe,' he hissed. 'We've extricated her. She'll never know how lucky she was. She's with the cops.'

'The cops? Deenie?' I asked.

'They've got someone for killing Sullivan.'

'Deenie? They've got –?'

Ken turned away from Nathan and looked at me again briefly. 'Some bloody sick nutter,' he announced. 'What else would you expect? He's an import. He's some expendable gang freak from Christchurch. Imagine bringing in some total hopeless clueless homicidal maniac from –'

We were talking at cross-purposes. 'I was asking about Deenie,' I butted in desperately. 'What's happened to her? Why's she with the police?'

Ken shook his head, as if he couldn't believe my questions. 'Deenie's got a lot of explaining to do,' he said. 'She's a bloody trimmer, is Deenie . . .'

'A trimmer? What do you mean?' I demanded. 'Where is she? I've got to talk to her.'

'She doesn't want to talk to you just yet,' Ken said. 'She's got other things on her mind she has to talk about, okay?'

That was enough for me. I was suddenly very angry. I stood up. 'What are you getting at, you filthy little . . .'

Ken stepped towards me. His fists were clenched and the sinews stood out in his neck. His eyeballs looked as though they were about to pop. For a moment I thought he was going to punch me – his own father – but he just reached out and shoved me in the chest so that I fell back onto the chair.

'Stop all that name-calling shit, will you, or so help me God, I'll crack you one,' he said. 'And get one more thing into your head, too. Deenie *is* a trimmer – and that's what Ralph and Brunning call her, too. She's exactly like you, you corrupt old prick. She's a main-chancer, an entrepreneur, a weasel, a stoat . . .'

'How dare you . . .' I began to say.

'Switch off for a change, will you,' Ken snarled. 'She's got the same mean-minded grievances and giant delusions of grandeur that have buggered up your life from the day you were born – she's inherited a belief that she's the ruler of this town – queen of Mt Matheson, empress of Rownley – even when she lives in Wellington. But she's only a small-time user, just like her father. She's a nobody, a nothing. She learnt how to be one from you – the way you always puffed yourself up to be the prince of this place, when you've always been nothing more than piss and wind. You're all bluff and bluster. You're only a skid-mark running down the porcelain . . .'

'Stop it –' I began to yell.

But he cut me off. 'Shut up and listen for once in your life,' he said. 'The fact is that she's my sister, and Ralph's, and what with blood being thicker, and all the crap – which really happens to be true – we've got her out of deep trouble. Just like you always used to have to get her out of the scrapes she got herself into in the old days. But this time she's excelled herself and she's actually managed to nearly get herself killed. She's stirred up half the gangs in the country, upset the whole drug network, dropped the Granseys into the sewage works and she's completely ballsed everything up again, just like she always does. Imagine moving back in with Nathan, so he can work off his little fantasies about you over and over . . .'

'Moving back?' I repeated.

'Poor class,' said Ken. 'Though you could hardly blame her in the circumstances. She didn't know Tuggy was going to lose his small change and start hacking up bodies. She had to hide somewhere and she must have thought the old bastard's balls were safely out of commission . . .'

'She didn't. You're lying,' I shouted.

'She's a loser, Arthur,' Ken said. 'Just like you are. Why can't you just relax and accept it? You've always been a washout. Somewhere, somehow, early on, you came an all-time gutser. You've been a dead man all your life.'

'What?' Nathan said weakly. It was the first time since he'd fallen back in his chair that he had uttered a sound. 'What did you say about Deenie?'

'Stuff it, will you,' Ken said. 'We cut her loose and got her out.'

'No, wait a minute . . .'

I was aware only as the words tumbled out that I must have sounded as though I was pleading, but there really was something the matter with my voice for the second time in twenty-four hours. 'Say all that again,' I squeaked. 'What dirty little lies are you trying to tell me about her and Nathan?'

'Look,' Ken said. 'I'm pissing off out of here and I don't expect you'll ever see me again, so you two old farts can sort it out for the rest of your lives, any way you like. Where do you think Deenie was when you went on your wild goose chase around Rownley, trying to find me, when all you had to do was let me in your front door to talk to you?'

I looked at Nathan. He had gone an even darker shade of red. A kind of unhealthy purplish colour. As I watched him, he undid a button of his shirt and slid his right hand inside, over his heart.

'Deenie went to Bradley's first, because she was too hot to come here. Tuggy's enemies or the cops would've raced each other to pick her up the minute she dared walk into this house – they had your card marked right from the very beginning, and she knew it. Bradley put her up for three nights, not for Deenie's sake, but because he's a good friend of mine.'

'Brunning?' I said incredulously. She had stayed with Bradley Brunning instead of her own father?

'It couldn't last. He's too well known around town and it got too freaky, and he had to tell her to move on – so where else did she go, but straight into the arms of your best friend, Nathan.' Ken went on. 'She'd been there often enough before.'

'That can't be true,' I said stupidly.

'It gets even better. About the only thing you can say for Deenie was she wasn't silly enough to walk into that warehouse with her moron boyfriend. Imagine working over a corpse like that, knocking his teeth out and cutting his hands off, all over a ten thousand dollar debt, then thinking you must be Superman and you can stroll in and out of old warehouses and everyone's going to be scared of you. Tuggy must have been choked to the gills on his own product. He was away with the cuckoos.'

'Hold on,' I said, but there was too much to ask and I simply couldn't get the words out.

'No. I won't bloody hold on,' Ken announced. 'I don't take orders around here any more.'

'But Deenie,' I said. 'She didn't . . . She couldn't . . .'

'Get used to the idea, will you? She did.'

'But . . .'

'All right, since you've asked for it, I'll let you think about Deenie's masterstroke. It's a little stunner. You'll really like it.'

'No,' I said.

'Oh, yes, Arthur. I think you need to know. It may even help you wake up in your old age. Little Deenie dear and Nathan got their heads together and she suggested what a good idea it would be to tell Bill where the body was, then she got in touch with Bradley to say Bill had the information and would he check it out for her as a really big favour. Get it? She thought it would take the heat off her. See? Bradley gets the information at secondhand, and he's completely suckered. He'd been looking after her for three days and he's a really close friend, isn't he? Then she gets Nathan to ring the police to tip them off and, if only she gets the timing right, with a bit of luck, she'll drop him right in it. Not a very nice way to repay someone who's risked at least a good bashing to put you up for three nights, but after all it's a bright idea and worth a shot, don't you think? The odds had to be pretty good. You work it out. Pity she nearly dropped her old man down the pan as well – but that would've turned out to be a winning jackpot for Nathan, wouldn't it?'

'Not Deenie,' I said. 'She wouldn't have done that to me.'

'Just goes to prove. Kids can be little buggers, can't they? If that's an expression that doesn't worry you too much.'

'Stop,' I tried to say, but only managed a strangled cough. Then I finally whispered, 'She and Nathan. They wouldn't have, would they?'

'What's that?' Ken asked, cupping one hand around an ear in a stupid theatrical way, as if he was suddenly hard of hearing. 'What did you just say? You always thought Nathan was your best pal? Well, it just shows you, doesn't it? You don't know a thing about human nature, do you? Not Ralph, not Deenie, not Nathan – and definitely not me.'

The door opened and Brunning stepped in. 'Come on,' he said. 'We promised Deenie to get her a lawyer.'

'A lawyer?' I repeated, still whispering hoarsely. 'What does she need a lawyer for?'

Ken shook his head, then closed his eyes for a few seconds and breathed out heavily. 'Deenie's going to be all right,' he announced finally. 'She's had a hell of a fright, which she bloody well deserved, though God only knows . . .'

'There's no time now, Ken,' Brunning said anxiously.

For the first time Ken laughed. 'Jesus, when all the murdering silly bastards find out what a stupid bloody farce it all was,' he said, 'there's going to be one hell of a rush for the Prozac bottle . . .'

'Tell me,' I groaned quietly. 'Will somebody slow down and explain what it all means?'

'Ask Nathan. You've got all afternoon – and the rest of your lives.'

'Not that. I want to know, where do you . . .? I mean . . .'

'How do I fit in? You tell my father, will you Bradley. But make it brief.'

'Ralph brought Ken down – from Auckland,' Brunning cut in proudly, as if he was making things clearer. 'I knew where Ken was because I'm an old friend of Bob Watkins. He keeps in touch.'

'Who's he?' I said.

'Watkins,' Ken said with a sneer. 'You remember him. You remember the night . . .'

'Must go,' Nathan announced suddenly, though very quietly, trying to stand again. I'd just about forgotten he was still there. For a moment he held on to the arms of his chair, then his legs gave way and he fell back once more.

Ken picked up the bottle of Cloudy Bay, sniffed it and asked, 'Cloudy Bay '89 – any good?' Then he smiled and said, 'Well, I'll fill your glasses and leave you both to it.'

And with that Ken topped up our glasses, then walked out of the room and closed the door behind him. His hand had not trembled once and he had not spilled a drop.

50

'Well then, old pal, what's all this about Deenie?' I asked when perhaps five minutes must have passed. After all, there was a whole lifetime's friendship between us, so there was plenty of time.

Nathan took what seemed just about as long to answer. 'You wouldn't understand,' was all he managed to say.

'I promise you, I'll give it go,' I said.

He didn't reply for a minute or two, but just sat there with his hand still inside his shirt. Finally he told me in a voice so faint that I had to cup a hand over an ear to catch his words, 'You never really loved them,' he whispered. 'None of the children. Not Belle either.'

'Didn't I?' I asked.

'And certainly not Deenie. Not in a grown-up way. You couldn't. You were her father.'

'But you managed to love her in a grown-up way, even when she was a schoolgirl. Is that right?'

'I told you, you wouldn't understand.'

'Oh, I understand, all right. I've heard about these things.'

'You'll never have a clue.'

'You're wrong there, old friend. I've suddenly got clues to all sorts of possibilities. Deenie was never the same again after you got to her, was she? It all adds up, doesn't it? You had to insinuate yourself into the hearts of the women I loved, and debauch them, didn't you? Christ – and to think all my life I never saw it.'

I'd got my breath back again now, but I didn't shout or

rave at Nathan. I spoke steadily and straightforwardly. Almost neutrally – as though I was sitting there, before him, in judgement. 'But why did you do it? That's what I don't understand . . . The way you systematically wormed your way into my family. The way you always took their side when there was trouble. It's exactly as Ken said. Look at Ralph, and how you pretended to explain him to me and support him. And – come to think about it – what about Ken himself? What about the way you made sure he came to you when I kicked him out? You wanted to work on him, too, didn't you?'

I sat upright and stared at Nathan. 'Why?' I repeated harshly. 'Why did you have to do it? Systematically. Over the years. Why? What did I ever do to you? You used my own family somehow to score off me in some dirty little game you've been playing ever since you've known me. You've . . .'

We must have made an odd sight, sitting there, with Nathan staring at the wall in front of him in silence, hand over his heart, as if testifying to some deep private truth, while I found myself suddenly waving a fist at the air in front of me, as if I was trying to punch my way out of an invisible paper bag.

Almost out of the side of his mouth, still without looking directly at me, Nathan said, 'You'll never have any idea. You don't have the ability or even the capacity for understanding. You've always thought you were right at the top of the tree with God Almighty and the Christmas fairy. But you've been blind . . . deaf . . . dumb . . .'

'Bastard,' I said.

'You don't know a damned thing about any of them,' Nathan went on slowly, gasping between breaths. 'You've never had the interest or the time – and you've never had an ounce of the common humanity you need to enter someone else's life and share their feelings with them. You never came to my mother's funeral, did you? Small things like that. One after the other. You're a bloody zombie, Arthur. A robot.

215

You've never lived. That's what's always made me hate you. You don't know what real life and real passion are about. You never really knew what I went through. Did you speak to me once about my father? You couldn't bear to touch me or even come near me. Have you ever mentioned it since? Never, never, never . . .'

'But,' I spluttered. 'We didn't talk about those things in those days. It wasn't manly. We buttoned up. Everyone did. It didn't mean . . .'

'You're a mechanical doll. A man of tin. Like the one in *The Wizard of Oz* You've never had it in you.'

'Whereas you do have it in you? Passion. Hatred? Poison? Murder?'

'I happen to have lived.'

'Well, I'll soon attend to that,' I replied.

51

Now I look back on it, the oddest maddest most nauseating recollection that suddenly hit me as I was talking to Nathan was the way he had asked me for wine. That was what really got to me. It was the one detail that tipped me right over from anger into an insane rage. It was the devious treachery that seemed at the time to capture the essence of his evil. I could focus on it, whereas the fact that he'd seduced my wife and daughter and had tried to insinuate himself greasily into the lives of two of my sons was too big to grapple with. The sheer effrontery, the crooked wicked mendacity and hypocrisy of his lust for the trophies of my cellar were what really stunned me.

As I sat there I felt a cold fury, such as I had only felt once before in my life, sweep over me. Believe me, I do not exaggerate. The chill began in my feet and I felt it climb my body, course through my stomach, chest and arms, then send out fingers of freezing madness up from the back of my head and across my skull.

I went over to the place where my old rifle was kept. I took it out, tipped several bullets into a coat pocket, shoved one up the spout, slammed the bolt, and walked over to my old friend.

Nathan's gaze had still not shifted to right or left, but now he appeared to have relapsed into a paralysis. His muscles seemed to have locked into a rigid spasm. He had not only lost all function in his legs, no other part of him – hands, arms, chest, head – was able to move. He just stared straight ahead, as if he was no longer breathing.

'I loved Belle,' I said.

He didn't reply, or make the smallest gesture.

'I love Deenie,' I said next.

There was still no sound from him.

Then I astonished myself by saying, without thinking, 'And I love my sons, Ralph and Ken.'

This time Nathan made what I can only describe as a small dismissive movement with his right hand, halfway between a pat and a wave.

'You've got nothing else to say?' I asked.

Perhaps I imagined that he shrugged, or it may have been just a small shudder. But he still made no sound.

'Well, here's to Deenie, first of all,' I told him. 'And after that, I'll give you another one I've been owing you for Belle. The boys can sort out their own retribution.'

A twenty-two is a light rifle. You can hold it out and fire it one-handed, like a pistol, with no trouble at all – except the barrel is so long that it upsets your balance, you lose control, your hand sways about and you sacrifice accuracy.

So, holding the rifle as though it was a pistol, I pointed it at Nathan. But I took good care to place the barrel firmly against his temple to steady it. He seemed to lean against the barrel, as if to help me take aim, then I pulled the trigger.

217

52

When Ralph walked in, Nathan was slumped in his chair, with his head hanging sideways over one arm, and I was sitting just across from him. I think I must have blanked out. I don't remember having sat down again, but I was in my chair all right – still gripping the rifle.

'Ken and Bradley got here first?' he asked.

I nodded.

'Well, I got diverted. I had to have a bit of a jaw to your pal Hapwidd,' he went on. 'You'll have to front up to him a bit later, too. There's a hell of a stir over in Rownley. Cops and television and reporters everywhere. The whole circus is in town . . .'

Then he noticed the rifle. 'Oh no, not pop-guns again, dad,' he sighed. 'Have you fallen right off the bloody roof?'

I couldn't speak.

'Here, give it to me, you silly old bastard,' he said. I realised again that no one had ever used words like that to my face before these past few days, but I was beginning to get accustomed to the accusation. 'I'm going down to Ocean Beach and I'm going to chuck it off the rocks when it gets dark tonight, before you really do an injury to someone, especially yourself.'

One by one, Ralph prised my fingers from the rifle, in the same way I suppose that Grace had had to winkle James's hands off the steering wheel of my new Jaguar so many years ago. Then he took the rifle away and leaned it against the wall behind him. At last he, too, sat down.

'Deenie,' I managed to say. 'What's happened to . . .'

'Just like I always told you,' Ralph said. 'She was in it right up to her ringlets. But who knows – it looks as though with a bit of luck she's going to get away without ending up on a count. They need her as a witness, and – well, the odds are beginning to favour her. But it's all in the lap, as they say.'

'She betrayed me. She could've got me . . .'

'Her and Nathan? Ken told you?'

'Yes.'

'Well, you can blame her in one way, and you can't in another. She always had bad taste in men. Don't act so surprised. You've always known what she was like and what she got up to. She's got a kink that way. Same as mum.'

Trust Ralph to come out with a piece of meaningless stupidity like that, though I felt too ill and exhausted to point it out. 'I still don't completely see how you and Ken and Brunning . . . How did you do it . . .?' I started to ask.

'I think it was the brandy,' Ralph answered, sweeping both hands through his hair, as though he was making a gesture towards cleanliness. He must have been out all night. Even from where I was sitting I could pick up a whiff of sweat and stale drink. 'Well, it so happens that for one reason or another Bradley knows every monkey in this jungle. Great apes, little apes, and the ones with blue arses – he knows them all. So, it was just a matter of waiting till the penny dropped, I suppose. He and Ken and I put you to bed and then we got half pissed and the name of this slimebag here kept on coming up. Simple.'

'But, I still . . .?

'Give over, will you, dad? Can't you see how it's all to do with a certain way of looking at things? It's like those books of squiggles and dots – when you look at the pictures and allow yourself to go cross-eyed, the whole thing comes clear. Until these last few days forced us all to change our focus and look again we'd never have been able to make out the connections, would we? See what I mean?'

'No.'

'Bradley Brunning delivered the magic key – as simple as that.'

'Brunning?'

'He's one of them. Same as Ken and Bob Watkins.'

'One of what?'

'Oh, for God's sake, dad. A queer. Where have you been all your life?'

'A homo-what's-a-name?' I managed to ask.

Ralph laughed louder than I'd ever managed to make him do all the half-century of his life. 'A homo-*what's-a-name . . .*' he repeated over and over again, wiping his eyes and spluttering. 'Will you warn me before you come out with another one like that? I'll need to take one of your heart pills first.'

Then he managed to calm down for long enough to drain the last inch or so of Cloudy Bay straight from the bottle and add, 'It's a funny thing, but that day Nathan and I had our little sparring match and he pulled all that snot on me about Daphne, that's when I suddenly made the connection with Ken. I hate smartarses and I thought: I just wonder what Ken knows about you, you clever little prick. So I got onto Bradley. I called on him when I went over to Rownley to make telephone calls. Bradley's always a goldmine of information – not that I've ever cultivated his company, so to speak.'

'I don't have a clue what you're going on about,' I said. 'Nothing makes sense.'

'Oh, I dunno, dad,' Ralph went on lightly. 'I've been bloody impressed with you actually. I think you've begun to learn a lot, all in one big curve, just lately.'

'But Nathan and Deenie . . . I can't . . .'

'It was all that bullshit about a million dollars that put us off. I warned you not to believe it – when I told you about it, didn't I? I had the right hunch all along, do you remember? There was never that much money around. It was all small-time gang-war stuff, with a lot of strutting and showing off and boasting about big numbers and low-class killing. Very unsophisticated and unintelligent when you think about it, eh? Tuggy must've been whacking into something more powerful than just plain lawn clippings to make him fly over his handlebars the way he did. He killed that poor bastard you found on the beach, then got a fright and Deenie says he thought he'd make it look like a professional job and that'd hide his tracks. Can you believe it? Hacking and hammering away at a corpse like that? He must've been rocketing around the moon at the time. Of course, someone was sent in to shoot him. Simple as that. Or it should've been, but it never is. The next thing is there's a total breakdown in communication – just as you'd expect – and everyone hits the panic button and starts hiding their assets and snarling among themselves and it soon looked much worse than it was. Jason now thinks it's all a big laugh and he's very grateful to you, by the way, for extricating Tommy Farr for him. Just shows, doesn't it?'

'The bastards,' I managed to say. 'Look at what they nearly did to us . . .'

'It's a loony business, drugs and money. A scary mix,' Ralph agreed. 'That's why I'm sticking to piss and cigarettes and keeping no more pin-money about me than I could stuff in a sock. The other stuff fucks their sense of proportion and they all go apeshit from time to time. Every year it happens. Read the papers – every year there's a new outbreak. They shoot each other, and they burn the bodies or mutilate them. And they always talk in millions, even when there's no more real money in it than you'd make on a paper round. Makes you wonder, doesn't it?'

'But there's so much else I want to . . .'

'Don't let it worry you, dad. Why don't you invite Ken and Bradley and me out to dinner in a posh restaurant tonight and we'll tell you more. If you like, we'll make the details up as we go along, just to entertain you – you know us.'

'I think I may just be beginning to.'

'But we'll celebrate survival, how's that for the genuine article?'

'All right,' I agreed. 'If I feel better in an hour or two, I'll book dinner for four.'

'And just remember not to worry this time when the cops ask you for another statement. They'll be around soon to ask you questions to do with things you know nothing about, got it? And they'll be so busy they won't give you any hassle. This time, I promise, they'll be glad enough to leave you alone. They've got nothing on you. They'll go to a lot of trouble to keep you at a distance.'

'But Nathan's . . .'

'Don't give him another thought. We're keeping him out of it, too. We don't want more complications under the general heading of Deenie, do we? We staked him out to make sure he wasn't going to do any harm to the girl, then when he came over here we just walked in and let her go. She wasn't even frightened. Pissed off and very bored and angry, that's all. She thought he was going to put her through a few old-age pension specialities. You know, a Golden Oldies' workout. I don't think he'd really decided what form it was going to take, but it could've got quite serious. These bloody Greeks, you know, a long history of strange practices.'

'But Nathan's . . . It's the real thing this time . . .' I began to protest. 'I mean – I've finally buggered everything up. You don't realise what I've done to him.'

'He looks all right to me,' Ralph said. 'Except he's taken the count. How did you sideline him? Spike his drink?'

Suddenly Nathan moved out an arm and groaned.

I looked at him in disbelief. 'He's dead,' I shouted. 'I killed him. I shot him dead.'

Nathan opened his eyes, gazed blearily at us, then focused on the glass beside him, the one that Ken had filled. He clutched it very carefully with both hands, took it to his lips and drained it in one go.

'Dead?' asked Ralph. 'Pig's arse he's dead.'

'I tell you, I shot him,' I insisted. 'Right through the temple.'

Ralph swung around in his chair and picked up the rifle. He held the breach to his nose, then laughed again. 'That peashooter hasn't been fired since the Boer War,' he said. Then he added, 'The bloody safety catch is on.'

Nathan sighed and stood up. His eyes were glazed and he seemed to be in a state of trance. With his hands outstretched he went to the door.

'Stop him,' I told Ralph.

'Nah. Why be bothered? Ignore the silly little rat.'

So Nathan walked out of my house and out of my life. He left right on cue, with the word rat hanging in the air and an empty glass on a sidetable, which I later threw out with the rubbish. I didn't want to have anything he'd touched in my house.

Ralph, of course, went to the cellar and chose another bottle while we waited for Hapwidd and Brown to arrive. I noticed it was a Penfolds Grange. In any other circumstances I would have laughed. Perhaps the boy was beginning to acquire a little style at last.

53

In between knocking off a mere thousand buck's worth of my best Aussie wine, Ralph managed to phone around and intercept Ken and Bradley in their quest for a lawyer. Then after a bit more ringing here and there I eventually got in touch with Frank Pelley and he agreed that his firm would represent Deenie. Even though he'd talked a lot of utter rubbish of a personal nature when he'd dropped in to see me a couple of days previously, he was still the best legal brains in town, and I wasn't going to settle for anything less.

Just as I hoped, Frank rang back that evening after six to say that after a lot of palaver and a bit of bargaining by a hot-shot associate from Hamilton who'd just joined the firm he was 'quite pleased' with the way things were developing. Deenie was being sensible and co-operative, and the only thing he asked was that we left the details to him and didn't get directly involved, so that he had a free hand to winkle Deenie out of police custody and back into my care.

That was easy to agree to. I certainly wasn't going to interfere with his plans and procedures, and Ralph, Ken and Brunning were beyond messing things up. They had all passed out. Ken and Brunning had collapsed onto sofas in my den, and Ralph had gone to his room upstairs – to catch up on his 'beauty sleep', so help me, in order to be in top form for the celebrations that night.

I had the luxury of a wonderful few moments of real peace and quiet, and at last I had an opportunity to devote my entire thoughts to sorting out the important comments that had to be put in writing when the police arrived to ask me for a last definitive statement.

However, yet again, nothing turned out as it should have. Despite Ralph's gratifying prediction of a police visit, I was never to be offered a chance to have a final say. After the hell I'd been put through, and the way the outside world had felt entitled to roll right over me and bulldoze my entire existence, interest in me stopped that day as suddenly as if someone had switched off an engine.

There was no slowing down, no putting the brakes on – just silence. No one came near to ask a single question. Yet again, it was as if I had done some kind of mysterious disappearing act. I simply wasn't there any more. It was as if I had never counted.

Yet only a few days ago, when I'd found the body on the beach, I'd been the centre of the action, the man who held the keys. And now? The only attention I received, if you can call it that, was a quick visit from the police – two days later, as it turned out – to suggest to me that if I had any travel plans for the next week or two then I ought to cancel them because I would possibly be called to give background evidence.

Background evidence? Apart from the insolence of the message, it just so happened that I'd been right in the middle of a storm, an earthquake, a maelstrom. Men had been killed. A thug had been shot right in front of me, almost on my doorstep. On the previous day – a matter of only a few hours previously, when you came to think of it – I'd actually been living under police protection.

It was totally farcical, like floundering around in a dream. There was nothing I could get a grip on . . . So I suppose this was the reason why I had no resistance left, and when the taxi called at half past seven to take the four of us over to

Rownley, to the dinner that Ralph had conned me into, I surrendered without a protest and allowed Ken to take over completely.

As we drew up outside the Bamboo Sunrise, where I'd booked us in, he took one cool look at the place and instructed the driver to ignore my directions and drive on to an establishment called the Pickled Poacher. Apparently Bradley Brunning had recommended it to him as the best eating place in town.

Well, that was news to me. Grace and I had patronised the Bamboo Sunrise on special occasions for more than twenty years, mostly on the odd evening when we had guests but couldn't face entertaining yet again at home. It's a pleasant place, with nothing bamboo about it at all, apart from the name. Just tubular steel chairs and tables, starched tablecloths and a spectacular photograph of the Great Wall of China. And I could have told Ken, if he would have listened, that for decades it has maintained a reputation in Rownley for providing dependable food, without any oriental extremes or surprises, at very affordable prices.

All I needed to confirm my anxieties, as the taxi picked up speed, was to hear Bradley Brunning's last word on the high life these days in Rownley. 'The Pickled Poacher,' he announced, 'is where everyone goes for a gourmet experience. It's what you call the perfect celebration type of establishment.'

I leaned back on my seat and groaned quietly. Was Bradley Brunning's vision of perfection the goal that all my civic ambitions had brought us to?

54

It was just as awful as I expected. As soon as we walked in the door of the Pickled Poacher we were met by a man in a striped waistcoat whom I took to be some kind of bookie or cardsharp, though he turned out, in fact, to have the enormous responsibility of sorting out the seating arrangements and, after a lot of consultation with diaries and ledgers, he conceded that through some complex adjustments of the furniture and a bit of fiddling with the books he would be able to do us the favour of making a table available, whatever that phrase meant.

As if to worry me further he then let us know proudly that a young man, wearing a shirt emblazoned with the name of the establishment – as if I didn't by now know perfectly well where I happened to be – was known as Brian, and he'd be 'looking after us' for the night. So, what was I expected to do? Ask for a high chair and a bib?

As Brian waved an arm towards a table for four and fluttered around us, you could catch the gusts of garlic and some kind of male perfume wafting off him. The pickled poacher was right. Once upon a time a chap who stank like that would have been lucky to get a job on the council nightcart.

But the full extent of what Brunning had led me into came when I opened the menu. It was as endless as it was incomprehensible. Pages of utter bilge you needed a dictionary and gumboots to wade through. And don't talk about the prices. They were absolutely light-headed. A plate of chicken livers came in at about twenty-five bucks, and that's without the vegetables.

Twenty-five bucks for fowl offal? Who did these swindlers think they were having on? I began to argue insistently about heading straight back to the Bamboo Sunrise, but no one listened to my opinion – as usual these days. I may have been brought along because of my chequebook, but that didn't qualify me as a registered voter when it came to a question of where my own money was going to be splashed around.

The 'cheapest' food on the menu, at just on twenty dollars, was a vegetarian dish with a fancy Italian name, so I settled on that, without bothering about a starter, in the forlorn hope that the others would follow suit. Some hopes. They whacked into oysters and assorted garbage, followed by steaks topped with some sort of cream sprinkled with hedge clippings. Ken's one also arrived with what looked like raspberry jam slopped all over it. I don't suppose that without the three bottles of overpriced wine they ordered they would have managed to sluice the muck down their gullets.

And, as if eating wasn't penance enough, the noise level kept rising. For some strange reason, considering the cost of everything and the outlandishness of the food, people seemed to be extremely animated. It wasn't at all like the old days at the Bamboo Sunrise, where the conversation was always rather subdued and pleasantly discreet. The rowdy element always headed for the takeaway counter and left the decent diners in peace.

I couldn't help sitting there, listening to the cackle around me and watching all the weird carry-on about the wine and food, and comparing the scene with a mental picture of the plight of poor Deenie, still suffering in the Rownley police station while we were living it up. When would she get out? Tonight? Tomorrow morning? Ever?

I was inwardly fuming over the unfairness of it all when I looked up and caught sight of Frank Pelley and his wife. I hadn't noticed them come in, but there they were, sitting on their own, eating in a little nook, in an aura of candlelight, clinking glasses romantically over dinner – at their age – as though Deenie and her problems didn't matter a damn, and all at my expense, no doubt.

It didn't occur to me that I may have been staring at them until Ralph leaned across to me, tapped me gently on the shoulder and said, 'No, don't.'

'Don't what?' I asked in surprise.

'Don't go across and talk to Frank Pelley. Not in the mood you're in. And stop gawking at him, okay?'

Ralph was getting to know me far too well if he was going to be able to read my mind as easily as this. 'But he's here and Deenie's there,' I protested.

'And you're here, too, aren't you?' Ralph said. 'So just cool it.'

I looked at Ralph in amazement. What did he think he was up to? Playing father to the man? It was an extraordinary thought, and it shocked me so deeply that I ended up saying, a bit lamely, 'But he might have some up-to-date news.'

'He would've come straight over and told you, wouldn't he?' Ralph explained patiently. 'He must've spotted you sitting here. So just get on with enjoying yourself and leave him to handle the Deenie end of things like you promised. After all, that's what he knows about. It's his speciality, isn't it?'

'What's that?' said Bradley Brunning, taking his nose out of his glass for the first time in an hour, except to eat. 'Who wants to know about our gorgeous barmy little Deenie?'

'I do,' I said suddenly and decisively. 'And my own boy is trying to obstruct me.'

'Who, me?' asked Ken, turning around quickly from an intense conversation he'd been having over his shoulder with one of the waiters. 'Obstructing? Christ, no one's gone out of their way to do more for their mad sister than me. She could've got everyone butchered. Everyone was watching out for her all over town. That's how you and Bradley got spotted going into the warehouse, and how you got noticed driving through the middle of town. There wasn't a fruitcake in Rownley who wasn't giggling down the phone to the gendarmes. And when it wasn't the crazies, the crims and the thugs, it was our dear little sister herself.'

'A lost soul, your sister . . .' said Brunning. He was obviously more than half drunk already. His eyes were glassy and he had a rubbery loose-lipped grin. 'She nearly frightened me to death when I was hiding her. Some of the things she came out with. She was hell to live with. Utter bloody hell.'

'We all knew that from a long way back, so let's shut up about Deenie,' Ralph cut in.

'No,' I insisted. 'I want to hear about my daughter, and I've got a right to be told.'

'You've got no *right* to be told anything,' Ken said, with a tight little smile that I didn't at all care for. 'You've always managed previously to make your mind up without bothering about the facts, so why change now?'

'Anyway, if you want my opinion, it's not the kind of conversation a father should listen to,' Brunning added with a slobbery little giggle.

'I don't know I agree with you, Bradley,' Ken said. 'When you put it like that I can only think that after all it might do my dear old dad some good to listen.'

'Give it rest,' Ralph said. But he was looking at the other two with a smirk he only just managed to hold back from a full smile.

Brunning may have been very stewed but he picked up Ralph's expression straight away and took his cue from it. 'Give it a rest?' he asked with a hiccup. 'Well she certainly needed a rest when we found her, didn't she? That dirty old Nathan had her chained up, like an escap . . . an escap . . .'

'An escapologist,' said Ken, with a comical grimace. 'Except there was no way she would have escaped.'

'Okay, she's got a thing going for kinky wrinklies, so lay off, will you?' Ralph said, though now he was having to hold a hand up to his mouth to suppress the laughter.

'You should've seen her. Oh, la, la. The gear she was in,' Brunning snorted.

My two sons began to laugh openly with him, though without looking me in the eye. They looked exactly like grubby smutty little schoolboys.

'Wasn't she a picture?' asked Brunning. 'And wasn't she all het up and pissed off? I must say I wouldn't have cared to be all trussed up in those chains like Houdini . . .'

'I blame her father for everything,' Ken said, this time looking me right in the eye, but still managing a smile. 'If he hadn't made such a balls-up of bringing up his daughter, she wouldn't have been chasing all her life after dirty old men . . .'

'Father-figures. Let's be discreet and call them father figures,' Brunning bawled loudly enough to make several diners turn around. I thought for a moment he looked so pleased with himself that he was going to stand and take a bow.

'And she wouldn't have taken up with Tuggy Sullivan and there wouldn't have been a body on the beach and Tuggy wouldn't have had to die and no one would've been shot in the leg and you and I wouldn't have had to come to Rownley and try to save –'

'Funny old fate, eh?' Ralph said in a hard tone that made Ken and Brunning immediately shut up. 'All that distress and disaster, with my sister chained up like a dog and people being murdered, so a complete bloody reject like me discovers his destiny in life is to end up as nursemaid to his dad. If a gypsy woman could've gazed into her crystal ball and seen it all coming, do you think she would've had the heart to tell me?'

He shook his head at the strangeness of the thought, then ordered another bottle.

Out of the corner of my eye I noticed Frank Pelley get up and go to some trouble to guide his wife to the door, taking a long route around the wall to avoid passing near us.

Fair enough, I thought. When you looked at it his way, I'm sitting here with two homo-what's-a-names and a self-confessed reject, my daughter's chirping like a budgie to the police, and my ex-best friend is a sex fiend, so why shouldn't respectable people take a little detour to avoid contamination?

I almost burst out laughing too. When I came to think of it, I mightn't have a long life left, but it was certainly going to be an interesting one. It was a mystery to me how it had all come to pass like this. The son I hated turns up to save me, the one I despised becomes my guardian, the daughter I loved is the one I have most hurt and whose life I have most damaged.

The waiter returned with a bottle that Ralph insisted on slopping into all our glasses without so much as sniffing the cork. He proposed a toast to happy times and I raised my glass with a smile that I simply couldn't help.

Suddenly, without even having to close my eyes, I could picture Deenie in all her glamour, and there it was again –

230

that jagged silver lightning bolt at the corner of her mouth. A tiny ripple of scar tissue that leapt from beneath her make-up and flashed momentarily with a blinding beauty. A hairline fracture at the edge of her smile. A thin flickering serpent that struck its fangs into my heart. I stared at her image in wonder and I swear it was as though I'd died. Everything stood still. I heard nothing.

Then I felt myself breathing again. It was exactly as if something hard and frozen inside me had melted. I must have looked a bit odd, because Ralph leaned across the table and said, 'Are you feeling all right, dad?'

Only a few days previously, which now seemed as far away as the beginning of time itself, it would have been impossible for me to have answered him the way I did.

'I'm stuck with the lot of you, it seems,' I said. 'And I can't say I'm too thrilled about it. But I think I can just about learn to cope, if you don't rush me.'

'The alternative's a bloody sight worse,' Ralph said with more truth than I would have expected, considering the amount he'd had to drink.

'That's the point,' I agreed. 'Here we are, and there's no satisfactory alternative, is there?'

'Well, I'll drink to that,' Ralph said, raising his glass again. 'Once you can figure that out, you've got to believe things are definitely looking rosy again.'

'Oh, I wouldn't go so far as to say that,' I couldn't help saying. 'In fact, I've got a terrible certainty that from tomorrow a whole new set of troubles is only just going to land in my lap.'

'Don't be so gloomy,' Ken said.

I looked at him for a few seconds, then I gazed at Ralph.

'Just think about it, will you?' I asked quietly.